Deadly Secrets at Ballyford Castle

An Ariadne Winter Mystery

by
Ellen Butler

Power to the Pen

Praise For Ellen Butler

"Butler keeps the plot barreling ahead. Fans of intelligent escapism will look forward to more." – *Publisher's Weekly Magazine* [*Swindler's Revenge*]

"Ellen Butler's "Swindler's Revenge" is an unputdownable adventure that will take readers on an electrifying yet light-hearted and humorous journey." – *InD'Tale Magazine* [*Swindler's Revenge*]

Ellen Butler continues her bestselling Karina Cardinal mystery series . . . Don't miss it!" – Julie Hyzy, *New York Times* bestselling author [*Diamonds & Deception*]

The larger-than-life moments have a gripping sense of reality, and combined with the book's sense of whimsy and engrossing mystery, the novel is an excellent start to a new mystery series. – SPR Review [*Isabella's Painting*]

"I loved this book ! This was a fast paced read full of mystery in a historical setting! I loved the way the author made all of the book very atmospheric and capable to keep me on edge!" – Midnight Booklover [*Ink & Intrigue at Ivy Tree Inn*]

"A deftly crafted and fully reader engaging novel with many an unexpected plot twist and turn, "Operational Blackbird" by Ellen Butler will have a special appeal to readers with an interest in Cold War era spy novels." – Midwest Book Review [*The Brass Compass*]

"...thrilling and cinematic, with tension that will have readers eagerly turning the pages to see what comes next." – Manhattan Book Review [*Operation Blackbird*]

Novels by Ellen Butler

To my husband,

in remembrance of our Irish adventure.

Chapter One
Ariadne Winter

The deteriorating gray-stone castle rested precariously atop the scrubby knoll. Its menacing shadow loomed above the pearl white Georgian manor house like a giant bird of prey. The crenellations that once crowned the battlements for archers were jagged and broken. Moss and ivy clung to the walls, creeping over the eroded stones, adding an eerie sense of abandonment. The wooden doors, long since rotted away, left gaping entrances that echoed with the shriek of the fierce Atlantic winds.

That is how my story at Ballyford Castle would have begun...had I been in a Daphne du Maurier novel. Lots of foreboding warning signs foreshadowing the rather horrifying events that unfolded during my visit.

As it was, when my septuagenarian chauffeur heard I'd never visited Ireland, he took it upon himself to drive me along the scenic route—turning a six-hour trip, from Dublin to the Cliffs of Moher, into eight and a half hours. The sun disappeared below the horizon half an hour before we arrived at Ballyford, the derelict castle nothing more than a darkened silhouette in the distance.

I can attest, all the travel books and brochures that boast about the Kelly-green rolling hills of Ireland are indeed accurate. Sheep dotted the verdant countryside along with plenty of castles—some dilapidated and crumbled, while others were maintained and occupied. The tiniest hamlets feature gothic-style churches to rival St. Patrick's Cathedral in Midtown Manhattan. And we often crawled for miles behind Gypsy carts loaded down with pots, pans, and other trappings of their trade. Unfortunately, Mr. Murray failed to notice my urgency to reach Ballyford. He regularly stopped to pontificate upon the finer points of different country villages, or to purchase a toffee, or to have a wee dram, or a spot of tea.

Every time I asked how much longer the trip would take, he would answer, "Oh, not much longer, lassie."

I believe he continued to call me lassie, because he couldn't or didn't know how to pronounce my given name. I'll admit Ariadne is not your run-of-the-mill name, especially for native English speakers. Ariadne was a Cretan princess, the daughter of Pasiphae and King Minos of Crete. You see, Mother was on a Greek kick when she was pregnant with me. On the first day of school, teachers taking roll call who didn't know any better would simply call out my last name, "Winter!"

Then I'd stand up and pronounce my name phonetically, for the teacher and everyone else in the class—air-ee-ad-nee. I'd proudly announce, "I am named after a Greek princess." That behavior ended in high school when I found out how Ariadne had been fooled by that double-crosser, Theseus, during our Greek unit my sophomore year.

I found it unlikely that I would see Mr. Murray following our trip to Ballyford, and didn't bother to clarify my name for him. Besides, I quite enjoyed the way the word, lassie, rolled off his tongue.

The windows of Ballyford Manor shone bright with welcoming light. As soon as the Vauxhall Victor rolled to a halt, Julia threw open the massive front door and dashed out to greet me, all a fluff, with her crinolines rustling beneath a tea-length, ice-blue dress.

"Ariadne! Dearest, where have you been? You phoned from Dublin simply *hours and hours* ago. Mother was about to send a search party." She wrapped her arms around my neck, and her floral perfume enveloped me.

"Mr. Murray was kind enough to show me the sights between here and Dublin," I murmured into a cloud of blonde hair.

She held me at arm's length. "That is a very smart traveling suit you're wearing. Did you get it at the fashion show in Paris?"

My head rotated side to side. "At Bergdorf's in the city."

"Dior?"

I sighed, knowing Julia would keep pushing until she weaseled the entire history of the suit out of me. "Channel. It's from the '56 fall fashion line."

She frowned.

Ever since I joined *Ladies' Lifestyle Magazine,* Julia expected me to wear only the latest fashions, not something two years old. I'd recently gotten off the copy desk and began writing feature articles, and while the pay was nominally better, living in New York was expensive, and my bank account couldn't afford designer fashions. This suit was purchased for me by my mother, a truth I refused to confess to my cousin.

"But I did pick up a few things in Paris. I can show you later."

Her face cleared. "Ah, *c'est la vie.*" The underlying excitement returned to her cobalt gaze. "What a lucky break you were in Paris for the magazine this week. I'm thrilled you're able to come to the house party."

"Me too. Mother is devastated that she's missing out. But, as you know, she's chairman of the Junior League fundraiser this weekend, and she'd never pass the reins over to another member."

"Of course not!" Julia shook her head. "Why, it would be a dereliction of duty."

She turned her attention to the driver standing beside me, my luggage at his feet. Gripping his hand, she gushed, "Mr. Murray, thank you for bringing my cousin to us."

His features lifted with a smile, and the wrinkles around his eyes deepened. "It was a pleasure. I take any excuse to get to Dublin to see my grandchildren." He tipped his hat and took his leave.

We waved, watching the Vauxhall roll away into the shadows. Two red lights blinked at us, then it rounded a verge and disappeared.

Julia clapped her hands. "Mother is dying to see you. Father, too, of course. And when was the last time you saw Cormac?"

"In the fall, when the two of you came up to New York."

My cousin met her boyfriend in Washington, DC, at the First National Bank where Julia worked as a teller. Cormac O'Connell came in to open a bank account. As the two of them tell it, their eyes met across the room, and they instantly fell in love. Cue the hearts and flowers. Needless to say, my cousin, who is six months younger than I, and often likes to point out my elderly status, is a hopeless romantic. For her sake, I prayed Cormac did indeed adore her as much as she adored him.

"That's right, we saw *West Side Story*. A brilliant love story, but what a tragic ending." Julia sighed with feeling. "Then you took us to that divey jazz club in midtown. I thought your mother was going to have a fit when Cormac and I arrived at her house on Long Island at two in the morning."

The stream of air, which continuously flowed across the island, began to gust in earnest. I shivered as the cold penetrated my wool suit.

"Come inside and warm up by the fire. Leave your bags. I'll ask Brian to fetch them." Julia tugged my hand.

"Who is Brian?" I followed her through the entry.

An iron and crystal chandelier cast a warm glow

throughout the cavernous foyer. The walls were painted yellowy cream, and our heels tapped against a black-and-white checkerboard marble floor.

"Brian Byrne. He's the estate manager. His family has been the caretakers of the castle and manor house for such a long time. He knows piles of history about the castle, the manor house, and every inch of the two-hundred-and-fifty-acre estate. Did you know the land goes all the way up to the cliffs? Although Brian's family hasn't been here nearly as long as the O'Connell's, of course."

"And how long is that?"

"Sixteenth century. The castle was built in 1542 or 62. Something like that." She waved her hand as if the date was unimportant. "It's a crumbling mess. Cormac wants to tear it down, but his father won't hear of it. Neither will Brian. Legally, I don't think it's possible. Cormac said something about a historic registry."

From the little time I'd spent in Europe, the depth of history in these countries continued to amaze me. No one *I* knew lived on the same land as their four-hundred-year-old ancestors. I'm not sure I could trace my family much past four generations.

"I imagine Lord O'Connell doesn't wish to erase family history," I commented.

The heavy tread of a male foot on the stairs had the two of us looking up.

"This must be the cousin you've been waiting for." The gentleman's frame towered above us. His broad shoulders filled out the tawny tweed three-piece suit. A gold watch chain draped across the chest of his vest. Gray liberally sprinkled through his full head of chestnut hair, and his florid features spoke of hours in the sun and Irish winds.

"Brian! Are your ears burning? As you can see, my cousin *finally* arrived. We were just talking about your history with the O'Connell's, and how you come from a long line of Ballyford caretakers."

Brian's face gave a funny twitch, but my cousin didn't seem to notice as she'd turned back to me to make the introductions. "Ariadne Winter, meet Estate Manager, Brian Byrne."

"Nice meeting you."

"The pleasure is mine." His meaty, rough hand encircled mine, and he made a slight bow. "We were beginning to worry."

"Apparently, your friend Mr. Murray took her over hill and dale, rather than the direct route. Her bags are on the porch. Only, I don't know where Lady Aisling wants to put her. Do you know?" Julia asked.

"I believe she decided upon the Viscountess Valentina room for your cousin." The soft brogue rolled out like warm bread from the oven.

"All the rooms are named after Irish royalty," Julia explained. "The Valentina room faces the cliffs."

"Indeed." Brian's head dipped. "You'll be able to see the magnificent sunsets from your windows."

"When it's not raining, that is." My cousin made a face.

The Viscountess Valentina room sounded grand to me, rain or no rain. "I'm sure it's lovely."

"I'll take your bags up." Brian strode to the front door and paused. "Why don't you fetch your cousin a drink in the Library?"

The way he said it, I could tell the room began with a capital letter L, much like the board game *Clue*.

"Whiskey? Something to warm the bones," he suggested.

"Oh, but the family is already gathering in the Withdrawing Room." Another capital letter room. "Mother is dying to see you. I'll take her directly." She gripped my hand again. "We can fetch you a drink there."

"Julia, I need to change and freshen up before I meet them." I tugged free, indicating my wrinkled skirt. I glanced significantly at her velvet frock. "Didn't you tell me the family dresses for dinner?"

"Indeed, they do," the caretaker pronounced.

"It doesn't matter. They'll understand you've just arrived," Julia insisted.

"It won't do, Miss Brennan," Brian warned. "Lady Aisling won't like it. Best allow your cousin to change."

Julia chewed her bottom lip in thought. "I suppose he's right. I'm still learning the, um, manor etiquette, and Lady Aisling can be a bit of a stickler."

Brian nodded in agreement.

"Come on, let's get you a drink." Julia pivoted and said over her shoulder, "Then, I'll take you up to your room to get changed."

"After I deliver your luggage, I'll let the family know you've arrived. Dinner is at eight sharp. Help your cousin unpack and dress, Miss Brennan. Don't be late," Brian suggested.

I followed Julia into the Library and realized this room had earned its capital letter. The two-story chamber held hundreds, if not thousands, of books soaring to the ceiling, with rolling ladders to access them. A few scattered lamps barely brightened the dark paneled room, heavy with brown leather furniture. A grand inlaid walnut table stood prominently to the right, an open atlas spread across its surface.

"What's your poison? Have you tried Irish whiskey yet?" My cousin minced over to the bar cabinet. A dozen crystal decanters were filled with gold, amber, and clear liquors.

"Not yet, but I'd prefer something lighter. Gin and tonic, if you've got it." I made my way to the fireplace, where the smoky aroma of peat bricks burned low. The opening was almost as tall as me. If I ducked my head a smidgen, I could climb inside.

"G and T it is." Julia poured the liquor and seltzer into a lowball glass and mixed it up with a long-handled silver spoon.

"Tell me about the other members of the household." I reached into my handbag to retrieve a cigarette until I realized I'd smoked my last Chesterfield at some pub in a tiny hamlet where Mr. Murray insisted on stopping for a wee dram.

"Cormac's brother Shane is here, of course." Julia handed me the drink.

"Older or younger?"

"Younger. And a bit of a waster, if you ask me. He spends half his time at the local pub. The other half, he wanders the hills, taking photos like some sort of Irish Ansel Adams."

"So, he's a photographer," I said with interest, since I was currently dating a fashion photographer from my office.

"For now, at least." The crinoline rustled as Julia plopped down on the tufted leather couch. "Three months ago, he was the stable manager for an estate up north. Before that, a sheep farmer, a failed pub owner, a wool exporter...you get the picture. Shane likes to try his hand at different jobs, but nothing seems to stick, and most of them are utter failures. After each job, he boomerangs back to the manor."

"Ballyford is a large estate. Isn't there something he can do for work here?"

She rolled her eyes. "According to Cormac, Shane doesn't want to be beholden to his parents for a job. He wants to make his own way in the world."

"But...he's not." My brows drew down as I sipped the tangy cocktail.

"So, you get the picture," she drawled, opening a lovely hand-carved box. "Cigarette?"

"What kind?"

"They're called Players. Unfiltered," she warned. I took the ciggy and retrieved a book of matches with a fancy crest on it from the clean ashtray. After lighting my own, I passed the booklet to Julia. "What about the O'Connells? I understand this is the first time your parents have met Cormac's parents. How is it going?"

She tapped a finger on her chin in thought. "Lord O'Connell is affable and good-natured, quite easy going. He's been recently ill and rather thin. Lady O'Connell...I mean Lady Aisling—she insists on being called—on the other hand, is, well, she's a bit stiffer and more reserved. It's probably a good thing Brian suggested you change before dinner." She lit her cigarette. "He's right. She wouldn't like it if you attended dinner in your travel clothes."

"I imagine your mother is giving as good as she gets."

Aunt Margaret was brought up in the same household as my mother and knew proper etiquette like the back of her hand. She simply tended to be kinder and more warm-hearted. As children, Aunt Margaret allowed Julia and I to style her hair and make-up. She'd get on the floor and play with dolls with us.

My mother laughed at me when I asked if I could style her hair. "Ariadne, I paid good money to have it done at the salon. I can't have you destroying a perfectly good shampoo and set."

"Oh, Mom is holding her own. My father is rather intimidated by Lady Aisling. He only answers her in monosyllables. She probably thinks he's as boring as a block of wood." Julia grinned.

"But they *are* here for a week. Things must be getting serious between you and Cormac."

A secretive smile played around her lips.

"I know that look. What's going on?"

She clasped her hands together, and her eyes danced. "We're getting engaged," she whispered.

"That's wonderful!" I plopped down next to my cousin, wrapped an arm around her shoulder, and squeezed. "Have you set a date?" I grabbed her left hand. "Where's the ring?"

"Shh." Her gaze darted about the room as if searching for someone lurking nearby.

"Why are we whispering?"

"It's a secret."

"But...why?"

"We plan to announce it tomorrow night at the party. Cormac will give me his grandmother's ring at that time. Oh, Ariadne, I've seen it—a gorgeous ruby and diamond ring in an antique filigree setting." She swooned against the couch cushions.

"It sounds delicious, but haven't you told your parents? Or Cormac's, for that matter?"

Julia shook her head. "Cormac wanted to make it a surprise."

"So, he's not going to get your father's blessing first?" I hesitantly asked. "You two just plan to spring it on everyone?"

"Cormac said he'd ask Daddy for his blessing right before the start of the party."

"I see. And you don't doubt he'll give it."

"Goodness, no. Why would he? I mean, look around." Julia flung out her arm.

I did, taking in the cavernous room. "You mean because Cormac is the oldest, and due to inherit all of this?" I waved my hand.

"Of course. Besides, Daddy will deny me nothing."

"Won't your parents miss having you in the States?" I gripped her hand. "Heck, I'll miss you."

"Cormac's family has business interests on the East Coast, and now the airlines have direct flights from

Shannon to New York. It'll be nothing to pop back and forth. They can come here, and I'll go there." Her eyes shone, and I couldn't help returning her excited smile.

"And one day, you'll be Lady Julia O'Connell, Baroness of Ballyford."

Julia grinned. "I have so much to learn, but between Mrs. Briggs—she's the housekeeper—and Lady Aisling, Cormac assures me, I'll quickly learn the ropes." Her smile slipped, and I read the uncertainty she tried to hide.

"I'm sure you will." I gripped her fingers. "You've always been a fast learner. Remember that first summer we went to riding camp? I was so jealous when you hopped up on that horse and cantered around the ring, as if you'd been born on it. It took me a full week before I felt comfortable climbing on the back of a horse."

"Heavens, yes. I remember the first time how you hunched forward, gripping the horse's mane with one hand and the reins with the other, and your horse went round and round in circles."

We laughed together over the memory.

Letting out a puff of smoke, she said thoughtfully, "I hope you remember how to do it, because I want to take you down to the cliffs tomorrow."

"I haven't gone riding in a few years, but I'm game."

Julia gasped and checked her watch. "Drink up. We haven't much time before dinner. I certainly hope you have something in your suitcase that's not utterly wrinkled, because there is no time to press it."

I slugged back the rest of my gin and tonic and pulled Julia to her feet. "Lead the way."

Chapter Two
Ariadne

Julia led me through a maze of corridors and down two different sets of stairs until we reached the Withdrawing Room, where a low hum of conversation greeted us. The room exuded elegance with its rich gold and deep green decor. Walls were adorned with champagne silk damask, and malachite moldings traced the edges, creating a fertile, textured backdrop. A large, gilded mirror dominated one wall, reflecting the warm glow of antique brass sconces. Plush velvet furniture in rich colors accented with gold brocade pillows spread throughout the opulent room, while thick, green curtains framed the tall windows, blocking out the drafty Irish winds. A crystal chandelier hung from the ceiling, casting a golden light over a richly patterned Persian rug.

"She's here!" Julia trilled, stepping into the room.

Conversations petered out as heads turned our way. I'd packed a polyester, emerald colored cocktail dress that brought out the green in my eyes, and didn't require ironing, but I couldn't help self-consciously tugging at the dress as the room silenced.

Aunt Margaret happened to be standing closest to the door. Her floor-length, silk dress swished upon approach. "Ariadne! Thank goodness you're here." She kissed me on each cheek and hugged me with one arm, as she held a cocktail in her other hand.

Uncle Gerald followed Margaret with a bear hug. "Little Ariadne. When was the last time we saw you?"

"It's been too long." I stepped back and smiled at my aunt and uncle.

She, an older version of my blonde, blue-eyed cousin, while my uncle was the opposite. Dark hair turning salty, hooded eyes, with a boxy physique, enhanced by his padded dinner jacket. When did his chiseled jawline develop into walrus jowls?

"I think it was the Fourth of July bash my parents held two years ago. How is Tommy doing?" My cousin Tommy, a few years younger than Julia, currently resided at the US Naval Academy in Annapolis, Maryland.

"He's doing well. In his senior year now, and he just announced his plan to attend flight school." Uncle Gerald puffed out his chest with pride. He came from a long line of Navy men and served on the USS Fletcher during the war.

"Wonderful. Be sure to give him my best when you see him. And I expect an invitation to the graduation," I declared. Knowing my aunt would be the one to be mailing them, I gave her a wink.

A subtle cough brought us back to the reality that there was a roomful of people who needed introductions.

Taking control, my aunt turned to the crowd. "Ariadne, you remember Cormac O'Connell."

He was, as I remembered. A smattering of freckles across his nose with a head full of reddish-brown hair, looking fit and handsome in a white dinner jacket.

"Miss Winter, it's lovely to see you again." He formally shook my hand.

"Why, Cormac! I thought we were on a first-name basis since your trip to New York. Call me Ariadne." *Especially since we're soon to be related.* I didn't say the latter aloud, but I certainly thought it.

Cormac's hazel eyes furtively darted in the direction of his parents before answering, "Yes, of course. Welcome to Ireland, Ariadne." He pulled me further into the room.

"May I introduce you to my parents? Lord and Lady O'Connell, this is Julia's cousin Ariadne Winter."

"Welcome to our home, Miss Winter," Lord O'Connell was tall and lanky—almost too thin—and there seemed to be a slightly yellow tinge to his skin tone and the whites of his eyes. The man's warm smile was inviting as he clasped my hand with both of his in a weak, papery grip. I noticed a cherry red spurt of spidery red formations on the backs of his hands. "I hope your drive from Dublin wasn't too taxing."

"Not at all, Lord O'Connell. Thank you for inviting me to join your house party."

Callum stepped out of the way and pulled his wife forward.

"Lady O'Connell, it's lovely to meet you." I smiled. "Your home is beautiful."

"Call me Lady Aisling. Everyone does. Brian informed us you had arrived." She was a vision of effortless grace, her beauty striking—an aquiline nose, dark hair, and high cheekbones framed a face of flawless porcelain. The only detractor—her thin lips perpetually curved downward, as if constantly searching for and expecting to find the flaws in the world around her. Her eyes—cool, piercing, and the color of storm-washed steel.

"You've seen your room? Is everything to your liking?" Her inquiry was solicitous, but the small smile seemed stiff and didn't make it to her eyes.

"The Valentina room is perfect. Your home is quite magnificent, and so...large. I'm afraid I'll lose my way getting back to it." I grinned.

"It won't take long to get used to it. Julia's been here only a few days and seems to find her way around," Lady Aisling replied absently, brushing a piece of lint off her peacock blue, satin gown. I wondered if she'd had it made to match her husband's vest or vice versa.

Julia nodded her head and agreed, looking up at her

14

soon to be mother-in-law a bit like a puppy searching for praise. "Lady Aisling is quite right. And Ariadne's room is in perfect order. I made sure she knows where the bathroom and towels are, too."

Lady Aisling glanced briefly at Julia before returning to gaze past my shoulder and announced to the room, "Very well. I delayed dinner by half an hour to accommodate our latecomer. But we cannot wait any longer. Cook will have a fit."

While I don't believe Lady Aisling meant it to be an insult, her comment left a sting. After all, it wasn't my fault that the drive took so long. Mr. Murray had been sent by the O'Connells, or, at least, by their caretaker. If I'd hired my own driver, I would have arrived hours earlier.

Lady Aisling's husband offered his arm to her and led the group across the hall. Julia's parents followed, with Julia and Cormac behind them.

A black-haired young man, his curly hair slicked with oil, wearing a suit that was too large, approached me. "Hullo, I'm Cormac's brother, Shane O'Connell." He slurred his S's and gripped my hand in a hard clasp.

I couldn't help the jerk-back as his whiskey breath blew at me. "Nice to meet you, Shane. Julia told me about you." I pulled myself free of his damp grip.

He blinked and offered his elbow. "Figured I'd do the pretty. Shall we?"

Before I could respond, I found Brian at my side. "Sorry, Shane, your mother asked *me* to escort Miss Winter into the dining room."

Relieved, I took Brian's proffered elbow and followed him into another opulent room—this one decorated in blue and gold. The place settings held almost a dozen pieces of silverware, and I prayed I'd be able to keep them straight. I didn't want to embarrass Julia. I could see that Lady Aisling would be a force to contend with.

Aunt Margaret sat to the right of Callum at the head of the dining table. To my surprise, Brian pulled out the chair to the left of Callum. I figured I would have been relegated to the middle seats. Brian sat to my left, while Shane sat next to my aunt, and Julia next to him. Lady Aisling was at the foot of the table with my uncle to her right and Cormac to her left. There was an empty seat between Brian and my uncle.

As soon as we were all seated, a middle-aged woman in a black dress began doling out the soup.

"Briggs, have Daisy clear the extra place. Imogene can have a tray in her—"

A petite redhead wearing riding attire with buff colored pants tucked into tall black boots, and a white blouse strode into the room. "No need, Mother, I'm here!" Her plump cheeks were pink from the cold, and freckles filled her wrinkleless face. I guessed her age to be around sixteen.

"You're late, and you haven't changed," Lady Aisling objected.

"Didn't have time." She pulled out the empty chair and plopped onto it.

Her mother winced and said in steely tones, "Imogene—"

The teenager plowed over her mother's admonitions. "Peanut threw a shoe. I had to walk her home the last mile."

Lord O'Connell glanced up from his soup.

"Imogene, you are *not* dressed appropriately for supper—" Lady Aisling reiterated.

"Ah, let her eat, Aisling. She's a growing girl," Callum contradicted before turning his attention upon his daughter. "Is the mare injured, Imogene?"

Lady Aisling's mouth turned into a straight line.

16

Imogene paid no attention to her mother and faced her father, who looked at her with the same loving forbearance my father had for me at that age.

"No, she's dandy." Imogene studiously laid the napkin on her lap. "Um, Dougray and I checked her over."

"That is a relief. If she'd been hurt, I'd have to pull her from the Killarney International."

"Thanks, Briggs." The teenager dug into her potato soup. "No chance of that. Peanut and I are going to win the Killarney Cup this year."

He shook his head. "I don't know, poppet—"

"Dad! You promised! You said, if I could make the mark you'd put me in!" she argued as only a young teen girl can, with a determined whine at the end.

"*Imogene,* that is enough," Lady Aisling stated in a tight voice. "Your father will decide if you are ready for the Killarney International Cup when the time is appropriate. You are being rude to our guests."

Imogene flushed and dipped her head. "I beg your pardon."

Lady Aisling's shoulders remained erect as she made introductions. "Miss Winter, I apologize. My daughter Imogene is quite excitable when it comes to her love of horses. She forgets herself. Imogene, Julia's cousin, Miss Winter, is joining us for the weekend. She arrived this evening from Dublin."

Imogene leaned forward, waggled her fingers at me, and grinned. "Hullo. Julia told me about you. Aren't you the cousin who works for *Ladies' Lifestyle Magazine?*"

I couldn't help returning the grin. "Hello, Imogene. Indeed, I am that cousin."

"She was attending a fashion show in Paris," Julia explained. "It's only a hop, skip, and a jump for her to come to Ireland."

Imogene's eyes lit up, and she said in reverent tones, "I've always wanted to travel to Paris. Was it wonderful and romantic?"

"*Oui.*" I nodded. "It is, as they call it, the City of Light."

"I adore Paris," commented Aunt Margaret. "We visited in '52. Julia, do you remember?"

"Of course." Julia tapped her lips with the napkin. "I remember you made us spend all day at the Louvre, and my feet bled."

My aunt frowned. "I don't recall that."

"I do. She insisted on wearing a pair of new heels, rather than the loafers you recommended." Uncle Gerald glanced at his daughter. "She got blisters."

Julia reddened but said nothing.

Imogene asked with wide-eyed innocence. "Did you have a passionate affair with a Frenchman while you were there?"

"Imogene," Lord Callum and Cormac chided at once.

Julia tittered. Shane gave a snort. My uncle seemed too intent on eating without dripping soup on his tie; he hadn't heard or ignored Imogene's question. My aunt hid a grin behind her napkin.

Meanwhile, Lady Aisling inhaled her soup which brought on such a bad coughing fit, she had to excuse herself from the room. "Carry on," she choked out.

I pinched my lips together to keep from laughing and answered with gravity, "No, Imogene. I did not. I have a boyfriend."

"Too bad." Her shoulders deflated.

I took pity on her romantic heart and added, "My boyfriend is a photographer at the magazine and was in Paris for the fashion show with me."

Shane, who hadn't touched his soup but had downed two glasses of wine, entered the conversation with a slurred, "I'mmm a f-f-fo, f-f-fo...I take pictures."

Imogene ignored her brother's interruption. "Did

you walk along the Champs-Élysées holding hands?"

I didn't know what to do with Shane's comment. Instead, I answered Imogene, "We did. We went up the Eiffel Tower, too."

She put a hand to her chest. "Did he kiss you at the top?"

I felt my ears beginning to burn. "It was quite busy with tourists." I failed to mention that Gavin did steal a kiss, maybe two, as we walked the Seine late one night after dinner. Imogene was correct, I couldn't think of a city more romantic than Paris. We certainly bypassed plenty of other lovers kissing along the river.

Lady Aisling returned, and conversation quieted as we observed propriety and stopped talking across the great expanse of the table. Briggs and a young maid removed our soup bowls and served the next course.

During dessert. Cormac clanged a fork against his glass and rose. The table went silent.

"First, I'd like to thank Mr. and Mrs. Brennan and Miss Winter for coming across the pond to visit us."

"We appreciate the invitation," Uncle Gerald responded raising a glass.

"I have something to tell you. I was planning to make this announcement tomorrow, but I've decided the intimacy of tonight's dinner is the perfect place." Cormac dug into his pocket and pulled out a small jewelry case.

Lady Aisling frowned and said in a questioning tone, "Cormac?"

"Earlier this evening, I gained Mr. Brennan's permission to ask for his daughter's hand in marriage."

Surprised, Julia stared up in wide-eyed wonder at her boyfriend. My aunt gasped in delight. Lady Aisling's lips flattened, but she said nothing.

Cormac shoved his chair back, got down on one knee, and presented the little red box to Julia. "Julia Brennan, my love, will you make me the happiest man on

Earth and marry me?"

My cousin pressed her palms together. "Oh, Cormac, yes!" she squeaked out.

Cormac opened the red box and placed the ruby engagement ring on my cousin's finger. After taking a moment to admire the glittering stone, she leaned forward and kissed him on the lips. The table erupted in cheers and congratulations.

Misty-eyed, my aunt hugged her daughter while my uncle shook Cormac's hand. Lord O'Connell leaned down to kiss Julia, gave his son a hearty handshake, and called for Briggs to bring out the champagne. Clapping her hands and hopping from foot to foot, Imogene waited for her father to step out of the way so she could hug her big brother. Calmly, I awaited my turn to congratulate the couple. Taking note, the only two people who did not get up to congratulate the couple were Brian and Shane. While Brian sat back with a distant smile, Shane stared moodily into his half-empty wine glass. Lady Aisling congratulated the couple with a diffident smile.

As I hugged Julia, Shane chucked back the rest of his wine, slamming the glass so hard on the table, I'm surprised the stem didn't break.

Rising, he announced in a sloppy voice, "Congratulash-shuns, brother. Always one sh-tep ahead of me." He gave a salute and stomped out of the room, ricocheting off the door frame as he went.

Lady Aisling began to go after him, but her husband gripped her elbow, and I barely heard him say, "Don't. Leave him be." In a jocular tone, he declared, "Here's Briggs with the champagne!"

Once we all had a glass in our hands, Lord O'Connell raised his into the air. "To my son, Cormac, and his fiancée Julia. Your happiness! Slainte!"

We echoed his sentiments. While everyone gazed at the happy couple, I noticed Brian remained in his seat, eyeing Lady Aisling and her husband with a calculating look.

"Isn't it wonderful, dear?" Lord O'Connell placed a hand around his wife's waist.

"Wonderful," she echoed, her smile wooden.

"We'll announce the engagement at the party tomorrow," Lord O'Connell said, clapping his son on the shoulder.

For most of the occupants, the atmosphere in the Dining Room for the rest of the meal was a merry one.

Chapter Three
Brian Byrne

Since the two lovebirds refused to be parted, instead of the men retiring to the Billiard Room or Library, everyone followed Aisling back into the Withdrawing Room. The newly engaged pair sat together on the sofa. The Brennans and Julia's cousin perched around them, while Imogene plopped down on a two-hundred-year-old loveseat, jamming a piece of paper into her tight pocket. Inwardly, Brian winced, knowing exactly what would come next.

"Imogene Fiona O'Connell! Go upstairs to change out of those filthy jodhpurs and clean up. I will not have my formal room stinking of the stables," snapped Aisling.

"But Mu-um," Imogene whined. "I want to hear about the wedding plans."

"*Out!*" Her mother pointed at the doorway.

With a huff and great exaggeration, Imogene dragged herself off the delicate silk damask and sloped out the door.

Cormac nodded at something Mrs. Brennan said and caught Brian's eye. He gave a slight headshake, and Brian lifted his chin. Brian was a patient man; after all, he'd waited this long. There would be time to let Cormac know, he would *not* be accepting his "terms."

A quiet but heated discussion between Callum and Aisling came to Brian's ears. He sipped the last of his wine as he eavesdropped.

"I'm going to go check up on him," Aisling insisted.

"He's a big boy. Cormac just got engaged. Your presence is required here," her husband responded. "I expect you to be kind to Julia."

"The girl has no idea what she's getting into," Aisling murmured gloomily.

"Callum's right, stay with the family." Brian approached the pair. "I'll go check on Shane."

"Much appreciated, Brian. He just needs to sleep it off. He should be better in the morning," Callum said.

Brian stopped by the kitchen to retrieve a strong cup of coffee before checking all of Shane's usual haunts. The caretaker found the young man playing pool in the Billiard Room.

"We need to talk, boy."

Shane slammed the cue ball so hard it bounced off the table and rolled under a chair. With a curse, he threw the pool stick down and spun around to face Brian. "I suppose this means the men are on the way. Did they send you to clear out the rogues?"

"The family is congregating in the Withdrawing Room. Here." Brian held out the coffee cup. "Drink this."

Shane made a face. "You're a bit late. Briggs brought me a cup ten minutes ago." He indicated a coffee pot and a mug sitting on a silver tray. "I've already downed one and am into my second."

Brian shrugged and took a sip of the strong brew for himself. "Shane, we need to talk. I have been through the books."

Shane spun away and picked up the other cup. "I don't know what you mean."

"Yes. You do. I am here to tell you, it *must* stop. *Now.*"

Shane slugged back a gulp of coffee. "I needed that money for my photography equipment. Cormac refused to loan it to me."

"Why didn't you ask your father?"

The mug clanged against the silver tray. "You know why! I will not take another dime from my exalted father! Money from him comes with strings attached."

"Perhaps. But there's a reason for that. He's given you quite a bit over the years."

Shane stiffened and his eyes slit. "A fact he sees fit to remind me, every time I come home."

Brian strolled over to the pool table, casually leaning against it. "What about your mother?"

Shane snorted. "She would have told Father."

"You took more than just the photo equipment."

Shane flipped open a box that held cigars and cigarettes. He chose a cigarette, lit it, and spoke with the fag dangling out of the side of his mouth, "I owed someone."

"Who?"

"None of your business."

"I can make it your father's business, if you like," Brian suggested with deceptive calm.

Shane paused and took the butt out of his mouth. He scrubbed his face.

"You might as well tell me." Brian eyed the boy.

His clothes hung off of him. He'd lost at least a stone while working the stables up north. Shane had never been fat, but a boyish pudginess that used to fill his facial features had disappeared. Now his cheeks were angled and sharp, enhanced by the messy cluster of curly hair framing his face. The hallows beneath his lashes spoke of sleepless nights.

"You know, there are other ways I can find out. I don't think you want me asking a bunch of questions around the village."

"Gambling debt," Shane confessed. "At the Sligo horse track."

Brian stared into his half-empty coffee; his head shook with disappointment. "Inherited your

24

grandfather's gambling streak, have you?"

Shane tsked. "It's no such thing. I had a tip. The mare was a sure thing. Even her name was Lucky Lady."

"What happened?"

Shane sucked on the cigarette. Smoke poured out of his nose as he spoke, "She came up lame. Bloody jockey didn't know what he was doing. He should be horsewhipped."

"I don't think I can cover this up."

"You've done it before!"

Brian's head snapped up. "A pittance, compared to now. Shane, you took a thousand pounds!" he thundered.

"Yeah, well, we've all got secrets to keep, don't we?" Shane gave Brian the side eye.

"What do you mean by that?"

"Who was that chap at the pub on Wednesday night? I saw you give him an envelope. Full of money, if I had to guess."

Brian said through his teeth, "That is none of your business."

"Perhaps, it's not mine. But is it my father's business?" Shane spun in a circle and jauntily trooped out of the room. "Well, hullo there. If it isn't our little American fashion doll."

"I-I was looking for a bathroom. This place is so confusing. I'm completely turned around," Brian heard Miss Winter reply.

"There's one through the Billiard Room, to the left of the fireplace."

Indeed, Shane was correct, Miss Winter looked like the epitome of fashion in a deep green dress that matched her eyes and hugged her curves. The incredibly high-heeled black pumps elongated her legs, and even though she'd spent all day in the car, nary a dusky curl was out of place on her head. She topped off the outfit with a very proper pearl necklace and matching earrings. If anyone looked like a future lady of the house, it was Miss Winter.

"Mr. Byrne, I didn't realize you were here. Shane, I mean, Mr. O'Connell said there is a bathroom . . ."

"Through there." Brian pointed.

Her heels tip-tapped across the room. He'd observed the differences between the two cousins during dinner. Miss Winter was dark and reserved, almost to the point of mystery, whereas Julia's blonde beauty and effervescence brightened any room she walked into. He could understand why Cormac fell in love with the young lady; however, he wondered if she'd be able to manage what was to come.

Brian observed Aisling's shocked expression when Cormac proposed. Her reaction hadn't gone unnoticed by Callum either. Brian hoped Aisling could learn to respect her son's decision and at least behave cordially toward Julia...especially once things changed. For change was undoubtedly on its way to Ballyford Manor. Brian wondered how Julia Brennan would endure it.

While he pondered the ramifications of Cormac's engagement, Brian retrieved the cue ball, replaced Shane's cue stick in the holder, and racked the colorful balls into a precise triangle. Pleased with his handiwork, he spun the triangular ball rack between his fingers.

"Why is Shane O'Connell angry about his brother's engagement?"

Brian jerked. The rack bounced and clattered onto the hardwood floor. "I didn't hear you enter."

"I didn't mean to sneak up on you." Miss Winter ran a finger along the polished wooden rail.

Brian hung the rack on a hook next to the cue sticks.

"Why is he upset?" she pressed.

"That is a complicated question." His shoulders sank with a sigh. "Do you play pool, Miss Winter?"

She shrugged. "I've played a few times. It's a very pretty table. Those claw feet look hand carved."

"They are." He brought her one of the sticks. "How about a game?"

She rolled the cue between her hands. "Shall I break?"

He made a slight bow. "Be my guest."

Chapter Four
Ariadne

I strode to the far end of the table and placed the cue ball just off center behind the head string. The cue stick hadn't been chalked, so I took a moment to chalk it before lining up my shot.

Mr. Byrne remained silent, casually leaning against the opposite side of the table, pool cue in hand with its butt resting on the floor.

I took a slow, deep breath, and released it. *Crack!* The balls scattered across the table. The solid red ball dropped into the corner pocket, and the cue ball settled into the center of the table.

"Lucky break," he commented.

"Looks like I'll play solids. Two, side pocket." I put the solid blue in the side pocket. "Tell me about Cormac and Shane."

"I think I've just been hustled." Amusement played around his full lips.

I grinned. "You're stalling."

Mr. Byrne shrugged. "When the boys were young, they were the best of friends. On Cormac's twelfth birthday, things changed. His father determined it was time for Cormac to begin learning about the responsibilities of Ballyford and what would be expected from him in the coming years."

"You mean when he inherits the estate?"

Mr. Byrne cleared his throat. "Um, right."

With the cue stick, I pointed to a corner pocket. A

moment later, in dropped the yellow ball.

"Nice shot."

Unfortunately, the cue ball landed against the rail, behind two striped balls, leaving me with no direct or indirect line to one of the solid balls. "Shane must have known his brother was set to inherit the title and lands."

I'm sure there was some sort of bank shot to be made, but I couldn't see it. I wandered around the table searching for the best place to put the cue ball to limit the caretaker's shot.

"Up until then, Callum spent time with both the boys, fishing, riding, you name it, they were a threesome."

"And Cormac's twelfth birthday offset the threesome's balance?" I barely tapped the cue ball. It rolled to a stop just beside the striped balls, making for a difficult but not impossible shot for Mr. Byrne.

"It's not as though Callum didn't spend time with Shane. Corner pocket." The green striped ball plopped into the leather net. "He just spent more one-on-one time with Cormac."

"Which made the younger brother jealous?"

Mr. Byrne nodded and set up his next shot. "Thirteen, side pocket. Shane did anything he could to gain more of his father's attention. Won riding championships and became a marvelous golfer. He desperately competed for his father's attention." He tapped the cue ball; the orange stripe fell into the pocket, clicking against the solid blue one.

"Did their father make an effort to have one-on-one time with Shane?"

Mr. Byrne chalked his stick and eyed the table. "His mother did her best to spend more time with Shane, in hopes of offsetting the rejection and jealousy he felt. She realized Callum needed time with his oldest but often argued that he could be showing Shane how to run the estate, too. Callum said it would be cruel to teach Shane, only to have everything go to his brother. He wanted Shane to go to university or learn a trade to keep him occupied."

"What's the age difference between Shane and Imogene?"

"Twelve years."

"Did Shane get a university degree?"

"Unfortunately, he was kicked out of uni in his second semester. Eleven, side pocket." Mr. Byrne's shot went wide, knocking my solid purple one into the side pocket instead. "Blast it!"

"Nice shot," I snickered.

The caretaker cringed and shook his head.

"Imogene must have been an adjustment for the family."

"When Imogene came along…Aisling didn't have as much time to give to Shane. And Callum…well, Imogene being the youngest and only girl…" Mr. Byrne struggled to explain.

"Wrapped around her little finger?" I suggested.

"Something like that," he agreed.

"Seven. Corner pocket." I pointed with the stick. "So, the middle child gets ignored. Left to the wolves?"

"It wasn't quite that bad. And it's not as though Shane is destitute. When he turns thirty, he'll gain access to his inheritance. In the meantime, the boy is hellbent on bouncing from one job to the next."

The seven fell into place. "What is he good at?"

"Horses. It's always the horses. It's in his blood. He's better with them than Cormac ever was. I can't figure out why he can't settle at a stable."

"Six. Corner. Why doesn't he run the stables here?" The green rolled into the pocket.

"Doesn't want to have to answer to his brother and father. I suspect he's biding his time until he gets his trust fund and will set up his own stables."

"Five in the side. How old is he now?" I leaned across the table to line up the shot.

"Twenty-seven, two years younger than Cormac."

"Three more years, then." The balls tapped against each other, and the five dropped into the pocket, clanking against two others. "I'm surprised he's not gadding about, traveling Europe or the States, for that matter. Just to get away. He seems the type."

"Already done. Years twenty through twenty-four," Mr. Byrne said matter-of-factly. "After the second arrest, Callum put his foot down. Hauled Shane back to Ireland. Forced him to get a job."

I processed his comment as I lined up my next shot. "Eight ball, corner pocket."

"There you are!"

Startled by my cousin's exclamation, I hit the cue ball too hard. "Damn!" The eight-ball rolled into the pocket, followed by the cue ball.

"Ariadne, you've been ages. I thought you'd gotten lost."

"I did," I stated flatly. "Found my way here."

"And Brian unwisely took up your offer to play a game?" She turned to the caretaker. "How much did you lose?"

"We aren't playing for stakes," I answered, gripping the pool cue with both hands.

"Don't let her hustle you," Julia warned. "When Ariadne was in middle school, Uncle Theo enclosed the back porch. He built a bar and bought a pool table. Her father taught her how to play, and she spent countless hours mastering the art."

"Only when Mom wasn't around. She didn't think it was a ladylike occupation." I placed the cue stick in the holder. "Thanks for the game, Mr. Byrne."

"Call me Brian."

"Ariadne." I held out my hand.

"You're a brilliant player, young lady." His firm grip was rough with calluses. Clearly, his job didn't keep him slaving over ledgers and wearing fine clothing, like what he wore this evening. No. Brian Byrne was a man who spent time working the estate.

"Keep it to yourself. I might try to hustle Lord O'Connell for the deed to the castle." I winked and wiggled my eyebrows.

Brian's full smile lit up his freckled features. His forehead wrinkles deepened as he guffawed at my joke. "I'll keep your secret," he whispered.

With reluctance, I turned to my cousin and sighed. "Well, Julia. I suppose we must return to the Withdrawing Room."

I had enjoyed my quiet game with the estate manager and wasn't ready to return to the stiff formality of Lord and Lady O'Connell.

"No." She gave a head shake. "Lady Aisling disappeared with Mrs. Briggs half an hour ago, and Mom retired to her room. Daddy, Cormac, and Lord O'Connell headed into the Library to smoke cigars and drink brandy." Julia made a face. "Ick. Those things stink. You'd best join them soon, Brian, before they smoke all the good ones."

Brian checked the time on his pocket watch. "I'll do that. Congratulations again, Julia. I know you'll make Cormac a happy man."

Chapter Five
Julia Brennan

Julia held out her left hand and stared at the new heirloom sitting on her finger.

"Was that planned?" Ariadne asked.

Julia shook her head. "No. I told you, we were going to do it tomorrow. Cormac said he wanted it to be a surprise, and he couldn't wait." She folded her hand into a fist. "It's a bit big. Cormac said we can go into town to have it properly sized, after the party."

"An excellent plan." Ariadne hooked her elbow through Julia's. "We can't have you losing the family's Koh-I-Noor before the big party. Shall we see if we can find some ice cream to filch and talk about your wedding plans? We can stay up half the night, like we used to when we were kids."

Julia's face fell, and her shoulders drooped as if the world rested upon them.

"What's wrong?"

"You missed the fireworks." She sighed. "Mom was talking about having the wedding at the Army Navy Country Club, and Lady Aisling acted appalled, like it was some rundown shack."

The Army Navy Country Club was a beautiful facility specifically built for active duty and retired officers. Julia's father was an excellent golfer and on the club's board of directors. Her mother chaired the Wives Bridge Club, while Julia played in the junior tennis league, and attended cotillion until she graduated from high school. Her grandfather played a pivotal role in designing the course. The country club was practically a Brennan family institution,

"Oh, dear. I don't suppose that went over well."

"Lady Aisling said we had to hold the wedding here, *of course*. As if it was a bygone decision. She said, since Cormac was the heir, he would be married at his ancestral home." Tears sheened in her eyes. "Then Daddy got upset and said his only baby daughter was going to be married in the US of A and that was that."

Ariadne wrapped an arm around Julia's shoulder and pulled her close. "Hoo-boy. I'm not surprised."

"Why? Lady Aisling has been kind to me."

Ariadne's brow rose, and her features turned skeptical. "I'm sure when Cormac brought his girlfriend, all was well and good. However, upon Cormac's announcement, she had a sour expression, which she quickly hid. Watch out for her. I believe she'll try to place a wedge between you two. You must remember Cormac is her eldest, and due to inherit the title and estate. Her expectations for his bride will be high. Think astronomically high, like the moon."

Julia chewed her bottom lip—a habit she had when working out a knotty problem. When they made plans to travel to Ireland, Cormac indicated his mother would love her as much as he did. Was Ariadne correct? If so, Julia had her work cut out for her to gain Lady Aisling's approval.

Ariadne interrupted Julia's thoughts. "What happened after your father put his proverbial foot down?"

"Oh. Mother and Lord O'Connell calmed everyone down. Mother said there would be plenty of time to work things out to everyone's satisfaction. Tonight was a night for celebration, not for family squabbles. Lord O'Connell agreed with Mom and kind of gave his wife this steely-eyed glare."

"I knew Aunt Maggie would be able to hold her own

against the haughty Lady Aisling. What did the Grand Dame say after that?" Ariadne pinched her mouth, and Julia could tell she was trying not to smile, which only sought to bring Julia closer to tears.

"Nothing. She closed her mouth with a snapping sound and sipped her champagne. Although I don't know how she achieved it, considering how tight she kept her jaw."

Her cousin supplied an inelegant snort. "My dear cousin, where do *you and Cormac* wish to marry?"

"Cormac says he'll get married anywhere. He doesn't care. As the bride, he said, I can have whatever I want. But I don't want to upset Lady Aisling. What a horrible way to begin our lives together." A tear dripped down her apple cheek. "Oh, Ariadne, I can't imagine all my friends will be able to come over here for a wedding. The bride's side of the pews will be *empty!*"

"Tut-tut. Dry your tears." Her cousin fished a handkerchief out of her brassiere and handed it over. "If Lady Aisling doesn't back down, you'll simply have to have two weddings. Or at least two receptions. Your parents can pay for one in the States, and if the O'Connells must have one at Ballyford, they can arrange it and pay for it."

The thought of having two weddings hadn't occurred to Julia. It seemed so decadent. Although...Cormac *was* a in line to become the next baron. She sniffed and tapped at the tears. "You think so?"

"I know so. Leave it to your mother. If I know Aunt Maggie, she'll have everyone sorted before the weekend is up. She is a formidable force when it comes to her children."

Julia blew her nose. "I suppose you're right."

"Of course, I'm right. Now, lead me to the kitchen. Do you think they'll have strawberry ice cream? You know that's my favorite."

"I-I don't know." Julia finished mopping up and held out the handkerchief.

Ariadne scrunched her nose. "Keep it. Tell me all about the kind of wedding dress you want. If you come up to New York, I'll get you an appointment at the most exclusive bridal salon on the East Coast. While we're there, you can pick out the dress you'll make me wear as your maid of honor."

Tears dried, Julia perked up, clapping her hands together. "Oh, Ariadne! You mean you *will* be my maid of honor?"

"Of course, you ninny. I was kidding when I said I'd think about it."

A giggle of happiness escaped Julia's lips.

"Now, are we supposed to turn off all these lights?" She indicated the half dozen burning lamps throughout the room.

"No, the staff will take care of it."

"Look at you, already playing the lady of the manor. C'mon, *Lady* O'Connell, show me the kitchen," Ariadne said in hoity-toity tones.

Julia tucked her elbow through her cousin's and towed her into the hallway. "First, I want to hear more about this photographer you're dating. Why haven't I heard about him through the Anna-Margaret grapevine?"

"Because my mother hasn't met him," I confessed.

Julia gasped. "Why on earth not? Isn't your mother still throwing men at you every Sunday dinner?"

"It's every other Sunday. And yes. She is. My father met him. Also, my Aunt Ruby. Considering Aunt Maggie doesn't know about him, it must mean my father kept his promise not to tell Mother."

"When did he meet—?"

"Gavin Turnbull," Ariadne stated primly.

"Ooo, Gavin. I love it. Very Irish." Julia's comment

received an eye roll from her cousin. "When did your father meet Gavin?"

"About a month ago. During one of our weekly lunches. They got on like a house afire."

"Why not bring him home for Sunday dinner?"

"I'm not ready to subject him to Anna Winter's Marriage-Babies-Family-Interrogation." Her cousin shrugged, and, glancing away, muttered, "I'm afraid he might bolt."

"Wait a minute?" Julia came to a halt and grinned. "Do I hear wedding bells? Has my cousin finally fallen in love?"

Ariadne's cheeks bloomed like a summer poppy.

Julia clapped her hands. "You have! You have!"

"You're being ridiculous." She strode ahead, almost stomping down the corridor. Over her shoulder, she called, "I thought we were getting ice cream. On our way, you can tell me about this mausoleum you'll one day inherit."

Julia decided to leave the conversation alone for the time being. She rushed to catch up. "The central part of the manor house was built in 1859, and additions have been made over the years. The part we're in now is part of the east wing, which was built in the 1880s. And the west wing at the turn of the century."

"Julia!" Cormac strode down the passage toward them. "Brian said you were in the Billiard Room."

Julia breathed deeply, loving the little tingle she felt every time she saw her handsome fiancé. Ha! She, Julia Margaret Brennan, was engaged.

She minced over to Cormac and threw her arms around his neck. "Did you miss me?"

He grinned down at her and delivered a perfunctory kiss on her lips. "I see you located your cousin."

Julia grinned back. "She was playing pool."

Cormac's brows drew down. "With Shane?"

"No, Shane was in there earlier, but he left when I arrived," Ariadne answered.

"Then who—"

"She was playing with Brian," Julia explained.

"Oh, Brian." Cormac's frown remained. "Did he...say anything?"

Ariadne tilted her head. "What do you mean?"

"Well, um, anything about the family perhaps?" Cormac hedged, tucking Julia to his side.

Julia's mouth tightened as she tried to figure out what her fiancé was hiding. "Darling, you needn't worry. I've explained everything to Ariadne."

Ariadne frowned but said nothing.

Cormac's features suddenly turned stormy. "Everything? What do you mean by that? *What is it you think you know, Julia?*"

Julia's face burned, and her heart dropped. Cormac had never spoken so harshly toward her. "I simply told her how Shane has trouble holding down a job. That he was a bit on the skids. I'm sure he'll find something soon," she assured him.

Cormac's features cleared. "I see. Did Brian also slip his tongue about our family secrets?"

"You mean about Shane?" Ariadne glanced down at her nails. "Not really. Why?"

Cormac cleared his throat. "My brother wasn't at his best this evening. Please, don't judge him by his behavior tonight. He's going through a-a...hard time."

"Ariadne understands. Don't you?" Julia's eyes begged her cousin to diminish Cormac's irritation. "It's not like she works for one of those awful tattling tabloids they have over here."

"Mm, yes. You needn't worry. I'm not here to blab your family secrets to the magazine. Frankly, unless your brother drunkenly stumbled across the Dior runway, knocking down one of the models, my magazine doesn't

38

care," Ariadne airily assured him.

Cormac's features lifted, and he grinned. "Five years ago, my brother was so wild, knocking down an entire fashion show of models would have been par for the course for Shane."

Julia tittered.

And Cormac pulled her closer. "Do you mind if I steal my fiancée? She and I have, uh, things to discuss." He gave Julia a lascivious smile.

Julia tittered, staring at him with devotion. "Do you mind, Ariadne?"

"Of course not. Off with you two lovebirds. Go, get lost in this mansion and 'discuss' things." Her cousin winked. "Feel free to use me as your alibi."

Julia blushed and mouthed *thank you.*

"C'mon," Cormac tugged Julia down the hall while she giggled, trying to keep up with him.

Chapter Six
Ariadne

"Ariadne, wake up." The noise filtered through my unconscious dreams, and my brain reluctantly rose from the depths of slumber.

"Yoo-hoo, Ariadne-ee," a sing-song voice called.

The jangle of curtains reached through the haze. Gray, pre-dawn light filtered through the cobwebs of sleep. The silhouette of a figure stood in the window.

"Julia? Is that you?" I yawned and rubbed the sleep out of my eyes.

"Time to rise and shine."

"What time is it?"

"Six-thirty."

I yawned again. "Why on Earth are you awakening me at this early hour?"

"I told you. We're riding out to see the cliffs."

"You told me we would ride out to the cliffs. You failed to mention we'd be doing it before dawn," I groused and pulled the counterpane over my head. "Go by yourself. I'll see them another time."

Her weight compressed the side of the bed, and she patted my leg. "It's better to see the cliffs at sunset—"

"Great. Let's go at sunset," I mumbled.

"—but we can't," she continued as if I'd not spoken. "The party will be well into the swing of things. And there is so much to be done to prepare, I'm afraid that if we don't do it now, it won't happen. You *must* see the cliffs. You can't come all the way here and *not* see the Cliffs of

Moher."

I made a last-ditch effort. "I don't have riding gear, Julia. I wasn't told to bring any."

"That's why I brought you a pair of my jodhpurs, and I found a pair of boots that should fit you. You wear a seven and a half. Right? The sizes are different over here, but I think I've got the correct ones."

I groaned, threw back the covers and squinted at her. "You're not going to leave me alone until I agree, are you?"

She shook her head. "Nope."

"Ugh. Fine."

"We'll eat breakfast when we return. Meet me in the foyer in twenty. Be sure to wear a coat." One more leg pat, and she quietly disappeared, closing my door.

Thirty minutes later, I stood in the foyer wearing a borrowed pair of riding boots, Julia's jodhpurs, a button-down blouse, and a robin's egg blue, wool, walking coat, with velvet collar and cuffs. The coat came from Paris. Needless to say, I wasn't pleased that it would soon smell like a horse, but I had nothing else warm enough to block out the morning breeze.

I was still grumpy, made even more so because Julia was nowhere to be found.

"There you are!" Julia trilled, clopping down the corridor in her shiny black boots and full riding gear with a tight-fitting black coat.

"You told me to meet you in the foyer," I stated drily.

"Did I? No matter. That's a gorgeous coat. Are you sure you want to wear it? It might get dirty."

"I've nothing else appropriate to wear," I said through tight lips.

"Oh! Why didn't you say so?"

I scowled at my cousin's obtuseness.

"Come with me. There are all sorts of things in the mudroom." She grabbed my hand and led me through the labyrinth of passageways and down a flight of brick steps.

The mudroom was a ten by twenty-foot, hallway of a room lined with coats, boots, gloves, hats, umbrellas, and even a few pieces of riding tack. The scent of earth and grass permeated every inch. Eventually, I settled on a black peacoat that probably belonged to one of the boys when they were younger, and a leather riding helmet.

"Let's go. Shane will be wondering where we are."

"Shane?" I said with surprise.

"Yes. I ran into him upstairs. He offered to saddle the horses and take us down to the cliffs."

"Not Cormac?"

"Heavens, no. Cormac has far too many responsibilities today. Here is a treat for your horse." Julia passed me a handful of carrot pieces.

I followed her out the side door into a cobblestone courtyard. The morning fog had yet to fully burn off, and there remained a dampness native to the Irish air. Two white ponies stood quietly; their reins wrapped loosely around a hitching post. Smaller in stature than the quarter horses Julia and I rode back in the States, their breath puffed out in plumes.

"Oo, they are beauties, Julia." I approached the closest horse, holding out a closed fist. The mare leaned forward and tapped its nose against my gloved hand. I flipped it over, opening it to reveal the carrot. Her lips nibbled the orange vegetable, and she allowed me to pet her muzzle. I cooed, blowing lightly at her nostrils. "What kind of horses are they?"

"Those are Connemara ponies, or Capaillín Chonamara," Shane allowed the Gaelic name to roll off his tongue.

He slid off a glossy chestnut quarter horse and threw the reins around the post. The ponies looked small in comparison to the tall, broad-chested quarter horse.

I stiffened. "Good morning, Mr. O'Connell."

Shane ducked under the wood and came around to Julia and me. "Oh, there's no need for such formality. Call me Shane." He gave me a wolfish smile. "After all, we're going to be related soon."

"Very well." I gave a reluctant nod.

His eyes were clear without the telltale redness I'd expected from all the alcohol he'd imbibed the prior evening. He hadn't oiled his hair this morning, and damp wayward curls tumbled across his forehead. He wore dark gray breeches with a long oilcloth raincoat. "Julia told me it's been a while since you've ridden. The Connemara ponies have a lovely, soft temperament. That one you're petting is Coconut, and the other is Marshmallow."

"Was someone hungry when you named them?" I grinned.

Shane rolled his eyes. "Father allowed Imogene to name them."

"Shane's right. They are lovely horses to ride. Marshmallow is my favorite, but if you would prefer to ride her, I'm happy to ride Coconut."

Coconut nuzzled my shoulder as we spoke.

"It looks like Coconut, and I have made friends. I'll stick with her." I pulled out another carrot piece and fed it to her. "What's the name of your mount, Shane?"

He mumbled something while checking the tightness of the saddle on Coconut.

"I'm sorry, I didn't hear what you said."

Shane sighed and said quite clearly, "Nutmeg."

I raised one eyebrow. "Another one by Imogene."

"Half the stable is named after food items. The nameplates read like the kitchen larder. I call him Nutter. He can be a bit of a handful." Shane bent over with his fingers laced together. "C'mon. Up you go."

I placed a boot into his cupped fingers, and he boosted me onto the back of Coconut.

A few minutes later, the three of us were mounted,

and, like the Pied Piper, Shane led us out of the courtyard onto the grassy hillock leading down toward the Cliffs of Moher, the avenue deeply shadowed by the crumbling castle behind us. It was my first good look at the ruins, and I reined in halting Coconut's plodding gait. Wisps of foggy cotton balls hovered about the lower portion of the crenelated structure while the rising sun gave a golden glow to the top battlements.

Julia stopped next to me. "Quite something, isn't it?" A frigid breeze blew the tails of her coat across Marshmallow's backside. "Could you imagine living among the drafty halls in the middle of winter?"

"I can't imagine living in such a place at all. The stone is so cold and unforgiving."

Shane, having noticed he'd lost his followers, turned his steed and joined us. "She'll stand another five hundred years." He pulled a camera out of his saddlebag. The shutter clicked. "Would the pair of you mind riding up to that verge and allow me to photograph you with the castle behind?"

Julia glanced at me. "Do you mind?"

I shrugged. "Why not?"

Julia made a clicking sound and dug her heels into Marshmallow's side, leading the way up the hill. We took a few minutes to arrange the horses to Shane's liking and waited while he futzed with the camera.

I glanced at the crumbling relic. "Is there a resident ghost in the castle?"

Julia shivered. "Heavens, I certainly hope not."

"Why? For four hundred years, generations of O'Connells passed through that castle. There's bound to be at least one or two unhappy entities sticking around for posterity. Maybe a heartbroken bride. Or a son who committed suicide. Or a disgruntled servant."

Julia laughed at my suggestions. "Outrageous. The O'Connells are mild-mannered folk. There wouldn't be any disgruntled servants or the like."

I allowed a skeptical brow to rise. "Maybe *now*. People were different during medieval times. Always at war. I imagine the O'Connells had to protect their property. Maybe they were bloodthirsty warriors, raping and pillaging."

My comments brought forth delighted laughter from my cousin. "Ariadne, you always did have the most vivid imagination!"

"Perfect! Toss your hair like that again, Julia!" A few more snaps of the shutter, before Shane finished his photographs and tucked the camera into his saddlebag. Trotting up to us, he asked, "Do you want to go inside?"

My brows furrowed in confusion. "You can go inside? Aren't the floors crumbling?"

His mouth twisted. "About sixty years ago, the roof on the west and north wings caved in, collapsing the second and third floors. But the southeast still has plenty of sturdy flooring and an old winding staircase to lead the way."

"Have you been inside?" I glanced at my cousin.

She shook her head.

"I expect you'll want to see the family estate your children will one day inherit," Shane commented.

I squinted at him, trying to determine his meaning. Was it a slight or merely a statement? I didn't have enough time to find out, for Shane dug his heels into his mount, and with a quick whistle, the chestnut charged up the steep incline.

Julia and I shared a glance.

She shrugged and gave Marshmallow a kick. "Might as well check it out."

Coconut handily followed the pony up the hill to the plateau where Shane awaited us. "Over there is where the carriages used to arrive."

Only an archway, half of a wall, and a pile of

weather-worn stones remained of the old porte-cochere. The once grand entry gaped hollowly, missing its twelve-foot, wooden, double door. Probably rotted away a century ago. Three distinct levels rose into the glowing sky. Towers on either side rose above the rest of the castle. The north side, having fallen in on itself, teetered only half a story higher than the rest of the building. However, the south tower, still intact, soared two more levels above the main building.

Leaning back, I held a hand above my eyes to block the rising sun. Dips in the stonework were evenly placed across the square turret, like dentil molding on a fireplace mantle.

When I said as much, Julia remarked, "That's where the archers would stand and protect the castle. Cormac told me about it."

"Would they dump boiling oil on unsuspecting travelers as well?" I inquired.

"Undoubtedly. We can't go in the front way." Shane stated the obvious, as we'd have to climb over the five-foot mound of portico rubble to do so. "Go around that way, there's a doorway on the south side where we can gain entry."

Since I was closest to the trail he indicated, I took the lead with Marshmallow and Nutmeg following. At one point, the track narrowed, and we rode close enough to the castle wall, I could reach out and touch it. Parts of the coarse, weather-stained stones had been smoothed to a dark shine with wind and rain.

Coconut rounded the corner. A bark-colored cloth at the base of the tower wafted in the breeze. As I brought the horse closer, I realized it looked remarkably like the oilcloth raincoat Shane wore. Another gust shifted the cloth, and a head of hair revealed itself.

Julia let out a cry.

"Stay here," Shane ordered, dismounting his horse.

Not being the best at blindly following commands, in a flash, I too dismounted and strode over to the pile of clothing, with Shane hard on my heels. A man's body lay there, one of his legs bent at such an angle that his foot faced backwards. Broken castle stones were scattered around the site.

Brian Byrne's damp flesh was bleached of color, his freckles barely visible against the pallid tones, and his head visibly dislocated from his neck. Milky, swollen eyes stared at the brightening sky. Deep scrapes on his gloveless hands and face marred the pale skin. Bloodstains darkened the gravel path beneath his head.

I'd like to say this was the first dead body I'd come across. Unfortunately, it wasn't. Only a few months ago, I'd run across another dead man at the inn where I was staying in Newport, Rhode Island. My past experience didn't make viewing this one any easier. My stomach clenched, and revulsion crawled up my throat. My heartbeat thumped in my ears. Clasping my hands together, I breathed deep and slowly to stave off the nausea.

"Who is it?" Julia asked.

"Brian Byrne," I answered, glancing at Shane.

His face paled, not as much as the dead man's, but enough for me to notice. For a moment, his features showed shock, but then they hardened as his jaw clenched.

"He-he's not moving. Is he hurt?" my cousin whispered.

With a primeval cry, Shane ripped off his gloves and fell to his knees. He reached out a sturdy finger to touch the man's cheek. Rigor mortis had set in through the night, stiffening the body. With a flinch, Shane pulled away.

"I'm afraid there's nothing to be done," I murmured, placing a hand on his shoulder. "I'm sorry."

47

Shane's head bobbed. "You're right. He's been dead for a while."

"Dead?" My cousin's voice rang two octaves higher than normal.

Realizing my sensitive cousin shouldn't get any closer, I swung around and strode over to where she remained mounted on Marshmallow. "Julia, please go back to the manor and fetch help. Tell Lord O'Connell there's been an accident. Someone at the house must phone the local police."

"Father Michael must be notified to give the last rites," Shane muttered.

Julia continued to stare, her mouth bouncing like a child's ball, up and down, the reins slack in her hands. Marshmallow's head shook, and he shifted.

"Julia!" I barked, pulling her out of her trance.

She blinked rapidly, coming back to herself. "Y-yes. Of course."

Nutmeg munched on a nearby crop of grass. Shane rose to his feet and captured the horse's reins, bringing him over to my cousin. "Take Nutter with you. Speak only to my father. Do *not* tell my mother...or Cormac. Do you understand?"

Taking the reins, Julia nodded.

"Go on now," I said in firm but kind tones.

The pair of us watched as Julia trotted out of sight.

"Why not tell your mother or Cormac?"

Shane's eyes narrowed, and he continued to stare into the distance. "It will upset her terribly. Brian was family. She'll need to lean on my brother to get through this."

I tilted my head back, my gaze raking the stone tower. Two glassless windows, one above the other, revealed a circular staircase up to the top level where the archers would stand along the roof line and look out beyond the parapet to guard the castle. The windows were probably four feet tall. Brian must have fallen out of one. Or, perhaps, from the rooftop itself.

I spoke my thoughts out loud, "What do you think he was doing up there in the middle of the night?"

Shane turned, allowing his own gaze to scan the tower. "What makes you so sure it happened in the night? Could've happened this morning."

I tried to hide my scorn. "The body has stiffened. That takes hours. Six, eight, up to twelve hours."

"How do you . . ." Shane stared at me with a mixture of horror and appreciation.

Like I said, this wasn't my first body. Not willing to get into details about the murder in Newport, I shrugged. "You'd be surprised at the type of research a magazine requires."

"Never mind," he muttered.

I waited for him to propose a theory.

Finally, he shrugged. "A few days ago, Brian had to chase off some local kids who tried to hold a séance in the tower. Maybe they came back."

I understood how an abandoned castle would be a morbid draw to local teens. If that was the case, perhaps they knew what happened.

Maybe they even witnessed his fall. Or worse, caused his fall. In so doing, they panicked and beat a hasty retreat.

I crouched in front of the corpse. His fists were closed tight, and far too stiff to open to see if they held any damning evidence. The overcoat flopped on either side of him, revealing a jagged rip and blood on his white button-down shirt. I tilted my head. Something wasn't right. Something was missing.

A memory of Brian just before he left the Billiard Room popped into mind.

"His pocket watch is missing."

Shane uttered something in Gaelic.

"He wore a gold pocket watch at dinner last night," I repeated.

"I know the one," he replied harshly. "You seem to have an unusual obsession with the dead."

I glanced over my shoulder.

Shane anxiously paced, one hand on his hip, the other running through his hair.

"I'm simply trying to understand why Brian would have come out here in the middle of the night. In the dark." I peered at the tower again.

"Maybe he couldn't sleep. Maybe he was meeting a woman. Maybe, like I said, local kids were fooling around in the tower. It's dangerous, he would have wanted them out."

Slowly, my knees unbent. "If it's dangerous, why were you planning to take Julia and me inside?"

"What?" His pacing increased. "No. I meant, it's dangerous at night. There are no lights."

"How would Brian have seen these kids? If it was dark?"

"I don't know. They probably carried torches and lit candles. I told you," he snapped, shaking his hands as he spoke.

Hoofbeats halted our conversation. Lord O'Connell, astride a snorting Nutmeg, bounded around the corner. He spotted Brian and pulled up short. The horse whinnied in protest and sidled sideways, but the master of the house didn't seem to notice.

Muttering under his breath, "No, no, no, no . . ." He slid off the horse's back and, with his trench coat flapping behind, rushed over to the body. "Brian!"

I jumped out of his way as his hands splayed across the dead man's chest.

Chapter Seven
Lady Aisling O'Connell

Aisling ran an unsteady finger down her list, her lips moving as she read each item. "Yes, it all seems in order, Briggs. The salmon is coming from Tappers?"

"Of course."

"I'll never forget the time we used that Mannerly distributor." Her lips twisted. "Ghastly."

Briggs shook her head. "That was almost eight years ago, ma'am. The kitchen knows never to order from them."

Aisling sipped the last of her morning tea, and her sleeve fell back, revealing bruising around her wrist. "Yes. Well. See that they don't." Surreptitiously, she pulled her sleeve back in place.

"Of course."

"Have either of my two sons shown their faces this morning?" Aisling glanced at the empty table. Two place settings had been used and cleared.

"Mr. Cormac has already breakfasted, and said he had a meeting with Brian this morning."

Her hand shook the tiniest bit as she replaced the teacup onto the saucer. "And Shane? I suppose he's still in bed," Aisling said with disgust, taking a bite of toast.

"Mr. Shane's down at the stables this morning," Briggs supplied.

Mid-chew, Aisling stared at the housekeeper in surprise.

"He's taken the two young ladies out to the cliffs this morning. Miss Julia wanted to show her cousin, but the

Land Rover's tire hadn't been patched yet, and Nigel took the shooting brake into the village. It being a bit of a walk, Shane offered to saddle horses for the ladies to ride down to the cliffs, instead. Miss Julia said they would eat breakfast when they returned."

Aisling hmphed. "That girl better be ready for the party this evening and looking her best. Especially since there will be an announcement about—" her features puckered as if she'd sucked a lemon "—the engagement."

Briggs' face remained blank and unreadable. The housekeeper had been at Ballyford as long as the lady of the house. She would never offer an opinion unless directly asked.

To the housekeeper's surprise, Lady Aisling decided to ask, "What do you think of Cormac's choice, Briggs?"

The older woman licked her lips, and her hands remained clasped at her waist. "It seems Mr. Cormac is head over heels in love with the girl. She's quite beautiful, isn't she?"

"I suppose she's pretty enough," Aisling grudgingly agreed. "But do you think she's suited to Cormac?"

"He seems to think so," Briggs again replied noncommittally. "Although she *is* a commoner *and* from America. I suppose it'll be quite an adjustment for everyone. Is Lord O'Connell displeased?"

Aisling's teeth snapped together with irritation. "You're dismissed."

Without another word, Briggs gave a short head nod and left the breakfast room.

Aisling couldn't care less if Cormac chose to marry a commoner. After all, she'd not had a title when she married Callum, though her father was an extremely wealthy businessman. But she'd expected Cormac's bride of choice to be Irish, or at least English. Instead, he'd fallen in love with a Yank. A fluttery meringue of a girl with big blue eyes and an empty head. Her parents seemed to be perfectly fine...for Americans, but the girl had grown up in the suburbs, probably in some quaint four-bedroom home. She had no idea what it meant to run a household like Ballyford. The high expectations to which the O'Connell name was held in the villages surrounding the estate. The day-to-day operations of the manor, not to mention the constant struggle to find enough money for the upkeep.

Money. The estate consumed money like a whale consumes fish—in huge gulps. Her dowry, a handsome payment made by her father, replaced the manor's leaking roof, wired the telephone lines in the house, updated the bathrooms, and increased the size of the stables. It was gone within their first five years of marriage. Callum's father, Albert, had done a good job generating income for the property, but after the war, the world changed, and the money stopped flowing the way it used to. Not to mention Albert's penchant for gambling on the horses. Luckily, he passed before his gambling habits towed the entire estate under water. Then Callum made two disastrous investments, forcing them to take out a loan to pay the taxes.

Not to mention the expensive medicine for Callum's condition. It came from Switzerland and held the illness at bay...at least for the time being.

Cormac had new ideas for expanding the stables, to increase room for more horses to trade, and to create a stud farm. A lucrative business if you could obtain the proper horses, which took money. Brian's ideas focused on expanding grazing rights for the sheep farmers and selling twenty acres of the south portion to the neighboring Dunlavey family, who'd been asking for the past dozen years. Shane, outrageous as always, suggested renting out the property for movie people to use.

Unfortunately, her stubborn husband opposed all the new ideas. He was stuck in his ways and believed that if they worked harder, the old methods would bear fruit. But a large payment on the note was due at the end of the quarter. Paying it would draw down almost all of their savings.

Callum simply must change his mind.

Aisling would do anything necessary to make sure Ballyford Manor remained in the O'Connell family for her grandchildren, and great-grandchildren.

Anything.

Her thoughts circled back around Julia. Would the girl be an asset, a liability, or simply another mouth to feed? Aisling would prefer the first but would settle for the latter. If Julia began proving herself to be a liability, Aisling would simply have to sit the girl down and force her to see reason. Her mother seemed frugal enough—the dress she'd worn last night was elegant but simple, as were her jewels. Hopefully, she'd passed that prudence onto her daughter.

Speaking of the Brennans. Aisling heard hurried footsteps in the passageway. She tossed the linen napkin on the table and pushed her chair back to rise.

"Julia, you look flushed. Is something the matter, darling?" Mrs. Brennan asked.

"Mother, something terrible has happened! You won't believe it!" Julia gasped in dramatic tones.

Aisling stepped into the passageway. "What has happened?"

"Oh!" Julia spun around, her eyes wild. Wisps of hair escaped the combs she'd used to pull it back, and her face was damp with sweat.

Ever proper, Mrs. Brennan greeted her, "Good morning, Lady Aisling."

"Good morning to you as well," she said dismissively. "Julia, tell me what has happened? I understood you were going to ride out to the cliffs. Did someone get hurt? Your cousin, perhaps?" *She didn't seem to be the type of girl who knew one end of the horse from another.*

"No, nothing like that." Julia chewed her bottom lip.

When the girl simply stood staring, Aisling prompted, "Well, then? What?"

"Yes, Julia, tell us what's wrong," Mrs. Brennan said in softer tones, rubbing a hand along the girl's back.

"It's just that...Shane, um, I think he wants to tell you himself," the young lady hedged.

Aisling frowned. She did not expect to be denied. "I see. I was under the impression Shane had gone to the stables to saddle your horses this morning. Has my son returned to the manor?"

Mute, the stubborn girl shook her head.

Aisling huffed, "Enough of this nonsense. Out with it!"

Julia's determination crumpled beneath Aisling's stern demand. "Th-there's been an accident. S-someone fell from the castle tower."

Mrs. Brennan gasped. "Goodness. We must call for an ambulance."

"Of course, we'll call for an ambulance. Where is Briggs? She was here just a moment ago." Aisling checked up and down the hall. "I'll have her gather first aid materials."

"I'll help," Mrs. Brennan offered. "I was a nurse during the war."

"Fine. In the meantime, Julia, go find Cormac. He is meeting with Brian this morning to discuss estate business. Check Brian's office, it's the room to the left of the kitchen. Tell them to fetch Dougray and the stretcher. There should be some left over from the war in the storage shed off the tack room."

"But, my dear, who fell from the tower?" Mrs. Brennan asked.

"It-it-it—" Julia fumbled.

"Was it one of the local children? They think it's a lark to climb around the castle," Aisling supplied with a shake of her head.

"N-no." Julia twisted a button on her coat. "It is Brian."

"Brian? Brian Byrne? What on earth are you talking about? You must be mistaken," Aisling dismissed in high-pitched tones.

"No, ma'am, I'm not. Lord O'Connell took one of the horses to the castle. He-he said to phone the parish priest. I'm afraid Brian's...dead," the girl squeaked out.

"Dear lord in heaven," Mrs. Brennan murmured.

Aisling charged down the hallway, striding briskly toward the kitchen. "BRIGGS! CORMAC!"

Chapter Eight
Shane O'Connell

Rattled from the past two hours and irritated by the crying, Shane could remain seated no longer. He bolted from his chair to pace the Parlor floor. Back and forth. Sunbeams streamed through the half a dozen windows, bleaching the deep red carpet to pink. His body created elongated shadows within the sunlit boxes. He couldn't erase the sight of Brian's body from his memory. If he stared directly at the sun, maybe it would erase the memories. A foolish thought, Shane immediately dismissed.

He never should have suggested visiting that damned castle today. Then someone else would have discovered Brian's body. Why, oh, why didn't he ignore the girls' curiosity and insist they ride directly to the cliffs?

The cliffs were safe. The castle was not.

With Brian gone, Shane needed to get into his office to "doctor" the books. If Cormac or his father found out he'd taken the money, there would be hell to pay.

He checked the Louis XV mantel clock—an example of the entire room's décor, all done up half a century ago in French antiques. Shane hated this room with spindly-legged furniture and lady-like chairs. The worst part was the ceiling, painted with flowers, vines, and birds intermingled with fat winged cherubs. The clock registered not yet ten in the morning.

He was desperate for a drink.

Perhaps no one would notice . . .

Pacing closer to the tray of decanters, his mother finally spoke, "Not now, Shane."

His mother, true to her frigid personality—except for her initial gasping cry when Father Duffy arrived to give the last rites—showed little reaction to Brian's death.

"I don't know what you're talking about," he replied sourly.

"Imogene, please stop that crying. You'll make yourself ill," his mother admonished.

Imogene noisily blew her nose, and her sobs quieted, but did not subside altogether. As his mother sat tense and upright in one of the ornate armchairs, Mrs. Brennan comforted his little sister, rubbing her back and handing over tissue after tissue. Little wads of tearstained tissues surrounded Imogene like puffy white dandelions.

Instead of the drink, he lit another cigarette, realizing too late, he hadn't finished the first one. Ariadne gave him a significant glance, as she picked up the half-smoked fag and stubbed it out in the crystal blue ashtray.

She sat on the loveseat next to Julia, who fidgeted restlessly with the center button of her riding coat; her baby blues staring sightlessly into the unlit fireplace. Mr. Brennan stood sentry near the doorway with a concerned frown. His former military days were made evident by his rigid, upright bearing.

"What could be taking so long?" Shane demanded with frustration.

His father, Cormac, the priest, and the inspector had been holed up in the Library *forever*. After Father Michael had performed the last rites, he'd suggested the body be moved into the house. A suggestion overridden by Inspector Quinn, who insisted the body couldn't be moved until the coroner arrived from Galway, which greatly displeased the priest. The inspector apologized and explained that the law overrode the church's wishes and that the death scene needed to be investigated. The men moved inside so Inspector Quinn could use the phone to call the coroner.

Meanwhile, even though Shane had discovered the body, he'd been shunted aside. Told by the priest to "go and comfort the women." And here he was, cooling his heels. No information. Not allowed a calming drink.

His mother checked her wristwatch. "Shane is correct. This is taking too long. I must be getting back to the kitchen. The flowers should have been delivered by now, and if I don't get started, they won't be ready for the party. Where has Briggs gotten to?" His mother twisted in her seat, searching for her right-hand woman.

The room went silent for a moment; all eyes turned to the lady of the house.

"Mother! How could you?" Imogene cried.

"How could I what?" she said with a touch of irritation.

"A man is dead, Mother," Shane replied.

"A fact I am well aware of, *Shane*."

"You can't seriously expect the party to go forward. You need to tell Briggs to phone the guests." He took a drag and blew the smoke toward the ceiling.

"Cancel the party! Heavens, no! Why, it is your brother's engagement party after all. We are introducing his lovely fiancée tonight. We simply *cannot* cancel." Her eyes blinked rapidly.

"Mother! It-it just isn't done—" Shane's admonishment was cut off by the squeaking wheels of the tea trolley.

A young lady with ginger hair and a smattering of freckles rolled the cart into the room. "Excuse me, milady." She performed a little curtsy. "Seeing as the American ladies haven't breakfasted, Mrs. Briggs thought you'd be wanting some refreshments while you waited. She put out a fresh loaf of brown bread, jam, and coffee, along with the tea."

"Thank you...erm..." Lady Aisling's eyebrows rose. When the girl didn't respond, his mother prompted, "Your name?"

"Oh," the girl tittered. "I'm Lucy. I came up from Doolin to help with the party. My brother sets up the fireworks, and seeing as you needed extra hands, he got me...uh, this job," Lucy ended in a whisper, as she realized nobody was paying attention except his mother, whose frown turned disdainful as the poor girl prattled.

"I see. We will serve ourselves," his mother icily replied. "When you return to the kitchen, tell Briggs I need her."

"Yes, ma'am." One more curtsy, and the girl retreated like she had wings on her feet.

His mother stared at the doorway where Lucy had exited, as if waiting for Briggs to magically appear on the spot. Her fingers gripped the arms of the wing chair so tightly they turned white. When she made no move to serve her guests, Ariadne rose from the sofa.

"Shall I pour, Lady Aisling?" the American inquired.

Brought to her senses, his mother returned her attention to the trolley cart. "How kind of you to offer, Miss Winter. That would be lovely."

Chapter Nine
Ariadne

I poured coffee for the Brennans, tea for the O'Connell ladies, and passed out bread and jam to Julia and Aunt Margaret.

"Imogene, dear, try a little of this bread with your tea. It will make you feel better." Aunt Margaret encouraged the teenager who had put on fresh riding gear this morning.

Uncle Gerald patted my hand and thanked me. Shane declined any refreshment and continued smoking and pacing. However, after passing out cups to everyone else, I poured Shane a cup of coffee and took it over to the restless man.

"Have this. Not as good as whiskey, but better than nothing," I murmured.

He stared at me for a moment before stubbing out his cigarette and taking the saucer from my hands. "Very well." Shane returned to the side chair he'd vacated earlier.

My stomach grumbled. Realizing I hadn't eaten since dinner last night, I cut myself a piece of the fresh crusty brown bread, topped it with blackberry jam, and took my place on the loveseat next to Julia.

Lady Aisling placed her teacup on a side table and half rose. "What on Earth is taking Briggs so long? That stupid girl from town didn't deliver my message. Shane, could you—"

Briggs entered the room—her eyes watery and red, and her nose pink-tipped from crying. "You were asking for me?"

"Briggs! There you are." Retaking her seat, the lady of the house demanded, "Where do we stand with the arrangements?"

"I've told the kitchen staff to pack anything they can into the ice box. As for the perishables that can't be frozen, I thought about donating them to the Limerick orphanage."

Lady Aisling rose from her chair, practically sputtering. "Frozen! Donating to the orphanage! What on Earth are you talking about, Briggs?"

Confusion crossed the poor woman's wrinkled features. "What would you prefer I do with all the food?"

"Why, cook it. Of course!"

"But-but milady...with Brian...well, I assumed the party was to be canceled."

"No such thing!" Lady Aisling's gaze swept the room at large. "I would appreciate it if everyone ceased to assume the party is canceled."

Mrs. Briggs stared, open-mouthed, at her employer.

"I am afraid, my dear, Briggs is right. The party must be canceled." Lord O'Connell entered, his face drawn and his shoulders stooped.

Cormac, a middle-aged priest all in black except for the collar at his neck, and a white-haired gentleman with a bushy mustache and rosy face, followed Lord O'Connell into the room. The stranger wore an overcoat, with a herringbone flat cap tucked under his arm.

"Mother, this is Inspector Ronin Quinn. He will be conducting the inquiry into Brian's death," Cormac announced.

Lady Aisling ignored the introduction, "But my dear, we cannot cancel." She turned to the lawman, "Don't misunderstand me, Inspector Quinn. I am devastated by Brian's death. I can't remember a time when Brian wasn't around."

The inspector's eyebrows rose.

"But you see, my son has become engaged. This is to be a celebration. I am positive, Brian *never* would have wanted the party canceled on his account." Finding the inspector unmoved, she turned her attention to the priest. "Father Michael, you *must* agree Brian would *never* have wanted this special occasion turned into a tragedy. The party is an annual tradition, and for many guests, it is the highlight of the year. We simply can't let everyone down. After tonight, the family can mourn him properly...in private," she rushed her explanations, as though every word she said made perfect sense. "Until then, we must carry on with a stiff upper lip."

Imogene's sobbing notched up again.

Cormac stared at Lady Aisling with appalled dismay. "*Mother!*"

Lord O'Connell delivered a warning look to his son. "Darling, I know how important this event is to you." He placed an arm across her shoulders. "However, it would be imprudent to continue. What will our guests think when they find out about Brian's death?"

She tsked. "How would they find out?"

"It is a small community, and Brian is a beloved member of it," Father Michael counseled. "I have no doubt the villagers have already heard, and the gossip mill is running at full speed. Callum is right, you must cancel the party."

She gazed back and forth between her husband and the priest. "You believe we should not hold the party?"

"I'm afraid not," Callum replied.

"But Cormac's engagement . . ."

"While the engagement is joyful news, today is not the day for parties and announcements. It is a day for mourning. Your guests will understand," Father Michael said in dulcet tones.

Lady Aisling looked at her husband.

He nodded in agreement with Father Michael. "I'm sorry to put a pall on your engagement, Cormac. We will send an announcement to the newspapers and have a small party. *After* Brian is laid to rest."

"Of course, Father. Julia and I understand, don't we, dear?" Cormac perched on the armrest next to Julia and took her hand.

"Oh, yes! It would be most..." Julia searched for the correct word. "Improper. Yes, and unfitting to hold the party."

Lady Aisling bowed her head in acceptance. "Very well. Briggs, see to it."

"Yes, ma'am." The housekeeper turned toward the door.

Inspector Quinn raised a finger. "Don't go, er, Mrs. Briggs, is it?"

She lifted her chin. "Yes, sir."

"I'd like you to remain." He continued, "It is my understanding you were here at the manor last night. Correct?"

"Of course. My quarters are on the third floor." Mrs. Briggs stepped across the Parlor's threshold.

"Do any of the household staff members also live on the estate? Besides, Mr. Byrne?"

"Our stable master, Dougray, has lodgings above the carriage house," Cormac provided.

"We haven't filled the butler's position since Timmons left us...a while ago. The maids and other, um, footmen live nearby in Doolin," Lady Aisling bitingly explained.

"Please, everyone, if you would, take a seat." The inspector indicated a nearby chair for Mrs. Briggs. "I need to clarify the timeline of events that led up to Mr. Byrne's death." He pulled a small notebook and pencil out of his coat pocket and flipped to a page.

"Inspector, is this necessary? Can't it wait? The

ladies are distraught and need counseling, *not* an interrogation," Father Michael gently chided.

I assumed the priest meant Imogene, because from my vantage point, the rest of the ladies were bearing up quite well. As a lapsed Presbyterian, I didn't find a need for counseling from a Catholic priest. Additionally, I was surprised by the priest's interference in Inspector Quinn's investigation.

There had been a bit of contretemps at the castle when Father Michael began insisting Brian's body be taken back to the house, in opposition to Inspector Quinn's direction to leave the body alone until the coroner arrived. The matter was settled when the inspector let it be known that he would arrest any person or persons who moved Brian's body before the coroner arrived.

Like earlier, Inspector Quinn did not take kindly to the priest's chastisement. His face turned pink, and his spine straightened. "It is important for the facts to be taken down immediately. Time often causes witnesses to become forgetful or misremember."

"Very well." Giving in, Father Michael sat on the other side of Imogene.

"Mrs. Briggs, it may take some time. Please take a seat," Inspector Quinn directed. Lord O'Connell sat in the matching chair next to his wife, while Cormac pulled one of the side chairs flanking the fireplace, placing it next to Julia.

Once everyone was in place, Quinn began his interview, "Now, Lord O'Connell stated that the family supped at eight last night."

"That is correct," the head of the house confirmed.

"Was it usual for Mr. Byrne to dine with the family?" Quinn inquired.

"Brian often ate with us. He is like a brother to me." Lord O'Connell went on to explain, "His father was my father's estate manager. Brian and I grew up together. When his father passed, Brian took over the position. Brian's family has lived at Ballyford for generations."

"Hm." Quinn scribbled away. "You gathered in the Withdrawing Room after the meal. What time was that?"

"I'd say, about quarter past nine," Cormac supplied.

"And Brian joined the family?"

When no one offered up confirmation, Uncle Gerald cleared his throat and answered, "Correct. I recall, he was in the Withdrawing Room with us following dinner. But only for a short time. I believe he offered to check on Shane."

The inspector looked up from his notes. "And where was Shane?"

Uncle Gerald shrugged.

Inspector Quinn glanced at Shane. I too stared at the O'Connell's middle child, wondering what he would tell the inspector about the conversation I'd overheard.

Shane crossed his legs. While lighting a cigarette, he responded, "In the Billard Room."

"Brian found you there?"

"He did."

"And what transpired between you two?"

Shane blew a cloud of smoke toward the ceiling. "He reprimanded me for behaving like an arse at the dinner table."

Father Michael tutted.

The inspector didn't respond, and Shane breezily explained, "You see, I'd had a bit too much to drink. I'm afraid I behaved badly." His smirk revealed how little remorse he felt for his actions.

"And you went directly to the Billard Room following dinner?"

"Directly after. Briggs here can confirm it. She brought me a pot of coffee. To dilute the booze."

Briggs nodded, and the inspector made a note of it.

"After a few cups of the strong brew, I saw the error of my ways." Shane gave a cocky grin. "I begged Brian's forgiveness."

Quinn finished scribbling in his notebook and asked, "Then what happened?"

"Nothing." Shane focused on tapping the ash off his cigarette. "I left the room."

Shane lied quite easily. Too easily. As if he believed the words he spoke were the truth. Perhaps, the coffee hadn't done its work, and he had been too drunk to remember the angry threats he exchanged with Brian.

"You were the last person to see Mr. Byrne alive?"

Shane glanced up; his eyes were full of innocence. "Not at all. I ran into Miss Winter in the passageway. She got lost on her way to the toilets. I told her she could find one through the Billiard Room. I imagine she ran into Brian while she was there."

Inspector Quinn turned his assessing gaze upon our loveseat. "Miss Winter, you were with Shane when Mr. Byrne was discovered?

"I was." I placed my cup on the coffee table.

While the inspector wrote in his notepad, he asked, "Is it true? Did you see Mr. Byrne in the Billard Room?"

"I did."

Those steely blue eyes popped above the notepad. "What time?"

"Oh . . ." I frowned in thought. "I believe it would have been maybe quarter to ten. I don't rightly recall."

"And how long did you converse with Mr. Byrne?"

"Mm...a little while," I mused, tapping a finger against my chin. "He invited me to play a game of pool."

"You played pool? With Mr. Byrne?" Quinn's bushy white brows rose skeptically, as if wondering why a girl like me would choose to play pool with Mr. Byrne.

"After all, Inspector, it *was* the Billiard Room," I stated the obvious.

Quinn ignored my facetiousness. "How long did you play?"

"I'm not sure." I turned to my cousin, who had taken to staring into her coffee as if it could offer the answers she sought. "Julia—"

Startled, she jerked, and her cup clattered on the saucer.

"Do you remember what time it was you found us in the Billard Room?"

Julia stared at me, then glanced at Inspector Quinn. "I, uh, don't remember."

"You are Miss Julia Brennan, Cormac's fiancée," Quinn stated.

Julia nodded.

He made a note, and continued, "Miss Brennan, you went to the Billiard Room looking for Mr. Byrne?"

"Brian? No. I was looking for Ariadne. It was late, and she had been gone for quite a while," Julia explained.

The inspector tapped his pencil against the pad. "And you can't remember the time?"

"Maybe ten thirty? Ten forty?" She gazed at me for confirmation.

I lifted my shoulder. Maybe? I had no recollection of the time when Julia arrived.

Her attention returned to the coffee cup. "I told Brian the men had gone into the Library to smoke cigars. He said he would join them."

"The men? What men?" The inspector asked for clarification.

"Why, Daddy, Cormac, and his father." She counted off with her fingers.

"And Shane?"

"No-o. I mean, I don't know. He wasn't around when I went in search of Ariadne," Julia tripped over her words.

Quinn's attention returned to the black sheep of the family. "Shane, where did you go after you left the Billiard

Room?"

Shane lazily lit a fresh cigarette. "To bed."

After being glued to her feet, Briggs' eyes shot upward, and she fixed her gaze upon Shane.

The inspector didn't seem to notice the housekeeper's keen stare. Instead, he turned to Lord O'Connell. "Brian joined you in the Library?"

"He did not. I didn't see him again until . . ." He gulped, covered his eyes, and made a gesture with his other hand. "This morning."

"I see." The inspector took note of that. "Mrs. Brennan, what were you and Lady O'Connell doing after the men retreated to the Library?"

My aunt straightened and said concisely, "I retired to bed. Lady Aisling had gone to speak with her housekeeper, and once Julia left to find Ariadne, I decided to allow the men to continue their celebrations on their own. It was ten-forty-six when I arrived in my bed chamber. I remember taking note of it."

Once Quinn wrote Aunt Margaret's information in his notebook, his questions paused as he wandered further into the room. His gaze browsed the inhabitants one by one, until those bushy eyebrows pulled low, landing upon the matriarch. "Lady O'Connell, what time did you leave the Withdrawing Room to speak with your housekeeper?"

"About half-ten, I'd say," she mused.

"Where did this happen? In Mrs. Briggs' room?"

"In the kitchen. We were going through the checklists," she responded in clipped tones.

"Did you see Mr. Byrne?"

"No," she snapped.

"Don't you remember, milady?" Briggs interjected, fidgeting with her apron. "He was in his office. He said he needed to speak with you, after we'd finished."

Lady Aisling gave Briggs a hard stare before

answering, "Why, you're correct, Briggs. Thank you for bringing it to our attention. I'd completely forgotten."

"What time was that?" Inspector Quinn asked.

"I've no idea. I wasn't keeping track," she threw out as if the inspector's entire line of questioning was silly nonsense.

"Mrs. Briggs, perhaps you recall," Quinn prodded.

"I would say it was almost eleven," Briggs supplied. "I remember Brian was quite keen to speak with you."

This was noted by the detective, and those astute eyes narrowed a tad. "What did you discuss with Mr. Byrne?"

"Details about the party," Lady Aisling replied in an offhand tone. "Honestly, I don't remember."

The inspector scribbled on his pad.

"Oh! Wait!" Lady Aisling snapped her fingers, and her features brightened. "I do remember asking if we had any more problems with teenagers sneaking into the castle."

"Ah, yes, the teens." He scratched his head. "Lord O'Connell mentioned you'd had some problems with kids playing in the castle ruins."

"That's right, Inspector." Cormac rose from his chair.

Quinn let out a phlegmy cough, retrieved a handkerchief from his pocket, and wiped his mouth. "Tell me more about the incident."

Lord O'Connell interjected, "Brian caught four teenagers—locals, from the village, fooling around the castle about two weeks ago."

The inspector frowned. "He reported this to the authorities?"

Lord O'Connell jerked his head. "We didn't see the need."

"Just boys being boys," Father Michael inserted.

Lord O'Connell nodded in agreement. "Precisely.

I'm sure you're aware of the rumors?"

The inspector's face went blank. "Rumors?"

"The castle is haunted by our ancestors. The teens thought they'd hold a séance in hopes of speaking with them," Cormac explained the latter with an accompanying eye roll. "Brian lambasted the group and threatened to tell their parents. Then he drove them back to the village. You know, put a bit of a fright into them."

Quinn turned to Michael. "You knew about this, Father?"

"Not about the séance," the Priest denied. "Brian simply mentioned he'd found some teenagers trespassing in the castle. He was worried they might get injured while roughhousing around the ruins in the dark. Had I realized what they'd been up to, of course, I would have spoken to their families."

The inspector squinted at Cormac. "Mr. O'Connell, you were aware of the...um...trespassing teens?"

"Of course. I am made aware of all issues pertaining to the manor that arise," Cormac replied as if the inspector's question had been an insult.

Quinn ignored Cormac's pique, simply writing down the information on his notepad. Silence reigned, except for the scratching of his pencil against the paper.

Julia brought the cup to her mouth but changed her mind and replaced it on the saucer. Shane tilted his head back, his cigarette pointing to the ceiling. My aunt shifted in her seat. Imogene sniffed and wiped her nose.

Lady Aisling uncrossed and recrossed her ankles. "I remember now. Brian said he was going to check on the castle," she asserted. "It being a Friday night, he was concerned they might try to get back inside."

"Mm, I see." Inspector Quinn flipped to the next page. "Did anyone see Mr. Byrne after eleven o'clock?"

No one offered an answer. A few of us shook our heads.

Quinn's face screwed up and he fidgeted with his mustache, flattening it down before asking, "Did Mr. Byrne seem unhappy or depressed? Might he have..." The man let the insinuation hang in the air like a dirty cloud of smog.

Imogene gasped. Cormac frowned, and Shane let out a bark of laughter.

"Absolutely not," cried Mrs. Briggs.

"Lord O'Connell, Mr. O'Connell?" Quinn prodded.

Both men shook their heads.

"Father Michael?"

"Over the years, I've had plenty of conversations with Brian. None that led me to suspect he might take his own life," Father Michael supplied. "He's as steady as they come."

Lord O'Connell uncrossed his legs and leaned forward, putting his elbows on his knees to explain, "Brian wasn't one to evade the hard things in life. I don't think you could find a more levelheaded bloke in all of Ireland. It was an accident. A terrible. Tragic. Accident." He hung his head in sorrow.

"What happens next?" Cormac asked.

Quinn finished his notes before responding, "I will conduct an inquiry. Investigate the site of Mr. Byrne's, er, demise. It should take a day or two."

"What about the teenagers?" Lady Aisling asked in imperious tones. "Were they there last night? Perhaps he ran into them, and they panicked when they were caught and pushed poor Brian over the edge."

"Aisling! You have no knowledge that those teens returned last night," Father Michael chided, rising to his feet. "It is a sin to cast aspersions. 'Ye shall not spread a false report.' Exodus—"

"I'll need the names of the teens," Quinn interrupted the priest. "Do you have that information, Mr. O'Connell?"

Cormac shifted uncomfortably in his chair. "Brian didn't see fit to tell me the names."

"I know who they are," Lord O'Connell spoke in a deadened monotone. "The youngest O'Shaughnessy boy, his girlfriend Jane Macgregor, Jacob Gilbert, and Finlay Stewart."

The inspector scribbled that last bit and shut his notebook.

Imogene gasped. "You're wrong! Fin would *never* date Jacob Gilbert! He teased us mercilessly in primary school. He is-he is worse than a scoundrel, he's, a-a sleeveen!"

"Shh, Imogene, you shouldn't—" Father Michael sank back down next to the girl.

Lord O'Connell turned his attention to Imogene. "I'm sorry, pet, it's true. Part of the reason Brian wasn't harsher with them is because he knows...knew you and Finlay are friends."

"But...*Jacob Gilbert*," she wailed, and proceeded to regale us with a fresh spate of tears.

Stunned by the young lady's hysterics, the inspector slowly inched away from the sofa and smartly chose to change tactics. "Erm, I'll need to get inside the castle."

"Of course, I can show you the way," Cormac offered, rising from his chair.

"Later." The inspector tucked his pad and pencil into an inside pocket of his trench. "Around lunchtime. I expect the coroner from Galway will have removed the...er, body by then."

"I'm at your disposal." Cormac held out his hand, and Quinn shook it.

"Thank you for your time. I'll show myself out."

Once the front door closed behind the inspector, Lady Aisling released a whooshing breath and said with irritation, "Well, I suppose now that's over, I must go about canceling the party. Briggs, please continue your work with the hired staff and start phoning the guests. Tell Cook to plan for a cold lunch service. See if she can do something with the salmon for our dinner."

"And the rest of the food?" Briggs asked.

Lady Aisling sighed. "Put what you can on ice. I imagine we'll need it for the wake." Her eyes darted toward Father Michael, and she said loudly above Imogene's sniveling, "Send someone over to the orphanage with the rest."

"That is very kind of you. What a treat it will be for the orphans." Father Michael bestowed a munificent smile upon Lady Aisling.

With that, Lord O'Connell rose to his feet as if he were a man twenty years his age. His features sagged, sallow and distraught. "I'll be in the Library."

"But darling, I need you—"

He cut off his wife stating baldly, "I must contact Brian's family. It cannot wait any longer. Father?"

"I'll come with you, to pray with the family." Father Michael followed Lord O'Connell.

"Yes, of course," Lady Aisling replied to her husband's retreating back.

"What can I do to help?" asked Aunt Margaret.

"Oh, I couldn't ask a guest to—"

"Don't be ridiculous," Aunt Margaret said in a no-nonsense tone. "Brennan's rise to the occasion. Besides, we are soon to be family."

Lady Aisling's lips pursed, and she swallowed hard. "Very well. Do you know anything about flower arranging?"

"Of course."

"We have dozens of flowers that need to be arranged. Only, it is too much now..." She trailed off, shaking her head.

"Perhaps there is a hospital where they can be donated?" Aunt Margaret suggested.

"That's a fine idea," Cormac declared. "Mrs. Brennan, if you can pretty them up into a few containers, I'll locate someone to take them to the hospital in Galway."

"And maybe the church?"

The pair exited the room with their heads together, discussing the best places to donate the flowers.

Uncle Gerald approached Lady Aisling with quiet dignity. "What can I do to help?"

The fact that people were offering assistance appeared to be a novel idea to Lady Aisling. Her mouth turned down in thought. "Someone needs to oversee the rental company staff as they break down the equipment in the Ballroom. Make sure they don't scratch up the wood floors, that sort of thing."

"Consider it done." Uncle Gerald straightened his argyle sweater and marched into the hall as if preparing for battle.

Briggs followed Lady Aisling out of the room as her mistress peppered her with directions.

My aunt left an empty seat next to Imogene, whose tears had finally stopped. She'd slumped so far down on the sofa her head was even with her knees, and every few minutes she sniffed. I nudged Julia's leg to catch her eye and nodded in Imogene's way.

Finally, coming to her senses, Julia jumped to her feet and replaced her mother. She patted Imogene's leg. "Come on, sprite. Let's find you something to eat."

Imogene stared at my cousin as if she'd grown a third head.

Julia tried again. "I don't know about you, but I haven't eaten breakfast, and I'm famished." She rose and held out her hand, encouraging, "Why don't you come with me?"

"But...Brian..."

"Brian wouldn't want you to starve yourself." She

dropped her hand. "There is going to be a lot for us to do in the coming days. You'll need your strength to help your mom and dad," my cousin coaxed.

Imogene refused to move. Instead, she shredded a tissue, allowing the pieces to drop onto the couch and floor.

Nonplused, Julia stared at me, her eyes wide, and tilted her head toward the obstinate teenager.

Shane stubbed out his cigarette and sloped over to his sister. "Come." He held out his hand.

Mutinously, Imogene refused to take it, crossing her arms over her chest.

Her brother said something harsh in Gaelic, grabbed her hand, and forcibly pulled the intractable teenager to her feet.

"Nobody in this house cares! Brian was family! You're all behaving as if he were one of the livestock!" she yelled, stomping from the room.

Shane watched her leave with an annoyed twist of his lips.

"Maybe I should go after her?" Julia suggested. Although the way she said it, I could tell she had no interest in tangling further with the upset girl.

"Leave it," Shane advised. "Imogene is notorious for her temper. It's the ginger hair."

Julia chewed her lip in doubt.

"If you wish to impress my mother, I suggest you find your way to the kitchen and be useful to her," he recommended to Julia before exiting the room.

Julia glanced at me.

"It couldn't hurt," I encouraged.

Taking our advice, Julia followed Shane.

They left behind a vacuum of silence. Even the little mantel clock had stopped ticking, because someone had forgotten to wind it. I took another slice of brown bread and poured the dregs of the coffee into my cup.

I purposefully didn't ask for a job. I had my own plans.

Chapter Ten
Margaret Brennan

"That's the last of it. Did you find someone to take these into town?" Margaret arranged the last yellow rose into the largest vase.

Six flower arrangements lined the well-worn wooden table. Since the kitchen was filled with people from the catering company breaking down what they'd brought for the canceled party, Briggs had the florist bring the materials into the staff dining room. With its brick floors, low ceilings, and dingy cream walls, the space conveyed a stark contrast to the elegance of the rooms upstairs.

Cormac picked up one of the heavy bouquets in his arms. "Yes, one of the crofters offered to take them to Galway for me. I've arranged for two of them to go to the church in Brian's name. He'll drop off the rest at the local hospital. They look smashing. Thank you for taking the time to arrange them, Mrs. Brennan. I appreciate your help in our family's time of need."

"I wouldn't have it any other way," Margaret said distractedly. Out of the corner of her eye, she saw Ariadne slip past the doorway and disappear. "I believe I'll go see if I can do anything to help arrange lunch."

Margaret moved quickly into the corridor to see Ariadne surreptitiously slip through a door to the left of the butler's pantry. If she remembered correctly, that was the door that Mrs. Briggs referred to as belonging to Brian Byrne's office.

What would Ariadne be doing down here in Brian's office?

She followed her niece, bypassing the busy kitchen where Lady Aisling barked directions at the hired staff like a drill sergeant during basic training. The half dozen workers moved in and out of the back door with glassware and China that was no longer needed for tonight. A girl wearing the catering company's black uniform carried a box toward the door. Oblivious of the worker, Aisling walked into her path. Trying to dodge her, the girl bumped into the corner of the counter and cried out as a box filled with glassware crashed to the floor.

"You little fool! We are *not* paying for that," Aisling snapped.

While everyone's attention was focused on the poor girl and broken stemware, Margaret slipped through the door to Brian's office.

Ariadne stood in front of a hefty, inlaid, walnut escritoire. Three drawers had been pulled out, exposing a secret compartment in the back. In her hand, she held a sheaf of papers.

"Ariadne," she whispered, "what are you doing?"

Her niece jumped with a tiny squeak and spun around on her heel. She put a hand to her chest and gasped, "Auntie Maggie, you scared the daylights out of me."

Margaret's brow rose. Ariadne stopped calling her Auntie Maggie at the age of thirteen, when she declared the rhyming name too childish and switched to calling her Aunt Maggie.

"What in the world are you doing? This is a private office," Margaret chided.

When Ariadne didn't answer, Margaret tried again. "Ariadne, tell me at once what you have found."

Sighing, Ariadne confessed, "I'm not sure." She laid the papers across the desktop. "It looks to me like sketches of the manor lands. They've been subdivided. Here, here, and here." She pointed as she explained.

"I don't know what these little boxes represent. There doesn't seem to be a key." Her head tilted this way and that, and she squinted. "Maybe...tenant houses? And over on these bigger sections are larger boxes. Stables?"

"So what?"

"I can't figure out why Brian would have hidden something like this in a secret compartment. Wouldn't he want to show this to Cormac and Lord O'Connell? Unless . . ." Ariadne held one of the papers up to the light. "What if Brian was moving forward on a plan without the O'Connell's permission? Or against their wishes?" she mulled to herself.

"I hardly think Mr. Byrne could subdivide the land without Callum's approval. Besides, that is *none* of our business, Ariadne," Margaret said, taking her niece to task. "Put the papers back. After Inspector Quinn's investigation is complete, the family will clean out his effects, take inventory of the ledgers, and-and paperwork."

"Aunt Margaret," Ariadne confided, "I'm...I'm not sure Brian's fall was an accident."

Margaret gaped. "Why would you say that?"

She allowed the little map to float onto the table. "Last night, I found Brian and Shane arguing over money. The caretaker told Shane in no uncertain terms, 'I will not be able to cover up the money you took this time.' He threatened to tell Lord O'Connell what Shane had done. And Shane did not take kindly to the threat."

"You think Shane's stolen money from Brian?"

Ariadne's head rotated back and forth. "Not Brian. The estate. Julia told me that Shane refuses to take money from his father. I believe he stole it from estate funds instead."

Margaret pinched her lips together. "Why didn't you

mention this to Inspector Quinn?"

"Why didn't Shane?" She glided away from the desk and spun around. "I was simply trying to find evidence of the theft. But I can't seem to find the ledgers. Which I would have expected to be in one of these larger drawers down here." She indicated the file drawers at the bottom of the desk. "They seem to be missing."

"Perhaps Lord O'Connell or Cormac has taken them."

"And why would Brian hide *these* papers if they were a new idea to make more money for the estate?" Ariadne shook the papers at her aunt.

Margaret needed to shut this down. "I haven't the foggiest clue, but I think you're jumping to conclusions." Her niece was poking her nose into other people's business. Utterly inappropriate as far as Margaret was concerned.

Ariadne reached her finger into the pigeonhole cubbies and pulled one loose, finding another hidden compartment in the escritoire.

"Ariadne, I really must insist—" Margaret cut off her admonition as Ariadne pulled forth a brown leather-bound journal. The front flap was soft and darkened from regular use.

Voices in the corridor penetrated the heavy door. Margaret's heart dropped to her feet. She couldn't believe she was about to get caught rustling around in the estate manager's office. Ariadne quickly scooped up the paper maps of the subdivided estate, shoving them into the journal. Then she replaced the wooden cubbies, closing the hidden compartments. However, Margaret realized she still held onto the journal.

"Ariadne!" She hissed, pointing at the pilfered diary.

"Follow my lead," her niece whispered.

To Margaret's horror, Ariadne jammed the item into the back of her pants and pulled her coat over it. Then, her niece scurried over to the door. Before she could open it, however, the voices receded as the speakers turned away from the office.

Both women released a sigh of relief, and Ariadne sagged against the doorframe.

"Put that journal and those pages back before someone notices they are missing," Margaret hissed.

"No one is going to notice they are missing. The owner of the journal is deceased. The front is embossed with Brian's name." Ariadne held it up for her aunt to see the flaked gold inlay.

"Then you should turn it over to Inspector Quinn," Margaret insisted in hushed but firm tones.

"I have every intention of doing so...when he arrives at lunch. In the meantime, I'd like to see what Brian was hiding." Ariadne flipped through the pages, her eyes scanning the slanted script. "This looks like it goes with the other charts. He's talking about subdividing the land for additional sheep grazing. There are numbers here that show the profits it will generate in the next five to ten years. Again, I don't understand why he would be hiding this."

A cabinet door in the butler's pantry slammed shut, startling both women.

Her niece came to her senses. "We'd best get out of here before we get caught." She smiled cheekily as if it hadn't almost happened moments ago. Ariadne peered out the door. "The coast is clear, come on."

Margaret slipped out of the room behind Ariadne and quickly scurried away from Brian's office. They ran into Cormac carrying the last of the flower arrangements out of the staff dining hall.

"Cormac." Ariadne waved her hand. "Yoohoo."

He paused his steps to greet the two ladies. "Hullo. Almost finished with these flowers."

"I was just telling Aunt Margaret, Brian mentioned

something interesting to me last night...while we played pool. I was debating the importance of the conversation and if I should relay it to Inspector Quinn."

"Oh?" Cormac's features turned wary, and the flower arrangement settled a few inches lower in his grip.

"He mentioned subdividing the land for sheep grazing. And adding housing, to bring in more money for the estate?"

Cormac made a face. "He really shouldn't have been discussing estate business with a guest."

Not to be deterred, Ariadne pushed for an answer. "Had you heard about his ideas?"

Cormac sighed and shifted the vase's weight to his right side. "Yes, he made suggestions about increasing grazing and forestry rights. I agreed with them. It would have brought in more money. Unfortunately, my father is stubborn. He refuses to subdivide the lands for additional grazing rights and doesn't want the trees cut. While Brian's ideas were good, I've provided my own suggestions on how to make more money. My ideas would also yield a higher rate of return without subdividing land for additional tenants."

Ariadne clasped her hands behind her back.

Interested now, Margaret picked up the carrot Cormac dangled. "Oh? And what would that be?"

"I recommended starting a stud farm for racehorses. I have some connections and could acquire some fine brood mares rather quickly," he said with pride. Then, realizing he was speaking to ladies, color bloomed in his cheeks. He coughed. "Also, if we increased the stables, we could retain more horses for sale, and I could take twice as many to the markets."

All this talk about money for the estate was beginning to worry Margaret. "Cormac, is the estate struggling?" she asked outright.

Cormac hesitated. His chattiness seemed to have

dried up, and he shifted uncomfortably.

"I think my aunt deserves the right to know if her daughter is stepping onto a sinking ship. Is Ballyford on the edge of ruin?" Ariadne pressed.

His lips twisted, and he let out a chuckle that held little merriment. "Don't be silly. There is a mortgage payment due at the end of the quarter. Recently, unexpected repairs have been making things tight. That's all," he said with assurance.

A calculating look crossed Ariadne's features. Margaret knew what that look meant and waited patiently for her niece to respond to Cormac's assertion, because she, too, was unsure if she believed the young man.

"That's not what Mr. Byrne indicated last night," Ariadne stated.

Margaret rolled her lips inward, believing Ariadne's statement to be an utter falsehood.

Cormac was quick to follow up, "My father believes we just need to work harder, doing the same old thing. He doesn't understand that the world has changed since the war. New innovations would benefit Ballyford. Brian and I were in the process of creating proposals. We simply need to convince my father that this is what Ballyford needs right now. As I said, Brian shouldn't have been talking to you about the estate."

"Oh dear, I didn't realize the estate was in trouble." In concerned tones, Margaret asked, "Does Julia know about this?"

Ariadne was correct. Margaret didn't want her only daughter to enter a marriage, only to find herself homeless within the first year.

Cormac seemed to remember with whom he spoke and consciously brightened his features, replying jovially, "I wouldn't say we are in trouble. We will be able to make the payment. You and Julia needn't worry your beautiful heads over something insignificant. The O'Connells have been living on the Ballyford property for hundreds of years, making it through upturns and downturns in the economy. This is no different. We'll come through it. We always do."

Margaret responded with a "humph."

Once again, Cormac shifted the weight of the heavy bouquet. "Promise you won't say anything to Julia. Worrying over this matter would be unwarranted. We'll soon come around."

Margaret didn't like hiding something so significant from her only daughter. However, if the estate *was* in financial straits, there was no way the O'Connells would be able to host a lavish wedding. Which would provide Margaret with the justification she needed to insist that the wedding take place at home in DC. All she had to do was wait for an opening the next time wedding plans were discussed.

"I won't tell her," Margaret warned. "But it isn't fair to leave her in the dark. The best marriages begin with the two Ts. Truth and trust. Your mate should share your burdens. You will find your marriage much stronger if you take my advice." Lecture complete, she swiped her hands together as if dusting off the lie of omission.

Chapter Eleven
Ariadne

Tilting forward, Cormac imparted in confidential tones, "I didn't want to say anything, because it's a bit morbid. But, until we hire a new estate manager, Brian's salary will clear a chunk of the payment."

I nodded. "Mm, yes, I can see how you wouldn't want that thinking to get around."

"Father would have my head if I said something so crass in his presence. Mother, too. Everything will sort itself out. You'll see." He winked. "I've got to get these flowers to Mr. Gallagher."

"Yes, you mustn't keep Mr. Gallagher waiting," Aunt Margaret affirmed.

I delivered a short finger wave, sending Cormac on his way. When he was out of earshot, I murmured, "Did Cormac just provide a motive for murdering Brian?"

Her aunt sucked in a shocked breath. "Ariadne, how could you think such a thing!"

"How can I not? A man is dead. A man who has lived here his entire life. A man who knows this estate, including that castle, forward and backward." I pointed in the general direction of the castle.

"It was an accident," Aunt Maggie insisted. "People slip and fall all the time. He'd been drinking. And that castle looks as though it could come down at any minute. A catastrophe waiting to happen."

"And I can tell you, as one of the last people to see Brian Byrne alive, he couldn't have been more sober. I'm wracking my brain—" I tapped my temple "—trying to determine why he was out there in the middle of the night."

"Those village children...horsing around..." her aunt supplied.

"Maybe."

"Listen, my dear, your mother told me about the murder you witnessed a few months ago." She placed a comforting hand on my shoulder.

I turned with dread. "What did she tell you?"

"Simply, that you discovered the body. It must have been quite upsetting for you." A frown marred my aunt's motherly features.

I gave a noncommittal shrug. "Mm, something like that."

"I'm terribly distressed that it has happened again. But I can assure you, this is not like that other murder. It was an accident."

My aunt placed a consoling hand on my shoulder, but I shrugged it off. "How can you assure me, Aunt Maggie? Were you there?" I said with a bit too much vehemence.

Shocked by the accusation, Aunt Margaret gasped, slapping that same hand to her chest. "What an impertinence from you, missy. You know very well I wasn't," she chastised.

But I couldn't stop the words that tumbled out of my mouth. "Neither was I. Therefore, we can't rule out foul play."

Perhaps it was due to the dead man I'd found at the Ivy Tree Inn, but since finding Brian, my brain had been whirling. Puzzling over the reasons a man like Brian Byrne would have gone to the castle in the middle of the night.

Was it the teens? Or was Mr. Byrne meeting someone, perhaps a lover? Was it an accident, or was it something more sinister? Did someone lure him to the castle?

Aunt Maggie scrutinized me. "You are out of your depth, Ariadne. This is not the United States, and you are not a local detective. I suggest you keep your opinions to yourself and leave the investigation to the professionals." With that, my aunt marched up the stairs.

The discomfort of walking with a book jammed down the back of my pants reminded me that I still carried Brian's papers. I determined it would behoove me to divest the ill-gotten journal.

Chapter Twelve
Ariadne

I burst through the door to my suite, startling the maid. "Oh! I didn't realize anyone was here."

Releasing the pillow, she clutched it to her chest upon my abrupt entrance, giving a soft giggle. "You frightened me, miss. You're the American fashion model, yes?"

"Not a model. A writer. I write articles for a fashion magazine," I clarified with some regret. Though I'd moved off the copy desk, into a full-time writer position for *Ladies' Lifestyle Magazine*—due to my now famous exclusive on Donna Morgan, Princess of Maldinia—the elusive investigative reporter role I craved, remained out of reach from my grasping fingers. I foolishly assumed, after the *New York Journal* printed my article about the murder at Ivy Tree Inn, that it would be smooth sailing into an investigative reporter role. However, one in-person meeting with the editor quashed that vision.

Even with Gavin backing me up, his friend Budgie refused to put me on the payroll.

"I can't put a dame in the bullpen. My publisher would never go for it," he'd said. "Freelance work. That's the best I can do. I'll pay you the going rate for more pieces like this." Budgie had stood up, throwing down a handful of bills on the table, and began striding away, before turning back to us. "Oh, using your initials was a good idea. Keep using them. Makes it more respectable."

The maid's voice brought me back to the present. "You're pretty enough to be a model."

I shook off the memory and gave the girl a wan smile. "That's kind of you to say. How much longer will you be?"

"About ten minutes. I can leave now and come back later if you like." The girl tugged the coverlet until it was straight and tidy.

"No, you can finish up. I'll wait in the hallway."

She giggled again. "No need to wait in the hall. You can sit on the sofa by the fire. I'll work around you."

I took her advice, picked up a book about horticulture that some former guest had left behind, and settled in to wait. Brian's ledger uncomfortably jabbed my backside. I would have been better off in the corridor.

The maid's name was Daisy, and for the next half an hour, I learned about her entire family—her three rambunctious younger brothers, two older sisters, her mother who took in washing, and her father who worked at a textile mill. She was pretty enough. Her dirty blonde hair was braided in a milkmaid updo, and she had striking hydrangea blue eyes, but the sack-like brown dress and apron she wore did nothing for her figure or coloring. Either she hadn't been told about Brian's death, or she'd been warned *not* to speak to the guests about it.

Finally, she left.

I turned in circles in the Valentina chamber. The room, like the rest of the manor, was beautifully appointed—gold silk covered the walls while the cream and royal blue bedding matched the curtains. Like Brian's office, the Valentina room had a desk. Unlike Brian's office, it was a small woman's desk, petite with no secret compartments. Simply sticking the journal under the mattress or a chair cushion seemed too easy for someone to stumble across. I decided to tuck it into an inside pocket in my suitcase, which I shoved to the back of the armoire.

Hearing a knock, I quickly closed the armoire. "Who

is it?"

"Imogene," came her muffled voice.

The door swung inward at my touch. "Hello, are you feeling any better?"

"I'm fine," she mulishly replied. Her puffy, red-rimmed eyes and pink chafed nose told another story. "Cormac told me to tell you that lunch will be served at noon in the Morning Room. Although I don't know how anyone will be able to eat," the girl mumbled the last.

When I didn't respond, she added, "I'm supposed to take you to it."

My diamond-studded Elgin watch read ten to noon. "Thank you. I know where the Morning Room is. You needn't wait. I will be down directly."

Without another word, Imogene flounced away.

The chamber was decorated in Wedgwood blue and cream colors—a less formal room than the Dining Room. The oval table had been extended and was set for nine guests. To complement the six matching chairs, three mismatched ones had been added. Opposite the table was a walnut buffet with meats, cheeses, breads, and other sundry lunch items laid upon it.

To no one's surprise, lunch was a subdued affair. Lady Aisling and Lord O'Connell had not yet joined the table. When I arrived, the room consisted solely of young people—Julia, Cormac, Imogene, and Shane. Imogene was just sitting down. The rest were already seated, eating their meals.

"Father asked me to take the inspector into the castle this afternoon," Cormac commented. "Shane, since you discovered the body, perhaps you should come as well."

"Fine." Shane nodded, biting into a sandwich with a thick slice of ham sticking out the backside.

"How is your father doing?" I asked, scooping a helping of lentil salad onto my plate, placing it next to a slice of ham.

"He's taking Brian's death hard." Cormac's brows furrowed. "He and Father Michael spent forty minutes on the phone consoling Brian's family. The bill will be astronomical."

"Did Brian have children?" asked Julia.

"No. He has a sister who lives in Kildare. And a younger brother who lives in Dublin. He runs a shoe factory." Shane wiped a blob of mustard off his pinky with his napkin.

I took a seat between Shane and Imogene. "No children then?"

Imogene poked at a lentil with her fork. "Brian never married."

"Father always said it was because he was married to the estate," Shane explained with a sad sigh.

"Lemonade?" Julia held up a cut crystal pitcher.

"Yes, thank you. What about nieces and nephews?" I gently prodded.

"Three nieces and two nephews." Cormac held his glass out, and Julia refilled it before sitting down again. "He usually spent the holidays in Kildare, where the family would gather at his sister's."

"I suppose father discussed funeral arrangements with Brian's brother?" Shane popped the last bit of the sandwich into his mouth.

"I understand his brother would like him to be buried closer to Dublin." Cormac took a gulp of lemonade. "However, father said Brian's will specifies his remains be buried on the estate next to his parents."

"Wonder if his brother or sister will insist he be buried nearer to them?" Shane mused, pushing his plate away and lighting a cigarette.

Imogene dropped her fork. "I can't eat with everyone discussing poor Brian," she bawled and jumped to her feet. The chair tumbled to the ground with a crash, and the teenager fled the room.

"Oh, sweetheart, don't go!" Julia rose.

"Leave her be." Cormac wrapped his hand around Julia's wrist.

While Julia waffled, unsure if she should pursue the teenager, I righted the chair she had knocked down.

"Imogene is known for her dramatic exits." Shane puffed on his cigarette.

Julia retook her seat. "She seems quite cut up over Brian's death."

Cormac released his fiancée. "Like I said, Brian grew up here. Except for his time at uni, he's never lived anywhere else. In essence, Ballyford is home. Growing up, he was like an uncle to the three of us."

I found Cormac's choice of words interesting: "growing up." Now that he and Shane were grown men, did they no longer view Brian in such a role?

"Considering Imogene is still 'growing up,' perhaps she feels his death more deeply," I reckoned. When no one responded, I probed further, "Did Brian have rooms in the manor house?"

"Not in the house." Cormac explained, "He has...had a small cottage beyond the stables."

"It's going to be strange having someone else live in that cottage." Shane tapped ash onto his empty plate.

"Who is going to live in what cottage?" Lord O'Connell walked into the room and began serving himself from the buffet.

"The future estate manager," Shane clarified.

Lord O'Connell stopped what he was doing and turned his eye on his middle child and asked in steely tones, "The man isn't even in the ground yet, and you're giving away his home to some stranger?"

Shane blanched and stuttered, "Well, I-I, just meant. . ."

"Meant what?" Lord O'Connell continued to stare.

Shane's eyes narrowed in angry embarrassment. He crushed out the cigarette and refused to speak further. A tense silence settled over the room.

I had the uncomfortable feeling that Shane had grown up facing embarrassing situations such as this, which put him at a disadvantage compared to the rest of the family.

Cormac tried to smooth over the awkward moment. "No one is putting a stranger in there. We are simply discussing how it will be wretched not having Brian living in the cottage. Goodness, I can't remember when he didn't live in that place."

Mollified, Lord O'Connell returned to picking at the buffet. "Brian was born in that cottage. He lived with his parents there until his father passed, and his mother moved in with his sister."

"I imagine the family will take Brian's personal effects when they come for the funeral," Cormac commented.

"I imagine so." Lord O'Connell gave a mournful sigh and wiped his damp forehead with a handkerchief.

"It would make it easier for us if we didn't have to do it for the future caretaker." When his father glared at him, Cormac hurried to clarify, "Not now. Down the road, of course."

Lord O'Connell took Imogene's seat, his plate only half full with a bit of corned beef, a slice of cheese, and three small pickles. "*If* we get a new estate manager, I doubt he will live in Brian's cottage."

"What do you mean, *if?*" Cormac held a full fork halfway to his mouth. "Who will take care of the day-to-day operations?" When Lord O'Connell didn't immediately answer, Cormac continued, "Father, eventually we will *need* an estate manager."

The master of the house bit into his beef, taking a moment to chew and swallow before responding. "Shane has taken his hand at running a successful set of stables for eighteen months, up there in Connemara."

Shane's eyes grew wide, and his jaw dropped.

"Just because you're not living in this house, don't think I haven't been keeping tabs on you, Son." Lord O'Connell wiped his mouth with a napkin. "When I spoke to Liam, he told me he was going to miss having you. Couldn't figure out why you chose to bugger off when you did. I told him you stayed in that position longer than any other."

"What does that have to do with a new manager for Ballyford?" Cormac questioned.

"Perhaps Shane can be the new estate manager."

Cormac let out a guffaw, and Shane's shock turned to anger. "A fine sight, I'd do better than you, big brother."

"Are you taking the piss out of me? You couldn't last a year," Cormac derided. "I give it six months before you bounce out of here with your tail between your legs!"

Shane slammed his fist on the table, and our plates jumped. "We wouldn't be worried about money if I'd been in charge for the past two years."

"Why you—"

"*Boys!* Where are your manners? There are ladies present," Lord O'Connell snapped, nipping the argument in the bud.

Both men sat back silently, fuming.

Shane mutinously crossed his arms. "I won't have time to run things around here for you. I've got a new job."

Lord O'Connell looked on in surprise. "Oh?"

"My photography, of course."

Cormac snorted. "Who has hired you?"

"I'll have you know, before this-this incident with Brian, I planned to speak with our American friend here—" he indicated to me "—about opportunities at her

95

magazine."

My fork dropped onto my plate with a clatter at Shane's announcement.

"Ariadne, *could* you find a job for Shane?" Julia inquired.

"Er..." I'd come to realize Shane was a bit of a punching bag between his brother and father. Perhaps the treatment was deserved. Perhaps not. Either way, I had no interest in becoming involved in that part of the family drama. The magazine didn't hire photographers with zero experience, but I didn't want to embarrass Shane any more than his brother and father had already done.

I infused my response with enthusiasm, "I can certainly ask when I return home."

"Have you ever been to New York, Shane?" Julia asked.

He smiled and lit another cigarette. "Once."

"Son, while I appreciate your new interest, photography won't put food on the table. Meanwhile, you keep talking about the stable you're going to build when you receive your inheritance. Why not spend a few years getting some experience under your belt managing the estate," encouraged Lord O'Connell. "You'll oversee the grazing, farming, rentals, and work with your brother on the horse sales. Everything you'll need to know for setting up your own household and stables."

Shane remained skeptical, however, a glimmer of interest passed over his features.

"Whose household are you talking about?" Lady Aisling glided into the room.

"Father was suggesting we hire Shane to take Brian's place," Cormac said with derision in his voice.

"Until I set up my own house," Shane clarified.

Lady Aisling began shaking her head. "I don't believe that's a good—"

She didn't get to finish.

Briggs walked in and announced, "Inspector Quinn is here to see you."

Chapter Thirteen
Lord Callum O'Connell

Wearily, Callum pushed to his feet to invite the inspector to join them, but his wife beat him to the punch.

"Inspector Quinn! We are just having luncheon. Make yourself a plate. Join us." She picked up a dish from the breakfront and held it out.

"Thank you, Lady O'Connell, but I must refuse." Quinn gave a minute bow.

"Surely, you can take a moment to eat," Callum encouraged, gratefully returning to a sitting position. While the medication helped with the nausea, it only put a minor dent in the extreme fatigue. Every day it felt as if Callum was dragging himself through a bog. Every night he tumbled into his empty bed exhausted, feeling both guilty and relieved Aisling had taken to spending nights in her own room following the diagnosis.

Quinn remained firm. "I'm afraid I have some disturbing news regarding Mr. Byrne's death."

The china plate clattered on the buffet.

"I had your stable man, Dougray, take me into the castle," he explained.

Aisling angrily cried, "He had no right to do such a thing!"

Aisling's outburst, so out of character for her, caused the room to turn in her direction. Her face reddened, and a loose curl stuck to her temple.

Callum frowned in concern at his wife. "Darling? Are you quite yourself?"

Pushing the loose hair aside, she collected herself and continued in calmer tones, "What I mean to say, er, it was our understanding you would be visiting the tower after the lunch hour. With my husband or-or a family member."

"That was the original plan. Yes." The inspector scratched his nose. "However, after the coroner removed Mr. Byrne's body, I changed my mind. It was important to see where Mr. Byrne fell from."

"Did you find anything of interest, Inspector?" Julia asked.

"As a matter of fact, I did." From his pocket, he withdrew a small piece of gold chain with links broken at either end. He laid it on the table at Shane's elbow. "Does anyone recognize this?"

The boy recoiled as if it would bite. His wife turned pale. But it was Miss Winter's gasp that captured Quinn's attention.

One bushy brow rose as Quinn eyed the dark-haired girl. "You, Miss Winter?"

"I can't be sure," she hesitated, "but it looks like the chain to Mr. Byrne's missing pocket watch."

The other brow rose to meet the first. "You say it's missing?"

"Well, I didn't see it on...um, the body, when we discovered it. I even remarked upon it. Didn't I, Shane?"

"What?" Shane glanced up from studying the golden chain. "Oh, yes, the pocket watch. Miss Winter is correct. I don't recall seeing it on Brian. But then again, I didn't remember him wearing it last night."

"I do." Julia raised her hand like a schoolgirl. "I remember remarking what a pretty piece I thought it was, during dinner."

"Yes, of course," Callum agreed. "Brian usually wore it for formal evening meals. It belonged to his father. I'm sure he had it on last night. Does this mean those rapscallions *were* in the tower last night?"

"No," the inspector stated.

"Oh? You seem quite sure of yourself. How do you know?" Lady Aisling turned her back on the room and began filling her plate with meats and cheeses.

"I have ascertained, three of the four youngsters are at a tournament in Dublin this weekend, and the fourth worked down at McGarrity's Pub until two in the morning. Making it impossible for them to have been on the property last night."

Confused and frustrated, Callum slammed his glass on the table. "I don't understand. Why was Brian in the tower last night? He knows how dangerous it can be. The stairs become especially slippery when wet, and it rained last night. It's the reason he ran off those teenagers a few weeks ago."

Quinn remained calm in the face of Callum's frustration. "That is what I am trying to work out."

"Did you find any other clues?" Miss Winter asked. "Fingerprints?"

Inspector Quinn thoughtfully studied the young lady. "I have a man working on that now. Unfortunately, with the rain, it's doubtful we'll find any from where he fell."

Cormac's head popped up from his dish. "You've determined where he was when he fell?"

"I believe so. There were scuff marks in mud, and the moss was torn to bits. Exhibiting signs of a struggle atop the archer's platform."

To Callum's surprise, Miss Winter formulated a rather morbid question, "How easy would it be for someone to throw Mr. Byrne over?"

Quinn remained unflappable. "He needn't have been thrown. The stones on the ledge are loose, some missing. There's very little to grab hold of. A single push could put a grown man off his balance," Quinn gravely explained.

Julia gasped, putting a hand to her throat. "What man would *do* such a thing?"

"From what Inspector Quinn said, the killer didn't necessarily have to be male. A woman could give a shove as easily as a man," Miss Winter commented in an offhand manner, then taking a sip of lemonade.

Callum's stomach turned to knots, and his fists clenched. He glanced around the table at his family members, then shook his head. *No. It was an accident. Nothing more.*

Aisling took the empty seat next to Cormac. Her face pale and taught, she verbalized Callum's thoughts, "What utter nonsense. You think someone threw Brian off the ramparts? And now you're interrogating us? The family? Really, Inspector Quinn! Someone spoke rather harshly to me earlier today about throwing accusations around. It's almost criminal," she sputtered in disgust. "Why would any of us want to hurt our estate manager? He's practically a member of this family."

"I made no such accusation, Lady Aisling," the inspector demurred.

"Darling, Inspector Quinn is not accusing anyone. He is simply doing his job to investigate Brian's death," Callum assured her. Although he wasn't certain if his comments were made to assure his wife or himself. "You don't believe Brian was murdered, do you, Inspector Quinn? It was an accident. Correct?"

"I can't say either way at this point in the investigation."

"Um." Cormac coughed.

Callum turned to his son. "Have you something to say?"

"I didn't want to mention it, because it seemed like spreading rumors. However, a fortnight ago, I witnessed what I can only describe as a...*clandestine* meeting between Brian and a stranger in Galway." He helped himself to a cigarette from his brother's pack.

Callum frowned. "Galway? What were you doing in Galway?"

"It was nothing, just, um, business." Cormac brushed aside his father's question. "As I was saying, when Brian realized I was heading north, he asked for a ride. Said his sister was in Galway visiting a friend." He lit the cigarette and took a drag before continuing. "I dropped him at a house in town and agreed to pick him up at the same place in a few hours. Imagine my surprise when, half an hour later, I found him sitting with a strange man, in the back corner of a café on Eyre Square. I saw the man hand over a manila folder, and Brian passed him—" Cormac uncomfortably shifted in his seat and rubbed the back of his neck, "What looked like an envelope full of money."

His mother's fork clattered on the table. She cleared her throat and mumbled an apology.

While Cormac spoke, the inspector removed his pad and pencil from an inside coat pocket and took down the story. "What did you do then?"

"I left." Cormac shrugged. "Figured he was performing an errand for his sister. None of my business. When I picked him up at the house where I'd dropped him, there was no sign of the manila folder. I didn't mention I'd seen him at the café."

"Did Mr. Byrne display any other strange behavior that day?"

"As a matter of fact—" Cormac pointed at the inspector with his cigarette "—now that I think about it, Brian remained unusually quiet on the ride home from Galway. Seemed to have his mind on other things," he mused. "When I asked about his sister, he didn't have much to say."

"That is strange behavior to be sure. Usually, Brian

is full of stories about his nieces and nephews after a visit with family," Aisling observed.

"She's right. Brian always shares news about his family. Since he was, uh, discovered, I've been wondering more and more about that day at the café, and the man I saw him with. I even wonder if Brian's sister was in Galway at all." Cormac shrugged and tapped ash off his cigarette onto an empty bread and butter plate.

Aisling cast a calculating gaze at Cormac, but he didn't notice—nor did Quinn, who was too absorbed in scribbling on his pad. "Easy enough to find out. Can you describe the man you saw with Mr. Byrne?"

"On the slighter side, slick dark hair, a bit of a pointed nose. Sharpish features with eyes close together."

"Eye color?"

"Didn't get that close." Cormac shrugged. "He wore a driving cap."

"Age?"

Cormac's mouth screwed up in thought. "Mid-thirties? I believe he might have been an American."

Daisy the maid entered, carrying a blue jug. "I've got more lemonade." She glanced at Shane and blushed. Everyone ignored her as she went over to lay the vessel on the buffet table.

"Oh? What makes you think that?" Quinn's brows glided north again. "Did you speak to him?"

"No, he wore one of those jackets in red and cream, with a two-tone design. You know, decorative stitching on the collar and chest pocket flaps like Ricky Ricardo wears. Very American."

"I saw him with a man who matches that description!" Shane exclaimed.

"When and where?" the inspector asked.

"The Green Pub in Doolin." Shane's mouth twisted in thought. "Two...no, three nights ago. He gave the man an envelope that night too."

Quinn finished his scribbles. "Right, then. I'm headed out. I've stationed Gardai at the castle. No one goes in or out without my authority. Understood?"

Callum cut across his wife's objection. "Thank you, Inspector Quinn. We'll inform the staff that the castle is off limits. Daisy, please see the inspector to the door."

Once the pair was out of earshot, Aisling tsked. "Imagine blocking access to our own castle."

"It's not forever, Mother." Shane stubbed out his cigarette. "Only until the investigation is finished. Cormac, I'm interested in learning more about this business you had to attend to in Galway."

"That would be *none* of your business, *brother,*" Cormac snapped.

"Apparently, if it is about the estate, then it *is* my business," Shane replied in dulcet tones.

Cormac's eyes flashed, and his mouth pinched.

Before the boys could get into a proper row, Ariadne stood up and excused herself from the table.

Chapter Fourteen
Ariadne

I hurried down the passages, taking a wrong turn, before righting myself and finding my way to the front door. Throwing it open, I spotted Inspector Quinn as he was about to get into his car.

I hailed him. "Inspector! Inspector Quinn! Wait!"

"Miss Winter?" he said with surprise.

I reached the opposite side of his vehicle and panted, "Inspector, there is something I feel I must tell you about the investigation."

"What would that be?" The inspector eyed me in that piercing manner he had.

"About last night. I-I haven't been completely honest."

He shut the car door. "Oh? What about?"

"You remember, I told you, that I played a game of pool with Mr. Byrne?"

"Yes. In the Billiard Room."

"I failed to mention . . ." I fidgeted with an earring. "I came upon an argument between Shane and Mr. Byrne. And I may have...uh, eavesdropped before making myself known to the two men."

His features drew down. "I see. And you heard something that might be relevant to the investigation?"

"Perhaps." I glanced left, right, and over my shoulder to make sure we were alone.

Quinn patiently waited for me to elaborate. Then he, too, checked the area for any staff or family members lurking about. He prompted, "Rest assured, young lady, nobody is about."

I cleared my throat. "I heard Shane and Mr. Byrne arguing about money. A lot of money."

"How much are we talking about?"

"Mr. Byrne said it was over a thousand pounds. And it sounded like this wasn't the first time Shane had taken money from estate coffers."

His mustache wiggled, and the corners of his mouth turned south. "I see. Anything else?"

"Well..." I hesitated, unsure why I was finding it difficult to rat out Shane. "...Shane kind of threatened Mr. Byrne when he told him he saw Brian give some fellow at the pub a bunch of money. Said he would tell his father. It felt as though Shane was insinuating the money was a bribe or something."

The inspector studied me. "You're sure, it was Shane speaking to Brian?"

"Of course. Brian didn't respond, and Shane left the room, and, uh, I ran into him in the corridor."

"Why didn't you tell me this earlier?"

"Well . . ." I hesitated, unsure how to answer. *Why didn't I tell him earlier? Am I afraid of what Shane would do if he knew I overheard their conversation?*

"I believed, like everyone else, that this was simply an accident. Now that you've brought forth evidence that it might be something different, I felt it my duty to inform you of the argument."

Thoughtfully, he nodded. "Thank you for informing me."

I released the breath I'd been holding. An idea occurred to me. "Was Mr. Byrne known for gambling?"

"Not that I'm aware. Why do you ask?"

I shrugged. "Thought maybe the money packets were gambling payments. Don't know if you have loan sharks here in Ireland..."

"Yes, we have such an animal."

"In New York, they are definitely individuals to avoid. If you don't pay them back, they'll break your leg," I confided.

The inspector's brows flew upwards. "How do you know this, Miss Winter? Have you had dealings with such individuals?"

I laughed at the suggestion. "Oh, no. Not me personally. My father once warned me about them when I moved into the city. He's an attorney, you see. Told me if I ever had money problems to come straight to him."

"Ah, a good piece of advice from a father."

It occurred to me; now would be the right time to reveal the journal and other papers. However, if I did so, I'd have to turn them over immediately and admit to how I obtained the items. I wanted to read more before turning it over to the police. It might reveal an important clue.

He tilted his head. "Miss Winter, is there anything *else* you wish to tell me?"

I stared down at Julia's borrowed boots as I made an arc in the dirt with my toe. "Why no. Just the information about Shane's argument."

He sighed. "If you think of anything else, here's my business card. You may phone my office and leave a message."

I retrieved the card, glancing at the black print. "Thank you, Inspector. I feel so much better having told you."

"Good day, Miss Winter." He tipped his hat and went on his way.

I entered the cavernous foyer to find it empty and quickly scurried up the staircase. My objective—to get to my room before anyone spotted me. Especially my aunt, who would want to know if I handed the journal over to the inspector.

Mission complete, I locked the door and retrieved

the journal from its hiding place. Flipping through the pages, I re-read the information about the grazing rights subdivision and the money the caretaker had predicted it would generate in one year. The amount seemed substantial to me. I couldn't understand why Lord O'Connell dismissed Brian's suggestions.

Allowing the pages to sift through my fingers, I randomly stopped near the end, on a page with names, phone numbers, and addresses written in different colored ink and not in alphabetical order. It appeared to be a list of contacts Mr. Byrne had collected over time. I ran my finger down the pages, recognizing no one. At the bottom of the page, I paused on the name Harold Kendall. His phone number and address were in America—Massachusetts, to be precise. No indication from the address as to Mr. Kendall's employment or relationship with Brian Byrne.

A knock at the door had me leaping from my seat.

"Ariadne? Yoohoo, are you in there?"

Jamming the journal beneath a cushion, I called, "Coming."

Julia opened the door before I reached it. "Here you are! We've been wondering where you'd gotten to."

"We?"

"Well, maybe just me." She'd changed into a heavy blue skirt, pink cashmere sweater set, and penny loafers.

"What is everyone doing?"

"Lord O'Connell is handling the funeral arrangements. Lady Aisling went back to the kitchen to make sure the final bits of the party were properly packed away, and Mother is spending time with Imogene. She's in a very delicate state right now," my cousin whispered the latter, as if Imogene might hear.

"I'm surprised Lady Aisling isn't more...upset. Lord O'Connell seems more distressed than she."

"Yes. She's a bit of a cold fish. Cormac assures me

this is how she hides her true feelings, and deep down, she is deeply mourning Brian's passing."

"After all, she was the last person to see Brian alive. Wasn't she?"

Julia's eyes widened and glazed over as she spoke, "I suppose you're right. How awful. I was thinking to myself, if only I had encouraged Brian to play another game of billiards with Cormac, or you, for that matter. Maybe, he'd still be alive." She choked upon the last word, and wiped a tear from her cheek.

"You can't think like that." I put my arm around her shoulder and brought her to sit on the fainting couch. Realizing, at the last moment, that's where I hid the journal. Shifting quickly, I sat on the lumpy cushion. "You sent him to have a cigar with the men, as you had been directed to do. Nothing *you* did led to his death."

She sniffed.

I handed her a handkerchief. "Now dry your eyes and tell me what I can do to help you and the family."

"I can think of nothing." Her shoulders lifted, and she glanced aside. "To be honest, I came for the company. Lady Aisling released me and told me to go and rest. I'm too wound up to relax, and I don't know where Cormac's gotten to."

I need to get Julia out of my room, away from the journal. But how?

"Um...why don't we...go for a walk? I could use a bit of fresh air...to clear my head."

"If you think so?" Julia picked at a loose string on her cuff.

"Absolutely. Let me change out of this riding gear. I'll meet you in the front hall in five minutes."

"Okay." She sighed, heaved herself off the chaise, and shuffled out of my room.

Chapter Fifteen
Julia

Julia directed her footsteps toward the stables, which she smelled long before coming upon them. Ariadne had paired slim black pants that ended at her ankles with a forest green angora sweater. She'd chosen to wear the black pea coat from earlier, and a pair of Keds, which would be good for walking.

As the two approached the arched opening of the big barn, a gentleman with sandy hair liberally sprinkled with salt, wearing britches and a gray knit sweater that had seen better days, stepped into the sunshine. His features were cracked with weather-worn wrinkles, and tanned brown as a beetle. His expression spoke of anguish.

"Hello, Dougray!" Julia hailed him.

Deep-set chocolate brown eyes brightened upon seeing the girls, and he quickly hid his pain as they approached. "It must be my lucky day. What are you two lassies doing my way?"

"Getting fresh air," she replied.

"Plenty of folks coming and going from the house today." Dougray took off his cap and scratched his head. "Why, I saw Cormac, not a few moments ago, come along this same path."

"I thought we'd stop and say hello to Marshmallow and Coconut. Are they in their stalls?"

He shook his head. "It's turned into such a magnificent day, I've sent them out to pasture. You're welcome to head back there." He indicated the fields behind the stable.

"Were you able to replace Peanut's shoe?" Ariadne asked.

Dougray's face clouded with confusion. "I don't know what you mean, miss."

"Oh, I thought Imogene said that her horse, Peanut, threw a shoe yesterday."

He scratched his head. "Not that I'm aware. Seemed fine to me."

Ariadne frowned. "Never mind. I must be confused. Come on, Julia, let's go see the horses."

As soon as the ladies approached the fence rails, the two cream Connemara ponies galloped over to them. Julia dug into her coat pocket and found a few carrot pieces left over from their morning ride that had been cut short.

Her shoulders sank as she thought of poor Brian. He'd been so kind since her arrival. Occasionally, she could swear he even looked at her with pity in his eyes. As if he realized the difficulties Julia would face marrying into a family with Lady Aisling as the matriarch of it. Julia was just beginning to learn what a harsh taskmaster her future mother-in-law could be. When the party was unceremoniously canceled by Lord O'Connell, Lady Aisling dealt with the staff and hired folks with ruthless efficiency. Barely a word of thanks or appreciation passed her lips. She wasn't sure how Briggs put up with it. Even if Cormac did claim his mother's behavior was simply due to grief over Brian's death.

You could have fooled me.

"Fooled you how?"

Julia stared at her cousin. "What?"

"You just said, 'You could have fooled me.'" Ariadne fed the last bit of carrot to Coconut and pulled out a handkerchief to wipe her hands.

"Did I say it out loud? It's nothing, I was simply daydreaming."

"Is that Mr. Byrne's cottage? The one the boys were talking about at lunchtime?" Ariadne gestured toward a whitewashed stone house in the distance, its thatched roof complementing the black-framed windows and a vibrant blue front door, with a stone pathway leading up to it. The house was situated in a dell between the stables and the castle.

Julia shielded her eyes. "I suppose it is."

"I wonder who will be charged with cleaning it out?" Ariadne commented.

"Maybe Cormac, or one of his siblings." Julia's attention returned to the horse nudging her shoulder. "I'm sorry, Marshmallow, I don't have any more carrots. I'm all out." She patted the horse's muzzle.

"Shall we wander over that way?" Her cousin didn't wait for Julia's answer, she simply began walking in the direction of the cottage.

Their minds on other things, the two ladies strolled silently shoulder to shoulder deep in their own thoughts. Arriving at the stone pathway, Julia realized the cottage door was ajar.

"Perhaps somebody is already here cleaning out his belongings," suggested Ariadne.

"I would be surprised if that were the case." A shiver ran up Julia's spine. "Cormac said his family is supposed to arrive tomorrow."

Before she could stay Ariadne's steps, her cousin approached the entry. The door's hinges protested with a creak as she pushed it open. "Hello, is anyone here?"

"I don't know if we should . . ." Julia started.

"Hello? Inspector Quinn, are you in here?" She gently stepped across the threshold onto a rag rug, and Julia couldn't help but follow.

The musty scent of dampness and old furnishings

hung heavily in the air. At first glance, the cottage displayed a distinctive lived-in appearance. A pair of men's shoes had been kicked off and left just inside the front door. The random-width pine floors showed scratches and stains from years of use. A handmade Afghan was thrown across a jacquard print couch that dated to the Victorian era. The cushions on the easy chair in front of the gray stone fireplace had lost their fullness, giving the chair a deflated appearance. The threadbare carpet runner on the stairs leading up to the second floor had worn down so much, the diamond pattern was unrecognizable. Thick dust settled across a shelf of knick-knacks like a gray blanket.

"Has this cottage been around as long as the castle?" asked Ariadne.

"I'm not sure, but it does look very old. A few hundred years I would say." Julia sniffed the air, catching the faintest hint of sandalwood. *Brian must use the same aftershave as Cormac.*

She picked her way over to the fireplace to study a black-and-white photograph of Brian as a child, accompanied by his sister and brother. The three of them were dressed in their Sunday best and stared at the camera with very serious expressions. The photo was one of the few items not covered in dust across the mantel.

Ariadne joined her. "Wow. Look at Mr. Byrne. How old do you think he is in this photo?"

"Maybe eleven or twelve," Julia guessed.

A sound came from the back of the cottage, and the girls froze in place. Julia's heartbeat galloped in her chest.

"Hello, is someone there?" Ariadne called.

Crash!

Both girls started. Julia grabbed her cousin's hand.

"Hello?" Ariadne called again.

Little by little the pair tiptoed towards the back of the cottage where the kitchen was situated. A tortoise shell, striped ball of fur darted past them leaving white footprints in its wake.

Julia let out a yip of alarm before realizing the creature meant no harm.

With its tail raised high, the cat hissed and sprinted out of the house.

For a moment, the room remained silent as the cousins stared after the feline intruder. Then, Ariadne burst into relieved laughter, and Julia joined her mirth.

"Did you know Mr. Byrne had a cat?"

"I didn't." Julia put a hand to her thumping heart. "The barn has a couple of mousers. That might be one of them."

After the cousin's giggling subsided, Julia took a moment to observe the kitchen. Ariadne wrinkled her nose at the faint smell of sour milk. A dried bowl of half-eaten cereal had been left in the sink with an empty coffee mug next to it. Half a dozen clean plates were in the dish drainer. The cat must have opened one of the cabinets. A packet of flour had been knocked to the floor, and little, white powdered, kitty prints scattered all over the kitchen—on the floor, across the counters, even over the black AGA range.

Except for the footprints, the kitchen seemed relatively tidy, everything in its place.

"Do you think we ought to clean this up? I'd hate for Brian's family to find it this way when they arrive."

Ariadne nodded. "I'll help in a moment. I'm going to take a look around the place."

"Ariadne," Julia tutted, "we really shouldn't pry."

Her cousin drifted out of the kitchen. "I'll only be a moment."

"You're too curious for your own good!" Julia chided.

A ghost of laughter floated back to her.

Chapter Sixteen
Ariadne

It didn't take me long to pick my way through the cottage. The bungalow had two bedrooms upstairs, a bedroom on the main level, and one bathroom. As I made my way back to the kitchen where Julia was cleaning up after the cat, I noticed a small door beneath the stairs. I figured it was a coat closet. Imagine my surprise when I found a staircase leading down.

"Julia, come look at this."

My hand fumbled around the wall until it found a light switch. A lone bulb hung from an extension cord that was strung up in the center of the stairwell.

"You're not going down there. Are you?"

"Sure. Why not?"

"I don't know. It's probably full of spiders."

"If I come running back up the stairs screaming, you'll know you were right."

The stairs led down to a damp cellar with a brick floor compacted down onto the earth. I found another lone light bulb and pulled the chain. Rows of wooden shelves, half empty, lined the walls of the room. One shelf was full of mason jars. I held one up to the light and determined it had some sort of berry jam. Others were filled with tomatoes and vegetables. A floor-to-ceiling wine rack held half a dozen bottles, leaving a good portion bare. Some of the bottles were dusty, but none of them heralded decades of dust, like a forty-year-old vintage.

I wiped the dirt off my hands with a handkerchief. There was very little to see in this dungeon of a cellar, and

I began to regret my decision to come down. While no large spiders had jumped out at me, plenty of the empty shelves were covered in cobwebs, and I had no interest in acquiring a furry eight-legged critter in my hair.

Turning back to the stairs, my foot tapped something hard. It rolled across the floor, landing against one of the shelves. Bending down, I retrieved a dull red apple.

"Now, where did you come from?" I murmured.

"Ariadne? What did you find?"

"Not much. Bunch of shelves filled with canning jars." My gaze swept in a circle, landing on a crate of apples at the base of one of the racks. I bent to place it inside. A draft displaced one of my curls and tickled my cheek. Pushing it aside, I investigated further. The shelf was pulled a few inches from the wall, and I felt a slight breeze. Squinting at the floor, I observed a deep groove in an arc shape along the brick pavers.

"Julia? Are you still up there?" I called.

"Yes. What's wrong?"

"Nothing. Can you find a flashlight?"

"I saw one earlier...now where was it? Hold on."

While Julia searched for a flashlight, I tugged at the rack, mildly surprised as it effortlessly swung into the cellar. The caster made a grinding noise, and the shelf halted halfway.

"Found it!" Julia called from the top of the stairs.

"Bring it down, please."

"Um, are you sure you can't come and get it?"

I sighed at my cousin's fear of spiders. "You're not going to want to miss this!" I infused the sentence with as much enthusiasm as I could muster to pique her interest.

Moments later, I heard the hesitant tread of her loafers against the raw wooden steps. "Where are you?" She drew in a breath. "Is that..."

"A secret passage?" I nodded wiggling my brows. "I

believe so. I can't find any sort of light source, or electrical outlet for that matter. Please pass me the flashlight."

My cousin held it against her chest as if it were made of precious metal. "I believe they call it a torch in Ireland."

I rolled my eyes. "Torch, schmorch, just give me the light, Julia!"

The torch lit about a dozen feet into the tunnel. Ducking my head, I trod down three stone steps into the corridor. The rock walls felt damp to touch, and the ground was packed earth interspersed with stone. Fresh air gently whistled down the passageway. A broken candle lantern lay on its side, small glass shards littered around it, as if someone had dropped or accidentally kicked it.

"Where do you think it goes?" Julia whispered, as if someone might be listening.

The stone steps had developed a concave dip in the center from centuries of footfalls. I surmised the passage had been carved centuries ago. "If I had to guess, this is under the kitchen, which faces the castle. I bet my last dollar this is a secret tunnel that leads to it."

"Ariadne!" Julia called with alarm. "Where do you think you're going?"

I glanced back at my cousin, lighting her pale features with the torch. "To investigate, of course. Where is your sense of adventure?"

"What if there's been a cave-in and it's blocked?"

"Then we'll turn around," I said matter-of-factly.

"What if it's a maze of tunnels down here and we get lost?"

"Hm, you have a point." I chewed my bottom lip in thought. "On the right-hand side, you'll see some jars with lentil beans inside. Grab one of those, and we'll drop them as we go. That way we'll know how to get back here."

"But...what if the door closes?"

"It's not going to close," I said with a dismissive

wave of my hand.

"But, what if it does?" she asked with a high-pitched whine.

"Fine." I huffed and stomped back into the cellar. "Help me move this crate of apples. We'll leave it in the doorway, so it won't shut."

Finally satisfied, Julia, holding tight to her jar of lentils, followed me down the steps into the passageway. Every few feet, I heard the plink of a bean on the ground. Our tunnel angled downward, and I could feel the slight temperature change the further underground we traveled.

Approximately fifty yards into the tunnel, we entered a roomy cave, where the gentle sound of trickling water reached my ears. Raking the cavern with the light, we spotted an ancient wooden bridge spanning a small brook. The bridge was made of hand-hewn logs assembled using joints like mortise and tenon, with wooden pegs to secure the connections. A well-worn path lay before us over the bridge into another tunnel on the other side of the water.

"I don't have a good feeling about this," Julia's voice wobbled. "I think it's time we turned back."

"Nonsense." My words echoed and bounced around the cavern walls. "We must be more than halfway to the castle. We can't stop now. Besides, you've left us a perfectly fine road of breadcrumbs should we need it." As I spoke, the flashlight flickered. My stomach dropped. If we lost the light, we'd be in pitch blackness, unable to see a hand in front of our faces. It flickered again, and I checked the battery compartment.

"Uh, Ariadne? What's wrong with the light?"

"I think it's just a loose battery." I screwed the compartment tighter, then gave it a shake. This time, the light remained solid. "See. Nothing to worry about. Come on, let's get over the bridge," I cajoled.

While I'd been futzing with the light, I'd heard a rustling of what I feared were bat wings. They probably lived on the ceiling, and I did *not* want to mention them to my skittish cousin.

Our footsteps echoed, making it sound like there were more people than just the two of us. Reaching the other side of the bridge, I shivered with unease, and the hairs on the back of my neck rose. It was probably nothing, but I picked up the pace.

"I think we're getting close," I said over my shoulder entering the next tunnel.

This part of the passage had no stone underfoot, only the damp, packed clay. The light flashed onto a white shimmer, and I stopped.

Julia bumped into me. "Oof. Sorry. What's wrong?"

"Nothing." I bent closer to investigate. Pinching the round shimmering item between my two fingers, I straightened and held the light on it. "It's a pearl."

The pearl was an average size, roughly seven or eight millimeters by my estimation—ideal for an earring, cuff link, or tie tack.

"I have a pair of pearl earrings about that size. Mom and Dad gave them to me for graduation."

"Every woman has a pair of pearls about this size. They are practically a compulsory gift for a girl in her late teens," I commented.

"Let me see." Julia put down the jar of beans and held out her hand.

I dropped the jewel into her palm. "What is it doing down here? It's not dirty. Was it dropped recently?"

I felt rather than saw movement behind Julia. Before I could react, my cousin shrieked and hurtled into me, knocking me back a few feet. I came up hard against the rock wall. My left hip and elbow took the brunt of our weight. The flashlight flew out of my hand.

Utter darkness descended.

Julia's screams repeated, over and over, right into my ear. And she gripped my jacket as if it were a lifeline.

Fear in its most basic form flooded my system. We were in the dark, with a menacing presence. I didn't know if it was human or animal. Either way, with my cousin shrieking like a banshee, *it* certainly knew where *we* were. My hand found her mouth, and I placed it over the top.

"Julia! Julia!" I hissed. "Stop yelling. It knows where you are."

My cousin's screams shut off like a faucet, and I removed my hand.

"Is-is he-he s-still h-here?" she whimpered.

"It was human?"

"I felt a hand grab my arm, and I ran into you trying to get away."

"Shh, listen." Replacing a hand on her mouth, I cocked my ear. I barely heard the sound of retreating footsteps. "Do you hear that?" I whispered.

I felt her nod beneath my hand.

"I think whoever it was, we scared him off." For a moment, I could have sworn I saw the shine of a lantern, then it rounded a corner and disappeared.

My cousin let out a breath and pushed herself off me. "Ariadne?"

"Yes?"

"Do you see that? Up on the ceiling. The little green lights?"

Indeed, green stars glowed above us, blinking on and off. I didn't know what they were, but it gave me a sense of relief knowing we weren't completely in pitch blackness. "They look like fireflies. Fluorescent rocks, maybe?"

Watching the tiny lights flickering seemed to calm Julia, and my own heart slowed from a dead run down to a jittering trot.

"We didn't see them before because the flashlight

made it too bright."

"How are we going to get out of here?" Julia asked in a high-pitched voice. "I can't see a damn thing."

My cousin must have been out of her mind with fear, because in all the years I'd known her, I'd never ever heard her swear.

"Just a sec, let me think." Then I remembered. "Wait, I should have..." I dug into my coat pocket. Thanking my lucky stars, my fingers encountered a half pack of cigarettes and a book of matches that I'd filched from Brian's cottage. I struck one, and it flared to life. "Help me find the flashlight."

I held the match low to the ground, slowly moving it back and forth.

Three matches later, Julia spotted it. "There!"

As she picked it up, I heard the awful tinkling of broken glass. Her lips turned down.

"I think it's broken." She flicked the switch up and down.

"Oh, dear." There were only a few more matches left in the book, and I didn't know if they would hold out until we reached the castle entrance.

"Oh, my goodness! I'm so silly! I can't believe I forgot...." my cousin mumbled and felt her pockets. "Yes, it's still there." She pulled out the most beautiful thing I'd ever seen. "I took the candle out of the broken lantern!" she crowed, holding aloft her prize like she'd won a gold medal at the Olympics.

"Oh, you beauty! Bless you for your foresight, Julia Brennan."

While my cousin clutched the candle, I put the match to the wick, and it sprang to life.

"Pick up the beans. I'm leading us the rest of the way. If someone comes from behind, they can grab *you* next time," she stated with authority and firmly stepped past me, shielding the flame as she went so it wouldn't blow out.

The pearl was forgotten, and we continued our trek.

Finally, after what seemed like hours, but was probably less than ten minutes, we reached a circular stone staircase. Up and up, we went until we stopped in front of a crumbling wooden door studded with rusty nail heads. The cracks in the timber were wide enough to stick a hand through. The door was at least nine feet tall and heavy but gave way easily as we pushed it forward.

Stepping across the threshold, we found ourselves in a circular antechamber that could only be inside Ballyford Castle. Across the way, the base of a second circular staircase rose up and up. Breathing deep, I realized we were in the tower from whence Brian fell.

Whence. Such an old-fashioned word.

Standing in the five-hundred-year-old castle, the word whence seemed apropos. I pictured a woman in Renaissance garments passing across the floor, a blue train elegantly dragging behind her. Perhaps it would catch one of the rough stones, and she'd give a tug to release it. I could almost see the tiny piece of cloth left behind. The vision disappeared from whence it came.

There it was. That word again.

Whence.

My lips lifted of their own accord. Laughter bubbled up my throat, and I placed fingers across my mouth, but I couldn't seem to hold it back.

Chapter Seventeen
Julia

She was laughing!

Julia couldn't believe it. *We barely escaped these horrible, dungeonous tunnels, and Ariadne has the temerity to laugh when we are finally freed. As if the entire episode is a great lark!*

"What do you think you're laughing about?" Julia snapped, stomping her foot. "We almost *died* down there! And *you* think it is *funny!*"

Ariadne slapped a hand over her mouth to mask her mirth, but it still escaped through her fingers, making Julia even angrier.

"I'm sorry," Ariadne gasped and bit her bottom lip. Her body still shook from silent laughter.

"Get a hold of yourself!"

Ariadne drew deep breaths to calm the giggles. When she seemed under control, she explained, "It's just...I mean...I think it's a reaction from the, er, encounter."

Julia glared at her.

"Sorry." Ariadne barely held back a grin.

She looked ridiculous. Her hair was mussed, with something white—probably a spiderweb—clinging to it. The jar of beans was clasped to her chest and her borrowed coat damp from the dripping walls of the tunnel.

A sigh escaped, and Julia allowed her features to soften. "Very well. Now that we're free, we'd better find a safe place to exit."

"Shane told us the North and West wings were dangerous. We're in the south wing, so it should be okay." Ariadne wandered over to the circular staircase and stared upward. "Do you think we should—"

"Absolutely not!"

Surprised, Ariadne turned to her cousin. "You don't even know what I was going to say."

"You were going to ask if we should go up the tower to investigate."

"Okay, maybe I was going to ask that." Sheepishly, Ariadne stared down at the jar. "We still have some beans left. I'm sure we could find our way back down." A grin peeked out at Julia.

"You are...you are...the *worst cousin ever!* Completely *incorrigible!*" Julia huffed and sputtered.

Ariadne put on a rather humorous frown, and Julia couldn't help the giggle that escaped.

"Do you think, one day, someone will be walking the tunnels wondering what on earth those beans are doing there?" A childhood memory occurred to Julia, and she snapped her fingers. "I know, they'll begin to sprout and grow up and up, like that fairy tale, *Jack and the Beanstalk.*"

Ariadne gave a snort. "I doubt it. More likely, mice or rats will eat those beans first."

"Ariadne! Ew! That's disgusting!" Julia's nose scrunched, and she stuck out her tongue. "Did you see mice down there?"

"No, but I think I heard them," Ariadne distractedly replied, staring at something on the stairs.

"Dear heaven. I cannot *believe* I let you talk me into going through that tunnel."

"Oh, pooh. You know you wanted to see what was down there. Besides, one day you'll be Baroness of Ballyford. Don't you want to know the castle's secrets?" Ariadne placed the jar on one of the steps.

Julia thought about that hand grabbing her arm, and she shivered. "No, Ariadne. I could have done without knowing that secret."

Pinching something between a thumb and finger, she held it up to the light. "Hm."

"What have you got there?"

"It looks like a piece of fabric." She tsked. "Not even, more like a few threads woven together."

Julia gasped. "Does it match something Brian wore last night?"

"No." Ariadne frowned. "I don't believe it does." She tucked the fabric into the cigarette box. "I'll give it to Inspector Quinn when we see him."

"Very well. We'd better find our exit. I hope we don't get caught by the police. Inspector Quinn told us the castle was off limits until the investigation is finished." Julia checked her gold watch. "Believe it or not, it's been less than twenty minutes since we went into Brian's cottage. It felt like we were down there for hours and hours."

"It certainly did. Well, milady, lead the way." Ariadne made a goofy curtsey and pointed in the direction of the doorway that must lead to the rest of the castle.

"Oh, stop!" Julia scoffed.

Ariadne suddenly stiffened and shivered.

Noticing the strange behavior, Julia asked, "Somebody walk across your grave?

"I-I just had this feeling, like we are being watched." Ariadne's gaze scanned the room, searching for a being or entity that might be observing the two girls.

Julia didn't wait for her to find it. Marching across the room, she headed toward the exit. "Let's get out of here."

It took the pair a few minutes to find a windowless opening which they could climb through and drop down onto the ground. They were surrounded by trees, enveloped in the scent of evergreens and fresh sap.

Julia dusted off her backside and glanced around. "I think if we go through there, we'll find our way back to the stables."

Her sense of direction turned out to be correct. After a short hike through the woods, the forest began to thin, and they soon emerged near the paddock.

"See. I told you. Oh! There's Cormac." Relief flooded through her body. "It looks like he's just come from the cottage. He's probably searching for me."

"I don't think—"

"Yoohoo! Cormac!" Julia ignored whatever her cousin was about to say and waved frantically at her fiancé. "Here we are! *Cormac!*"

He spotted her and pivoted from his current course. Coming to a halt, he waited for her to catch up. Julia hurried toward him almost at a run, while Ariadne strolled at a slower pace.

Julia finally reached her fiancé and threw herself into his arms. "Were you looking for me?" She went up to her tiptoes, her lips pursed for a kiss.

"Um, sure, I mean, yes, of course. Not here, people can see us," he murmured, redirecting Julia's enthusiasm by rotating her to his side. "Where have you two been?"

"Oh, Cormac! You won't believe what we found," Julia said with excitement.

Ariadne caught up to the couple and drily commented, "I have a feeling your fiancé is well aware of our find."

Julia's eyes widened. "What do you mean?"

"He's grown up here. As a young boy, I wouldn't doubt the cave tunnels were a place to play or perhaps hide from a scolding nanny," she drawled, tipping her head.

Chapter Eighteen
Cormac O'Connell

Cormac did his best not to flinch as Ariadne spoke of the hidden caverns beneath the castle.

He cleared his throat. "You discovered the tunnels, did you?"

"Yes! And Ariadne suggested we check them out," Julia breathily replied. "There is a passage that goes all the way from Brian's cottage to the castle!"

"This area is a warren of caverns and tunnels. You shouldn't be exploring them by yourself," Cormac warned.

"We weren't alone. We had each other," Julia scoffed. "But you're right, it is confusing when you're down there. I didn't know if we'd get lost, so we dropped beans all the way, like Hansel and Gretel dropping their crumbs in the wood." Julia turned to her cousin. "Ariadne! What happened to the beans?"

Ariadne didn't flinch or even glance at her cousin. Her sharp green eyes stared straight at Cormac. He felt as though she could see into his soul.

"Ariadne? Where are the beans?" Julia repeated.

"What? Oh, the beans." She turned her empty hands over and stuffed them into her pockets. "I must have put them down and forgotten them back in the castle tower room."

"You didn't go up the tower. Did you? I stressed how dangerous going up there would be when Inspector Quinn was here," he scolded.

"Good heavens, no! Especially *not* after the tunnel

incident," Julia shivered beneath his arm.

Cormac schooled his features. "What incident?"

"It was nothing," Ariadne spoke up, staring hard at her cousin. "I dropped the flashlight, and it broke."

Ariadne's response was not what Cormac had been expecting, and he couldn't help the flash of surprise that crossed his features. "That must have been...troubling."

Julia opened her mouth, but Ariadne cut her off. "You have no idea. It was black as pitch down there. Luckily, Julia had the foresight to bring a candle, and I had a matchbook. And all was well."

Julia glared at Ariadne. "Yes, but we haven't told you the best part—"

"I'm sorry, Julia, but I think the stable master is trying to catch Cormac's attention." Ariadne pointed.

Cormac squinted over his shoulder. Sure enough, the older man beckoned him. *What now? Could anything else go wrong with this day?*

"Excuse me, dearest. I must speak with Dougray. Before I go, I wanted to see if... you two would like to visit the cliffs. The shooting brake is back and..." He rubbed his jawline. "I thought you could use some time away from the house."

"Yes, of course. Ariadne hasn't seen them yet. We were supposed to go this morning..." Julia trailed off, realizing what she'd been about to say. Her cousin came to the rescue.

"I'd love to see the cliffs." Ariadne nodded. "I think we could all use a bit of...distance."

"Very well. As soon as I finish my business with Dougray, I'll meet you at the Carriage House."

As the ladies walked away, he watched them hold an intense, whispered conversation. Cormac wondered if Julia's dusky-haired cousin would cause trouble. He felt incredibly relieved when he found them coming from the castle grounds. He worried they'd backtrack and come back to the cottage. What a fright they would have had if they'd found the entry to the tunnel closed tight.

He'd have to have the castle entrance nailed shut and barred as well.

"Coming straight away, Dougray." Cormac waved and loped toward the stable master.

Chapter Nineteen
Ariadne

"What was *that*?" Julia hissed at me.

"I don't know what you're talking about."

"You cut me off at every turn. And completely downplayed the fright we had in the tunnel. I didn't get a chance to tell Cormac about the man in the tunnels."

For a moment, I held my tongue, debating if I should tell my cousin that Cormac had the same red clay on his brown work boots as we had on our shoes. I recalled the eerie feeling of eyes watching as I walked across the bridge and again at the base of the tower.

Was it Cormac?

If so, I couldn't fathom the reason why he would not have announced himself. *Could he be the one who grabbed Julia? Did Julia's screeching panic frighten him? Why would he flee? If it wasn't Cormac, was he in collusion with the perpetrator?*

Or had there been someone else in the tunnels with us? Someone with an ominous motive. Someone who didn't want us to find that pearl.

The suspicious thoughts tumbled unbidden in my brain. All I knew, there was a dead man, and as an outside observer of the O'Connell family, several of the family members made me question how much Brian would be missed.

"Answer me, Ariadne," Julia snapped, halting our progress just outside the courtyard.

"I'm afraid the tunnel incident was a prank.

Probably by one of the local kids, messing around in the—how did Cormac put it—warren of caverns. More than likely, you're screaming fit scared him off. Cormac has enough on his mind with Brian's death. I didn't think our silly adventure needed to weigh upon him."

Considering my words, Julia tapped her nails against each other as if one were playing on an old washboard. "You're right, you know. This is a terrible time for Cormac, and I shouldn't be adding to his worry. I won't say another word about it."

"I think that would be best. At least for now. One day we'll laugh about the entire incident."

Julia's nail tapping ceased, and she glared at me. "Not for a *very* long time."

I cleared my throat. "I, uh, need to use the facilities before we head out to the cliffs."

"Good idea, I probably should as well." Striding across the stone courtyard, Julia looked down at her feet. "Goodness. Our shoes are a mess, from traipsing around the forest."

I didn't find it necessary to correct her assumption that the red clay was not from the forest floor.

"Hm, the cliffs can be muddy as well. We ought to change back into boots. Don't want to make these loafers worse than they already are." The doorknob twisted beneath her fingers. "Do you still have the boots I gave you this morning?"

"Yes."

"Leave your shoes in the mudroom," she said, kicking off her penny loafers and shrugging out of her coat.

"I'll tell Briggs to have someone clean them," she said with an almost lady-of-the-manor air. "Meet me at the Carriage House when you're done."

We heard Lady Aisling's voice in the distance, and Julia's shoulders tensed. Before I could ask here *where* this Carriage House was located, Julia muttered, "I can't let her see me shoeless." In her sock-feet, she bee-lined out of the mudroom.

"Wait." I stuck my head in the hall. "Julia?"

She'd disappeared. Shrugging, I figured I could sniff out the Carriage House on my own.

Passing the Morning Room, I noticed the chafing dishes had been cleared, and the room cleaned. Even the death of the estate manager didn't interfere with the efficiency of the staff. I wondered if it was Lady Aisling's doing or the capable Mrs. Briggs.

Once in my room, I placed the tiny swatch of fabric I'd discovered inside the pages of Brian's diary. The peacock blue stood out vividly against the white paper. I considered taking the journal with me, but decided against the idea, and again buried it inside the wardrobe.

The bathroom I'd been assigned to use was at the end of a rather long corridor. A thick green carpet with gold accents muffled my footsteps. The walls had been painted a soft cream color and were littered with oil paintings. Still-life paintings were interspersed with landscapes and portraits. Many with dark backgrounds were difficult to appreciate in the dimly lit corridor. Every door I passed remained firmly closed, and a single bulb burned in each of the double wall sconces. Much like my own room, many of the doors I passed had a plaque on the door and listed peerage titles—Countess of Kingston, Earl of Meath, Earl of Cork, etc.

Upon exiting the facilities, I discovered Shane staring intently at something in his palm while absent-mindedly closing the door behind him.

"Hello," I greeted.

"Oh!" He jerked and shoved his hand into his pocket. "You startled me. I didn't see you there. If it isn't our little *American* fashion plate," he said in a teasing manner, but I detected an underlying nastiness as he said the word American and loped toward me.

Ignoring his jab, I pasted on a smile and met him halfway down the passage. "I've noticed the upstairs hallways aren't very bright."

"A silly cost-saving measure my mother insists upon." He screwed down the unlit bulb of the closest sconce shedding nominally brighter light. Indicating my riding boots, he inquired, "You're not planning to go riding again, are you?"

I shook my head. "Cormac offered to take us down to the cliffs. He said the shooting brake is back. What is a shooting brake? Some kind of carriage?"

"No. It's a car. I suppose it is similar to your American station wagon, only it's got two doors instead of four." He grinned before his expression shifted into one of calculation. "Can't blame my brother for wanting to get away for a bit. A gloomy pall hangs over this house. Everyone is whispering and walking on eggshells."

"Are you surprised? From what I understand, Brian was like a family member."

"Like one. Not actually one," he asserted.

If I'd been a family member or staff, the audacity of his statement might have taken my breath away. Being a stranger, I could see his point. Although I do believe it was a rather harsh thing to say. I wondered if Shane spoke boorishly to see if he could rile the person to whom he spoke.

Refusing to rise to the bait, I asked, "Can you tell me how to get to the Carriage House? That's where we're supposed to meet up."

A half-smile lifted one side of his face. "You know what? I'll show you myself. Going down to the Cliffs sounds like a capital idea. Let me get a coat. Stay here." He strode down the hallway.

"Wait, where are you going?"

"To my room. I told you, I must fetch a coat," he

called over his shoulder. "You'd best put on something warm as well. Those winds can be unbelievably strong."

"But—"

He turned the corner before I could say more.

If Shane didn't come out of his own room, then whose room did he come from?

Hesitantly, I knocked on the Countess of Kingston's door. Getting no response, I placed my ear to it. Hearing nothing, I slowly turned the knob and peeked inside. A large bed chamber decorated in lavender and yellow greeted me. Knowing Shane would soon return, I didn't dare step foot inside. But I took a moment to give the room a cursory glance and vowed to identify who slept in the Countess of Kingston's enormous, canopied bed.

Moments later, Shane returned, loping around the corner, wearing a long black coat, and carrying a rectangular leather camera case. He held it up. "The weather is clear. I should be able to get some magnificent shots at the cliffs. Where is your coat?"

"Left it in the mudroom."

He took my elbow. "We'd best fetch it then and hie ourselves out to the Carriage House before my brother decides to leave us behind."

134

Chapter Twenty
Ariadne

The car bumped and jolted us along a dirt track as the blue waters of the Atlantic grew closer. Five minutes into the ride, I began to wonder if I'd been better off skipping this little jaunt, understanding why horses had been our original transport. We hit a particularly deep pothole, and I was thrown against Shane. Instinctively, my hand grabbed onto the nearest hold it could find, which, unfortunately, happened to be Shane's thigh. My nails dug in deep.

He yelped. "Bloody hell, Cormac! This isn't the Land Rover! Watch where you're going!"

With burning cheeks and a mumbled apology, I quickly readjusted to my side of the back seat and held on for dear life to the broken strap hanging above the window.

"I'm doing the best I can," Cormac said between clenched teeth. Another rain filled hole came into sight, and Cormac slowed to a snail's pace as the tires splashed through it.

"What's that mini castle-looking structure to the right?" Julia asked, pointing to a mottled stone tower in the distance.

"That is O'Brien's Tower. An observation tower completed in 1835," Shane supplied.

"Did your family build it?" My voice came out choppy as the car jittered over a particularly rutted part of the lane.

"No." His head shook negatively. "It's not part of our

property. Cornelius O'Brien built it. He was an MP for years."

Cormac spoke up, "O'Brien built it to attract more tourists. Help improve the local economy."

"Is it still open to the public? Are we allowed inside?" I lowered my sunglasses and squinted. I couldn't see anyone approaching the tower.

"It is open to the public. Quite a few visitors come in the warmer months. They're a little scarcer now. There is a parking area off the main road." Slowing the car, Cormac downshifted, and we bounced through a shallow pothole.

"We should go," Shane suggested. "It's a clear day. We'll probably be able to see as far as the Aran Islands. Maybe even the two bays, Liscannor and Galway. I'll be able to get some fine shots."

"How far away is it from where you plan to park?" Julia asked in an uncertain voice.

"Maybe a mile or two," Shane replied.

From where I sat, I could see Julia's profile as she chewed her lower lip. "I don't know. That seems far to walk. Your mother said she wanted us to return in an hour."

Shane snorted and crossed his arms.

"We can drive closer to the tower." Cormac upshifted, and the car moved faster as we hit a stretch of flat road.

"Maybe you can meet our local historiographer." At my confusion Shane continued to explain, "Fellow by the name of Dinny has fashioned himself a guide. Talks about the history, birds, and such things."

"Do several people visit the site?" I asked.

"Every year it seems more and more find their way. You'll see over to the right, there's a—" Shane's explanation was cut off as the car dipped. This time, Shane's hard body slammed into mine, ramming my shoulder against the car door.

I couldn't help the cry that escaped.

"Feck, Cormac! *Go dtachtfadh an diabhal thú.*" Shane muttered the Gaelic words as if putting a curse upon his brother. "You practically threw us out the window. If my camera's broken, you'll be footing the bill for it." He shoved himself back to his side of the seat.

"Aren't I already doing so?" Cormac ground out before saying loudly, "Are you okay back there, Ariadne? My buffoon of a brother didn't crush you, did he?"

"I'll be fine," I murmured, rubbing the injured joint. We hit another bump.

"Why is this track in such bad shape? I'm going to have a word with Brian about seeing to these bloody roads!" Cormac snapped.

The car went silent as if all the air had been sucked out. Realizing the name he'd invoked, Cormac's breath whistled through his teeth. The only sound was the grinding of the gears and the groan of the engine. Julia's lower lip wobbled, and she turned to stare out her window. Shane had the brains to keep his mouth shut the rest of the drive.

Cormac finally pulled the vehicle to a halt and broke the awkward silence. "This is as far as we go. The rest of the way is on foot. Button up, darling. The winds along the cliffs are quite fierce."

Shane went to the boot to mess about with his lenses and camera prep, while the rest of us began the fifty-yard trek out to the edge of the cliffs. Cormac's long legs ate up the yards, while Julia and I meandered at a slower pace.

"Julia," I said, "I've been meaning to ask you, who is staying in the Countess of Kingston's room?"

"Oh, that's Lady Aisling's room. Her husband is in the adjoining room, the Earl of Cork." She giggled. "Aren't they wonderful names?"

"Mm."

"All the rooms are named after some sort of Irish title," she explained.

"And what is Lord O'Connell's official title? I mean, I know he's a baron, but does he have some long, important title, like the English royal family?" I kicked a rock, and it skittered off to the left.

"He is Lord Callum O'Connell, Baron of Ballyford, twelfth Lord of Liscannor."

"That will make Cormac the thirteenth Lord of Liscannor."

She grimaced. "Ugh, don't remind me."

"What do you mean?"

"Unlucky thirteen and all that." Before I could reply, she flounced away from me and jogged the last few yards to catch up with Cormac, where he stood on the bluff.

With a contemplative silence, I witnessed the vista before me.

We were presented with a vast, breathtaking landscape that accentuated the unadulterated beauty of the Irish coastline. The towering, rugged Cliffs of Moher rose dramatically from the Atlantic Ocean where the waves beat over and over against the granite. They were the same waves that took thousands of years to carve the bluffs and overhangs. Bright sunlight bathed us with its rays showcasing the vibrant green vegetation against a clear blue sky, and the sparkling water below. A black seabird soared overhead.

"What is that bird?" Julia asked.

"Guillemot, they nest in the ledges of the rocks below," answered Shane, snapping a series of photos. "In the summer, you'll get to see the puffins. That's a skylark just there." He pointed his camera at a small brown bird with a speckled breast.

"What kind of camera are you using?" she asked.

"A Leica MP. It's what all the photojournalists use."

The pair wandered further down the cliff line. Shane

photographed more of the fauna, explaining to Julia as they went. Soon I could no longer hear what he said as his words were snatched away by the winds.

Shoulders hunched, Cormac turned his back to the ocean and attempted to light a cigarette, cupping one hand around the lighter to fend off the breeze. After half a dozen attempts, I cupped my hand around the other side, and the cigarette finally caught.

Cormac breathed in deeply. "Thanks. Can I offer you one?"

"Maybe later." I pushed my hands into the coat pockets and stared out to sea.

"Brian's death is a mess. I'm sorry you girls were here when it happened."

A mess? Not a tragedy? "I was wondering if you could answer a question for me."

"I can try." He lifted his shoulder in a half-shrug, watching Shane and his fiancée.

"I'm wondering why you were in the tunnels this morning. And why did you not tell Julia that you had been down there?"

His brows crunched together, and he removed the cigarette to study me. "Why would you think that?"

I stared down at the evidence on his boots. "The only place I've seen that red clay on your property is in the caves."

"Is that what you think?" He stepped toward me, forcing me to back up. "I'm not sure I like what you're implying."

Two more steps. The airstream blew hard against my back. He purposefully intimidated me. I'd never seen this side of him.

"I imply nothing. I'm stating facts. You have the same mud on your shoes that Julia and I acquired in the tunnels. Someone gave us quite a fright. And left us in pitch darkness to fend for ourselves."

He sucked on the cigarette and gave me a once-over. The smoke slithering from his nose was stolen by a gust as he spoke, "It seems you came out of it just fine."

"Were you down there? Did you hear Julia's scream of terror and do nothing?"

"I don't know what you're talking about." He glanced away. Dropping the half-smoked cigarette, he ground it out with the toe of his boot.

"Who does the pearl belong to? Friend of yours?" I don't know why, I said the latter in a taunting tone and smirk.

That comment got his attention, and he took another step towards me. No longer intimidating, cold fury raged in his steely gaze. I realized I'd pushed too far.

"I-I apologize. I didn't—" Shuffling back further, my heel hit rocks and pebbles. I hadn't realized how precarious my position had become until I heard Shane and Julia's voices calling me.

"Get back from the ledge!" Shane hollered, running at a fast clip. The camera was on a strap around his neck, and he held it to his chest as he ran.

"Ariadne!" Julia yelled.

The drop was only inches away, where hundreds of feet below, the ocean dashed against rocks. If I lost my balance—

Before I could scream, or even fully process the danger, Cormac grabbed my arm in a cruel grip, yanking me forward away from the edge.

I stumbled, managing to catch myself before falling to my knees.

Shane and Julia reached the two of us.

My cousin, breathing heavily, slung an arm over my shoulder. "Ariadne! What were you thinking? You were way too close to the edge."

"You scared the daylights out of us!" Shane admonished.

"If it hadn't been for Cormac . . ." Julia just shook her head.

If it hadn't been for Cormac, I wouldn't have been put into such a precarious position.

Releasing me, Julia cooed at her fiancé, "You're a hero, darling." And wrapped her arms around him. Lips puckered, she got on her tiptoes, and this time he bent down for the kiss.

"I say, Ariadne, are you quite all right?" Shane asked.

"Yes, thank you." I massaged the feeling back into my arm. It would be bruised by tomorrow.

Shane rounded on his brother, but before he could blast him with his wrath, Cormac interrupted, glancing at his watch, "Shall we head to O'Brien's Tower? We haven't much time before we're due back."

"Sounds good to me." Julia turned her attention to me. "If Ariadne is up to it?"

Even though I'd rather have returned to the house, in the face of Julia's excitement, I mustered up some enthusiasm. "Of course. Lead the way."

Julia and Cormac walked arm-in-arm back to the car. My cousin hung onto Cormac like Spanish moss on a Sweetgum tree. Shane and I followed at our own leisurely pace. There was no way I would turn my back on Cormac O'Connell during the rest of my trip.

Chapter Twenty-One
Lady Aisling

Aisling watched the last white truck roll away from the estate like a final nail in the coffin of her party. Her disappointment felt complete. Quite suddenly, the sleepless night she'd experienced, and the subsequent tear down of the canceled party caught up to her. Exhaustion filtered through her limbs. "Briggs, if Callum asks for me, inform him, I'm going up to my room to lie down."

Briggs masked her surprise, but Aisling couldn't help noticing the flared nostrils and saucer eyes. Unless she was ill, Aisling never rested during the day.

Briggs accepted her mistress' choice to retire with equanimity asking, "Shall I send up a tea tray?"

"No." Aisling checked her watch. It read ten after three. "I told the children to return by four. I'll have my tea with them in the front parlor."

"Very well."

Aisling remembered her duties and began to question her decision. "Do you know where the rest of our guests have gotten to?"

"The Brennans? I believe Imogene invited Mrs. Brennan to the stables to see the horses. Last I saw, Mr. Brennan was holed up in the Library with a pipe. Said he found an interesting World War I book about the German and English Naval fleets."

"That's fine then." Aisling nodded with relief.

Mrs. Brennan had taken to Imogene, and she was

happy to have her daughter entertain the American lady for the afternoon. As for Mr. Brennan, well, he never had much to say. Aisling assumed he'd be happy with a book and his pipe. "Have the fires been lit in the Library?"

Briggs bristled. Placing a hand to her chest, she defensively answered, "Of course, milady. Saw to it myself."

Realizing she'd offended Briggs' sensibilities by questioning the housekeeper's diligence in her duty, Aisling controlled the urge to roll her eyes. "Yes. I see. Good. I-I haven't been myself since we were told of the...accident." She yawned. "I'll head upstairs now."

Briggs gave a sympathetic nod. "I'll finish putting away the last of the dinnerware before starting tea."

"Don't bother making anything fresh. Heaven knows we've plenty of sweets going unused tonight. Since the fires are lit, let's plan to serve tea in the Library."

Briggs nodded and returned to the kitchen.

The door to Aisling's room creaked open. She'd need to remind Briggs to have it oiled.

The lightest scent of tea rose perfume hung in the air, a remnant from last night. In comparison to the cacophony of the past few hours, the room's noiselessness was almost jarring. She closed and locked the door, leaving the key in the lock. A tension headache squeezed her head, wrapping its tendrils from temple to temple. She pressed her cold forefingers against her scalp and breathed deeply.

Her gown for tonight, a black, silk, floor-length Balmain with pearl beading along the neckline, was draped across the bed, ready to be worn for a party not meant to be. She'd made a special trip to London to purchase the stylish designer dress.

With a sigh, Aisling scooped up the frock, taking a moment to view it one last time before returning it to the back of the wardrobe, murmuring, "What a waste of money."

Money Ballyford can ill afford. She couldn't bring herself to voice the thought.

Pushing the curtain aside, Aisling stood at her bedroom window. A single puffball cloud scuttered across the sky. The bright clear day allowed Aisling to view the soft humps of the Aran Islands from where she stood. A blue car traveled north, following the cliff line. It was being driven at a reasonable speed, and Aisling assumed Cormac must be driving. Shane, known for enjoying the thrill of speed, would have been racing the car at twice the speed, bucketing his passengers around like rag dolls. The car traveled past the O'Connell land boundary. Aisling frowned until her eye continued the line of direction and realized the foursome must have chosen to see the sights from O'Brien's tower.

She couldn't blame them. Aisling rarely allowed herself the time to appreciate the view of the cliffs and the ocean. The estate pulled her attention and time, and she seemed to always be running from one thing to another. Besides her daily duties running the household, there always seemed to be a matter to fix—leaks in the plumbing, crumbling plaster, a maid with a toothache, etc.

And she wouldn't give it up for anything. Ballyford was her lifeblood, and it would be her children's and grandchildren's.

Comfortable in the knowledge that the guests and staff were accounted for, she sat down in front of her Victorian-style, mahogany dressing table. The beautiful table had been a wedding gift from her mother when she married. Every day, Aisling sat in front of the mirror, she remembered her mother's excited smile when sharing the table's secret. How handy that secret had been over the years—hiding receipts from her husband, or letters that needed to be burned when there were no prying eyes around to watch.

Her hand reached out, but she hesitated. Did she need to do this now? Today?

It will provide peace of mind. I won't sleep a wink until I see it taken care of.

Removing the drawer to the left of the mirror, she reached into the void, found the finger hold, and pulled out the secret drawer. The wooden box landed on her lap, and she noisily sucked in a breath.

Empty.

It wasn't there.

She stuck her arm all the way to the back, her hand grasping, but her fingers met empty space. Getting onto her knees, Aisling peered into the void. Nothing.

Staring at the barren drawer, her mind raced, replaying her actions. She clearly remembered that she'd placed it in the hidden drawer.

Didn't I?

It was late.

Is my mind playing tricks? Was I too tired to remember?

"Did I put it somewhere else?" she whispered through the fingers at her lips.

She left the drawer on top of the dresser and hurried to the jewelry chest residing in her wardrobe. Removing a key from her pocket, she twisted the lock until the top released with a faint click. Relieved, Aisling found the damning sheet of paper still tucked behind the mirror. Thinking perhaps she'd been mistaken and had put it in the jewelry box with the papers, she meticulously checked each drawer and cubby.

No luck.

She moved to check the bedside table. Nothing.

The coffee table drawer. Nothing.

Under the couch cushions. Under her pillows. The floor beneath the bed. Beneath the couch. No. No. No. No.

With a racing heart and shaking hands, Aisling frantically searched the room. She pulled out clothing, tossing it willy-nilly from the dresser drawers. She tore apart the wardrobe, checking every shelf, clothing pocket, every nook and cranny, to no avail.

Eventually, Aisling returned to the dressing table, once more checking the drawer. But it hadn't reappeared.

One person knew about the secret drawer. Years ago, she'd been caught unawares when accessing it. Aisling assumed that person had kept her secret, but now realized she'd perhaps put too much faith in a young child's promise.

She replaced the drawers and sat back, wondering *who* had entered her room and taken it. *Why*? And *what* was to be done about it?

Chapter Twenty-Two
Ariadne

The venerable Mrs. Briggs met us outside the mudroom. "It's ten to four. You'd best hurry and change for tea. Your mother has requested it be served in the Library. Inspector Quinn is expected to join you."

Her voice remained steady, but her eyes were red and raw from crying, and I could tell it was a difficult façade for her to maintain. They'd both been working at Ballyford for many years, and it was obvious Mrs. Briggs held Mr. Byrne in high regard. This day probably seemed interminable, and I imagined if I'd been in her shoes, I would have wanted nothing more than to return to bed. However, such a weakness was not allowed to a woman in her shoes.

"Oh, almost forgot." She dug into her square apron pocket. "A telegram for you, Shane."

While changing into a gray skirt and blue cashmere sweater set, I decided it was time to share my discoveries with Inspector Quinn. I stuffed the journal and map into my skirt pocket. My watch read five after four, and I scurried out of my room, hanging a right and a left. It took a moment to realize, I didn't recognize the hallway. I'd taken a wrong turn. The stairs were not where I'd thought they should be. Backtracking, I heard voices coming from one of the rooms and was about to knock to ask for directions, when I recognized the speakers—Cormac and Shane.

The door to the chamber was cracked open, and I paused to listen. The brothers spoke in subdued tones.

"Just hear me out," Shane urged. "Support father's idea for me to take over Brian's duties, and I'll make your stud farm not only happen, but I can make it into a success."

Cormac scoffed. "And how do you think you'll do that?"

"Come now, you know I've a way with the horses. Better than you've ever been." Cormac snorted, but Shane continued, "Not only that, but I've also got a line on a stud that will be sure to bring us money."

"Really?"

"Bet on it. White Clover."

Cormac paused in thought before displaying his disbelief. "Pshaw. Paddy MacMahon would never sell White Clover."

"He would if he needed the money." Shane paced away, and I silently stepped out of the sight line.

"What?" Cormac snorted. "That man doesn't need money."

"That's not what I've heard. He's been living on credit for too long. That pretty, young wife he married five years ago? You remember."

"I remember. Nancy. The blonde with the big brown eyes."

Shane snapped his fingers. "That's the one. Nancy has expensive tastes, which Paddy has been catering to since they got married. Furs, jewels, new cars, and trips to foreign lands like Bali. Apparently, she talked Paddy into buying a place in Gstaad."

Cormac let out a crack of laughter. "I don't believe it. Paddy doesn't ski."

"I'm telling you, she talked him into it. Told him all

the important people winter in Gstaad, and that it would increase his reputation. She's got him wound around her little finger. Meanwhile, his horses haven't been winning like they used to—four, five years ago."

I chanced another peek. Shane had his back to the door.

Cormac rubbed a hand along his jawline, and his brows were drawn down in thought. "That's true. Ever since his trainer, Jeremy, left four years ago, Paddy hasn't seen the inside of a winner's circle."

"Now Nancy wants a place in the south of France, and he's selling White Clover to pay for it."

"I'll be damned." The conversation went quiet for a moment until Cormac continued, "If I do support you for estate manager, it still won't get us the stud farm. We need capital. Money we don't have."

"Like I said, I support you, you support me. That includes helping me obtain a quick infusion of cash."

"How?" Cormac gave his brother a skeptical look.

"In my pocket—" Shane tapped his left breast pocket "—I've got a telegram from that Hollywood movie studio I told you about. They want to start filming here in two months, and they're ready to put down a substantial deposit."

Before Shane finished speaking, Cormac's head was shaking. "Neither Mother nor Father would go for it."

"They'll pay us ten thousand pounds."

The room went silent. and I slipped deeper into the shadows.

"Ten thousand? Are you sure about that?"

"See for yourself." I heard a rustling of paper. "I sent the photos to a bloke in LA who works for the studio. Briggs just handed this to me."

The room went silent as Cormac read the telegram. I heard a door close somewhere in one of the corridors. At that point, I should have knocked. Instead, I glanced up and down the hallway to make sure no one was coming my way, then tucked myself further into the shadows. Which wasn't difficult considering only half the hall sconces were lit.

"I might be able to talk Father into it, but you know Mother would never allow vulgar movie people to darken her doorstep, much less give them the run of the place for what...it says here four weeks of filming."

"Don't worry about Mother. I've got something that will make her come around." The paper rustled again as Shane tucked it back into his pocket.

"What are you talking about?"

"Nothing that need worry you. At least not right now."

Cormac let out a deep sigh. "Fine. I'll support you in taking over Brian's duties."

Shane held out his hand, and his brother took it. "When will you speak with Father?"

"After dinner. "

I was about to beat a hasty retreat when Shane said one more thing that stopped me. "By the way, what was all that down by the cliffs with Julia's cousin. What were you two talking about?"

"Nothing of importance," Cormac said dismissively. "She wasn't paying attention. Neither was I, for that matter."

"She looked frightened."

"I'm sure she was. She almost fell off a cliff. Scared the piss out of me too," Cormac claimed.

"Still, I could have sworn there was more to it. She spent the rest of the trip warily watching you."

"You're imagining things."

"Am I?" Shane's voice was much closer.

I didn't wait any longer. On tiptoes, I fled round the corner.

Chapter Twenty-Three
Norah Briggs

The housekeeper sat on the hard stool, staring sightlessly at the closed butler's pantry door. Some years ago, it had been painted white. The paint was chipped on the corners and worn away around the tarnished brass push plate. She should have Daisy clean it and touch up the paint.

A job for another day.

Norah had never felt so drained, utterly depleted of energy. Even after her mother passed when she was twelve, Norah didn't feel like this. The tears from earlier—hidden from her employer—would not come now, when she was finally alone. The veins on her hands appeared prominent today, and she rubbed an age spot by her middle knuckle.

She began working at the manor, her first job as head maid, at the ripe old age of twenty-six, when Brian's father was the estate manager. Brian was only twenty-one and away, finishing his degree at uni. He came home for the winter holiday, bearing the handsomeness of youth. He teased and flirted with her, and she couldn't help falling a little in love with the intelligent young man. A mere three years later, his father passed, and Brian took up his father's position, while she was promoted to housekeeper. Brian became a good friend and confidante.

Initially, he feared he wouldn't be able to measure up to his father. Norah assured him he could do the job but advised him not to fill his father's shoes. Instead, to put his own stamp on the position. Initially, a difficulty for Brian, as the former Lord O'Connell didn't care for change. Six months later, when Callum came into the title, he realized the modifications Brian suggested would yield better returns for the estate. Brian finally made the position his own.

At the age of thirty and firmly "on the shelf," Norah knew there would be no marriage, no children, and no grandchildren. After putting off Brian's advances for years, she allowed a reckless passion to sway her better judgment. For nine months, she and Brian carried on a secret, but sizzling affair. Her stomach tingled at the memory of his broad hands upon her body.

When they were almost caught, in this very room, Norah recognized the dangerous line she walked. If their affair was discovered, Brian, being the man, would keep his job. Lady Aisling would dismiss Norah, even if she preferred not to. Moreover, since Brian was so much younger, Norah would be branded a wanton woman, leaving under a cloud of scandal without a reference. She'd never be a housekeeper again. At least not for anyone with means and standing in the community like the O'Connells. Though upset, Brian understood her fears, and they agreed to end their rash love affair.

Over time, their relationship grew into a deep and abiding friendship. Norah wondered how she would do without it. She couldn't quite believe he'd never walk into the kitchen and filch a biscuit off the tea tray. Never again would she rub his shoulders after a long day bent over the estate books.

Norah closed her eyes and pictured Brian hunching over his office desk. She remembered a few days ago, he'd hinted that he had some big news to share with her.

When she pushed for more of an explanation, he laughed and shook his head at her. "Not yet. Soon." He caressed her cheek. He did that every so often. She'd once made him promise never to do it when others were around. But then he went further and kissed her. Something he had not done since they'd ended their affair so many years before.

"Norah," he said, "it's going to change our lives forever."

Norah wondered if he spoke about changes to the estate. The ones Lord O'Connell was stubbornly against. She'd heard their arguments through the walls. Brian told Cormac to work on his father, or they'd have to start selling off portions of the estate.

The jingle of the front door startled Norah out of her reverie. Glancing at the clock above the door, she realized it was ten past four and knew she'd be in for a lecture from Lady Aisling. Even though her best friend was dead, there would be no shirking of duties today. Not as long as Aisling Gallagher O'Connell still drew breath.

Lady Aisling. She'd been acting oddly all day. Angry at having to cancel the party. It was a surprise since Norah knew Lady Aisling and Brian had gotten along well. When she arrived as a first-time bride, Aisling relied on Norah to run the household. And she often turned to Brian for advice on modernizing the manor with the funds from her dowry.

There was always respect between the two women. However, today, she had been shooting Norah looks, sometimes irritated, but at other times almost...

Norah couldn't put a finger on it. It was more than agitation and distress. Had it been...fear?

The front door chimed again.

"*A dhaibhail!* Where is Daisy?" In the absence of a butler, responsibilities for answering the door had fallen to Norah and her staff. The housekeeper hauled herself upright on aching feet, straightened her apron, and pushed against the tarnished brass plate of the swinging door.

❧

Norah escorted Inspector Quinn into the Library at quarter past four, only to find it empty. *Where is everyone?*

"Why don't you have a seat, Inspector? I'm sure the family will arrive soon, and I'll have Daisy bring the tea tray directly. Lady O'Connell—" The phone in the hallway buzzed, distracting Norah from what she was about to say. "Excuse me."

She bustled down the hall to the telephone table. "Ballyford Manor."

"This is the operator. I have a call from Gavin Turnbull."

Gavin Turnbull? Norah had no recollection of that name, but perhaps it was one of Shane's friends or a businessman for the estate. Though they normally called on Brian's phone line. Again, like a tidal wave, she remembered Brian was dead, and he'd never answer his office phone again.

"Hello? Can you hear me?" the operator practically yelled in her ear.

Norah blinked. "Yes, I hear. Put the call through."

After a few clicks, a distinct American accent asked over the crackling of the lines, "Hello? Is this Ballyford? The O'Connell residence?"

"Yes, it is. This is Mrs. Briggs, the housekeeper. Who are you calling for?"

"I'd like to speak with Ariadne. Ariadne Winter, that is. This is Gavin Turnbull. Her...uh...co-worker."

"It may take a moment. I'm not sure where she is," Briggs said.

"Please hurry, this call is costing me a pretty penny, and I don't think the magazine is going to reimburse me for it."

Norah laid the handset on the table and headed for

the front staircase. Turning a corner, she was practically ploughed over by her quarry. "Whoa! Slow down." Norah gripped Miss Winter's forearms to steady them both.

"Oh! Mrs. Briggs, I do apologize. I fear I'm late for tea," she whooshed out the explanation in one breath, her face flushed. "I hope Lady Aisling isn't upset with me."

"Well, she won't be, seeing as she hasn't yet come down."

"Oh! What a relief." Miss Winter's shoulders relaxed.

"But you've got a long-distance call waiting. An American chap. Claims to work with you."

She hurried to the phone. "Hello? Gavin? What's going on? Where are you phoning from?"

Norah should have been off to direct the tea or fetch the mistress. Instead, she lingered, wondering who would spend so much quid on a phone call to this young lady.

"In Shannon? You don't say? For how long?" The young lady twisted the cord around her finger.

Her face flushed, and a secretive little grin played around her mouth. If Norah had to guess, Gavin Turnbull was more than a colleague to Miss Winter.

"You should come here and see the Cliffs of Moher. You'd get some fantastic shots...I don't know. Not too far, I think." She turned and spotted Norah, and her eyes lit up. "Just a minute, Gavin, let me ask."

Pulling the phone from her ear, she motioned for Norah to come closer. "Mrs. Briggs, the plane my, er, coworker was on, had mechanical trouble, and they were forced to land at Shannon Airport. How far is it from Shannon to Ballyford?"

"Oh, not much more than an hour and a half, miss."

"Hm." She frowned in thought. "Do you think there is a...hotel or room my friend could rent in the area until Monday, when the next flight leaves? He's a photographer with the magazine and would like to get some photos of the cliffs."

"We've plenty of rooms here that were made ready and are going to waste now that the party's been canceled. Have your friend come here. I'll let the mistress know."

"No, no." Her head rotated back and forth, her curls bouncing. "I wouldn't want to impose on the family. Especially not right now," she whispered the last, as if Brian's death was a secret to be kept.

"Balderdash. Besides, Mr. Shane will be interested in meeting a professional magazine photographer. Tell your friend to take the A Six Eight bus to Ennistymon. And I'll send Dougray to fetch him at The Grey Haven Pub."

Ariadne put the phone to her ear. "Mrs. Briggs said to catch the bus to Ennis—uh?"

"Ennistymon." When Miss Winter gave her a blank look, Norah held out her hand. "Give it here. I'll explain it to him."

Ariadne handed over the phone, and step by step, Norah explained to Gavin how to get to Ennistymon and The Grey Haven.

"But how will I know your man?" Gavin asked.

"He'll know you. I'll tell him to search for a lost Yank."

Gavin laughed. "That shouldn't be too hard."

"I'll put Miss Winter back on to say goodbye." Briggs handed the phone over to the girl. "It's all set."

"Gavin, I'm so glad you're coming. You're not going to believe what's happened. I'll explain it when you arrive." She hung up and gave Norah a winsome smile. "Thank you, Mrs. Briggs. The poor man would be taking the wrong bus if it weren't for you."

"It's no problem, miss." Norah turned to go.

"Mrs. Briggs, may I ask you a question?"

"Of course."

Norah looked at Miss Winter in expectation of being

asked for a service. To her surprise, Miss Winter asked, "How long have you and Mr. Byrne worked at the mansion?"

"Oh, many, many years, miss. Decades. I knew Brian when he was a young lad of twenty-one."

She scrutinized Norah. "Would you say Mr. Byrne had enemies...among the family?"

"Among the family?"

"Did any of the O'Connells resent Mr. Byrne?"

"Resent him?" Norah said with shock. She shook her head. "No, miss. I can't imagine anyone resenting Mr. Byrne. Why the O'Connells treated him like family—"

"Like family." Miss Winter said at the same time as Norah. "Yes, Mrs. Briggs, I've heard that from quite a few people today. The fact remains that Mr. Byrne is dead, and according to the inspector, he may have been murdered. You are an intricate part of this household. I imagine you know many of the family's secrets."

Norah stiffened at the girl's forwardness.

Oblivious to her faux pas, the girl blundered on, "For instance, it was you who brought the coffee to Shane in the Billiard Room last night. Knowing he'd had a little too much of the sauce and could use something to sober him up."

"Shane has always been a bit volatile, but to imagine he'd want to hurt Bri—Mr. Byrne is ludicrous," Norah said coldly.

"Can you recall Mr. Byrne arguing with anyone of late? Or being secretive, perhaps?"

"Mr. Byrne rarely ever raised his voice. Certainly, he wouldn't do so against a family member. As for secrets..." Norah trailed off, remembering Brian's recent excitement and his words, *"It's going to change our lives forever."*

"I can tell by your expression, you've thought of something."

Norah's fingers went to her cheek. She could almost

feel Brian's touch there and spoke as if from a distance, "It was odd. He said he had some information. Something that would change our lives."

"Whose lives?"

Norah returned to the present, focusing on Miss Winter, whose face was bright with curiosity. The housekeeper realized she'd said too much, talking to this stranger, this chit of a girl, about the family business, and Brian! She was impertinent and too curious by half, trying to get Norah to gossip about the family. Norah silently scolded herself for allowing Miss Winter to draw her into such a discussion. It was time to nip the conversation in the bud.

Lifting her chin, she frostily replied, "I'm sure I don't know. I must be off to see about the tea service. You'd best hurry to the Library. Lady Aisling will be arriving at any moment."

Norah swept down the corridor, leaving the nosy Miss Winter to her own devices.

Chapter Twenty-Four
Ariadne

The excitement of Gavin's arrival dissipated a bit from Mrs. Briggs' snub. The faithful retainer clearly disliked my inquisitive questions about the family.

Honestly, I am surprised I got as much information out of the housekeeper as I did.

What was Brian Byrne so excited about that he thought it would change their lives forever? Whose lives? His? Mrs. Briggs? The O'Connells' lives?

Or did Brian Byrne have a secret so large, it would change the lives of every person involved with the estate? A secret that the O'Connells would kill to remain buried?

Chewing on those thoughts, I arrived at the Library to find it empty, except for one person. "Hello, Inspector Quinn."

The inspector turned from his perusal of a leatherbound book. "Hullo, Miss Winter." His bulbous nose was flushed red, and his cheeks were chapped from the cold.

"Are we the first two?"

"It would seem so." He replaced the book on the shelf.

"That's fine. As a matter of fact, it fits perfectly into my plans."

An eyebrow rose. "Plans?"

"Yes," I said, pulling the journal from my pocket.

At this point, I realized it was going to be difficult to explain how I'd found it, and why I took it. I hesitated a moment before deciding on a half-truth. "Today, Julia and I visited Brian Byrne's cottage."

The brow and its mate turned downward. "Why did you do that?"

"We uh...saw the door had been left open and we...well, Julia felt we should investigate. Make sure no one was stealing Brian's things."

His frown lightened a bit but remained skeptical.

"I found this diary, and some schematics, or a map of the estate, that I thought should be brought to your attention." I handed it over.

Quinn flipped through a few of the journal pages. "What makes you think this is valuable to the investigation? All I see here is estate business." He unfolded one of the maps, giving it a cursory perusal.

I chewed my lip. "Yes, well, it was more the back of the book, I thought might be of interest."

He spun the papers until he reached the back.

"You see, it's a list of contacts. Specifically, there is a fellow with a US address and telephone exchange—Harold Kendall. Perhaps that is the man Cormac and Shane saw with Brian?"

The only change in expression I could detect was a slight puckering of the inspector's mouth. "I'll follow up. But you must stay away from Brian's home. And don't take any more of his things," he scolded.

Chastised, I stared down at my pumps. "Yes, you're right. It-it was wrong of me to take those things. I-I only wanted to help."

"You need to leave the investigating to me, Miss Winter. It could be dangerous for a young lady such as yourself to stick your nose where it doesn't belong."

My head popped up. "Dangerous...because you believe Mr. Byrne was murdered?"

Quinn harrumphed, and his features remained stern. "The inquiry is ongoing, but, yes, if it is murder, it could be dangerous for you to be investigating on your own."

I tried a different track and said brightly, "Did you know about the passageway from Brian's cellar to the castle?"

The brows furrowed even more, almost touching. "I believe I told everyone, the castle is off limits."

"Oh, you did. Indeed. It was quite by accident that Julia and I found the passage and ended up inside."

The man put his hands on his hips and ground out, "What did you find?"

In all innocence, I responded, "What makes you think we found anything?"

"Intuition."

"Very well." I sighed. "If you turn to page forty-four in the book."

The inspector did as I suggested, and picked up the merest scrap of fabric, just a few pieces of thread, between his blunt fingers to examine it.

"That tiny piece of fabric was caught on a rough stone in the rotunda of the tower."

"This could have been left there at any point in time." He held it up to the light.

"Yes. I suppose it could have, but..." I paused and sucked in a deep breath. "Lady Aisling was wearing a blue dress last night. Lord O'Connell had a blue and white striped vest."

Both of his eyebrows rose to his hairline. "I'll take it back to the office to inspect it further." He replaced the threads in the journal and pocketed it.

"Did you get a chance to review the ledgers, yet?"

Quinn hesitated before answering, "Cormac turned them over. One of my men at the Gardai station is looking at them as we speak.

At Cormac's name, the frightening interaction at the cliffs rose to my mind. *Are the brothers in it together?*

Did they both want to see Brian gone?

"Anything else you'd like to share, Miss Winter?" The inspector tucked his hands behind his back.

How do I explain what happened? After all, nothing actually happened. Yet, there had been something menacing in Cormac's reaction to my question about the pearl.

My thoughts were interrupted by the squeak of the tea trolley being rolled in the doorway by Daisy. Julia and her mother came in behind the maid, closely followed by Cormac, Shane, and Lord O'Connell. Covering my frustration at having my tête-à-tête with the inspector curtailed, I plastered a smile on my face.

"Sorry, we're late," my aunt trilled.

Lord O'Connell glanced around the room. "Where is my wife?"

"Mrs. Briggs sent word. Lady O'Connell has a headache and is resting," Daisy replied.

"Has anyone seen Imogene?" Aunt Maggie asked.

"I believe she's still down at the stables, ma'am." Daisy's gaze rested on Shane a tad longer than necessary, and her cheeks flushed. I realized she'd done something similar at lunchtime.

Does the maid have a crush on Shane?

The young man ignored Daisy and busied himself absently perusing a bookshelf.

Lord O'Connell recalled the maid's attention, "Daisy, call down to the stables and have them send Imogene back to the house."

"Yes, Lord O'Connell." She dipped a short curtsey and exited the room.

Uncle Gerald arrived, scratching his head. "Is it time for tea already?" He snitched a cookie off the cart and sat down in one of the tufted leather chairs by the fireplace. The fire sparked and crackled, warming the room.

"Shall I pour?" My aunt didn't wait for a

confirmation; she flipped a cup onto a saucer and began the ritual of pouring tea, handing the filled cups to Julia or me to pass around to the men.

"What news have you, Inspector?" Lord O'Connell asked, accepting a cup of tea from Julia. "Thank you, dear."

"Any word on this stranger Brian met with?" Shane sipped his tea and watched the inspector as if he expected news on that front.

"As a matter of fact—" Cormac jumped to his feet and pulled a slip of paper from his pants pocket. "—I wanted to give this to you, Inspector. I found it in some of Brian's papers. It seems to be a demand for five hundred pounds. It doesn't say for what or from whom. Just the initials H.K."

My hand bobbled the tea, and the brick colored liquid splashed into the saucer, before I could pass it to my uncle. "I'm terribly sorry, Uncle Gerald. Let me mop that up and get you a fresh cup."

"No need." He pulled out a red handkerchief and sopped the liquid.

"Is that the man from the bar?" Julia asked in her innocence.

Inspector Quinn scrutinized the crumpled sheet of paper. "I don't know that I'd classify this as a demand. Seems to be an invoice for something. It says right here, for services rendered, £500. And at the bottom, it's marked paid in full. Where did you find this?"

"Told you, amongst his papers." Cormac busied himself by plucking cookies and a scone from the tea tray and placing them onto a dainty pink flowered dish.

Inspector Quinn delivered a calculating look. "In his estate office here, or at his cottage?"

Cormac bit into a cookie, and crumbs sprinkled his tweed jacket. "Don't recall. One or the other."

"So, you've been through his things at the cottage?"

"Merely looked through his papers. Father asked me to locate his legal documents—will, banking information, etcetera. That sort of thing." Cormac took his goodies and perched on the arm of the chair Julia had taken.

"I would have appreciated it if you had waited for me before going through Mr. Byrne's private files. I believe I requested to see *all* his files. I will need to see those documents, as well."

Cormac charged back with, "I would argue that the ledgers you took belong to the estate, and therefore they belong to the O'Connell family. Not Brian."

"Cormac!" Lord O'Connell thundered at his son, then turned to the inspector. "Don't be so hard on the boy, Quinn. I asked him to do it. I've got the documents right here." Callum rose and approached the antique desk situated by the window. "I planned to give them over to Brian's sister and brother when they arrive tomorrow." He retrieved a key from his vest pocket and stuck it into the lock of the bottom drawer. The heavy drawer slid open with a mousey squeak.

"Be that as it may, you have been tampering with evidence," the inspector warned.

His gaze briefly flickered in my direction, letting me know I was included in his accusation.

"Evidence? Bank statements and a will?" Cormac scoffed.

"The banking materials could reveal information that would lead to a motive for murder," Quinn explained.

Cormac shrugged, as if it didn't matter to him whether or not the inspector wanted the materials.

Lord O'Connell handed over two file folders with paper corners sticking out of them. "That's everything Cormac found. I asked him to retrieve the materials before you told us Brian may have been..." He visibly swallowed.

"Murdered?" Inspector Quinn finished for him.

"As you say." Lord O'Connell returned to his seat and picked up the teacup.

"Yes, I do," Quinn reiterated. "I also say, from now on, Mr. Byrne's office and his cottage are *off* limits to anyone but Gardai."

"For how long? His family is coming tomorrow. I imagine they were planning to stay in the cottage," Lord O'Connell pointed out.

He spoke sharply, "For as long as I deem it necessary." Inspector Quinn's features turned a mottled red color, highlighting the whiteness of his bushy brows and mustache.

Callum frowned at the inspector's sharp tones.

It was clear that at least three people—Julia, Cormac, and I—had been through Brian's cottage. There was no telling who else had been in it.

"I assume there is plenty of room for them to stay here—" he waved his hand in the air "—in the manor house," Quinn amended with less severity.

"Here you go, Inspector." Aunt Maggie handed him a cup and saucer. "Why don't you sit down?" She indicated one of the empty brown leather chairs. "Can I offer you a scone, or perhaps a cookie?"

"Biscuit," Shane replied, filching one off the tea cart like a small boy.

"Yes, a biscuit, as you say on this side of the pond," my aunt corrected and proceeded to pile a plate with cookies and a scone.

"Thank you, ma'am, I'll be fine." He slapped the files onto the side table, plunked the cup and saucer on top, and sat down with a huff.

"That is better, isn't it?" She handed him the plate.

Quinn must not have remembered his initial refusal, for he tucked into the cookies. Some of the crumbs caught in his mustache as he bit down.

"Now, Inspector, why don't you give us an update on the case?" My aunt stood by the fire and sipped her tea.

Lord O'Connell put down his cup with a distinct clank. "Yes, I would like to hear how it is coming."

We watched the inspector struggle internally before replying, "We have searched the castle, and we did not recover Mr. Byrne's watch."

"What are the next steps?" Julia asked.

"As we speak, your rooms are being searched."

That little bomb was met with silent shock as if the room expanded like a set of lungs taking a breath. Then Cormac jumped to his feet, shouting an epithet. Lord O'Connell barked. Shane visibly paled.

Uncle Gerry kept his cool. "I say, Inspector, is that necessary? You don't believe one of us stole Mr. Byrne's watch and pushed him off the ramparts?"

Relieved that I'd handed over my ill-gotten booty, I had the temerity to say, "Search away, Inspector. I've nothing to hide." My response garnered a frown from Uncle Gerald.

"Don't you require a warrant or-or something?" Cormac challenged.

"You're right, son. Now, where did I put it?" Quinn made a show of searching all his pockets, finally producing a piece of paper from an inside one. He held it out. "Compliments of the local magistrate."

Cormac marched over, snatching it from his hand. After reading it, he huffed and passed it off to his father.

Lord O'Connell rested a pair of reading glasses on his nose and perused the document. "I don't know what you plan to find. None of us wished Brian ill, much less for his death. He was practically family."

A commotion and the clattering of boot heels in the hallway garnered our attention.

In walked a young man wearing a dark police uniform, followed by Mrs. Briggs. "Inspector Quinn, I believe we've found it." He held out a pocket watch in a white gloved hand.

Quinn towered above the officer, squinting at the watch. "Mrs. Briggs, can you confirm this is Mr. Byrne's watch?" he asked.

"Yes, s-sir," her voice shook. "It does look like it. His father's name is engraved on the back."

"We found it amongst Shane O'Connell's things," the Garda's voice rang with accusation, and he pointed one long finger at Shane.

Julia and her mother both gasped. Lord O'Connell let out a gurgling sound. Uncle Gerald murmured something under his breath. But his brother Cormac showed very little reaction, merely a slight narrowing of his eyes. Finally, my gaze swept over to the accused.

Shane hunched down in his wingback chair; his coloring turned a shade of pea green, and his hands gripped the arms of the chair.

"Briggs you're dismissed." Lady Aisling stood in the Library doorway. "What is it you've found in my son's room?"

My shoulders jerked at her voice, so silent had she appeared.

Though her tweed skirt, sensible low-heeled oxfords, and sweater set were in order, her features appeared a bit wild, and the chignon at the nape of her neck was askew with pieces of hair sticking out of the sides.

"I was unceremoniously awoken from a nap by one of your Gardai. What *exactly* is going on, Inspector Quinn?" Her voice held an imperious yet strained note to it. "I've had an extremely trying day dismantling a party *you* insisted we cancel! I was finally resting to gather my thoughts about this tragedy, when one of your people burst into my room! Without knocking! As if they owned the place!"

The officer holding the watch blanched at Lady Aisling's accusations.

However, the veteran detective did not cower beneath her haughtiness. Instead, he rolled his shoulders back and puffed out his chest. "Apologies, my lady, if my Gardai were a tad overzealous in their duties. They were searching for this." He indicated the pocket watch.

Lady Aisling's body stiffened straight as a fence post. "Indeed?" The heat left her tone, and she spoke as if ice chips dripped from her words. "And what does our *new estate manager* have to say for himself?"

I cringed at her assignment of Mr. Byrne's title to her son, sensing it sought to shine further attention on a possible motive for Shane to commit murder.

At her use of the words "estate manager," Shane's head tilted, and the slightest smirk passed over his features. Her question did not make him cower, as I'd expected. Instead, I witnessed what seemed to be a silent exchange between the pair. He pulled himself upright, his spine cracking at the elongation.

"I can explain." His hands busily searched his jacket pockets for a cigarette pack and subsequently lit a fag. "Anyone?" He held out the pack, but no one answered him. "No? Suit yourselves."

"Shane, you were about to explain why you had Brian's watch?" His father prompted.

"Yes, well, this is rather embarrassing to admit." His face flushed. "I found it...next to the body...Brian's, I mean." He sucked deeply on the cigarette, holding his breath for a moment before pushing the smoke out through his nostrils.

"Go on," Quinn encouraged.

He bobbed one shoulder in a half-shrug. "I pocketed it."

Quinn sucked his teeth as he considered Shane's words. "And why did you do that?"

Shane made a show of tapping off the ash. "I need the money."

"Son! You can always ask—"

Shane cut off his father's chastisement, "It's for a photography contest. You've made your feelings quite clear on that front." Lord O'Connell closed his mouth shut so hard his teeth made a snapping noise. The young man returned his attention to the inspector. "I figured I could sell it for enough punts to purchase the special paper and cover the entry fee."

Lord O'Connell rubbed his temples and shook his head. "Ah, Shane, why'd you go and do something so foolish?"

Shane put on a good show of embarrassment.

From what Julia had told me, and what I witnessed last night, it would be quintessential of Shane to do something so crass for money. Nevertheless, I wasn't buying his story. He was lying about something.

Stealing the watch for money? If that is the case, where did the thousand pounds Brian accused him of pilfering go?

That type of money would more than cover photography and developing equipment, with plenty left over for a paltry contest entry fee.

Or is he lying about finding it at the base of the castle?

Perhaps Brian followed Shane, or vice versa, to the castle. There was another contretemps between the two men. A final row. In anger and fear, Shane pushed Brian over the edge.

How did he obtain the watch? Did he pick it up after checking on the body?

I recalled the pitch darkness upon my arrival yesterday evening and shook my head, changing the scenario.

Perhaps Shane lost his temper and pushed the older

man. Brian lost his footing. Realizing what he'd done, Shane reached out to pull Brian back onto secure footing, the way Cormac did with me at the cliffs. But he was too late, and all he could grab hold of was the chain and the watch.

"Miss Winter? Miss Winter!" Inspector Quinn brought me back to Earth.

"Yes?"

"I believe you discovered Mr. Byrne's body along with Mr. O'Connell. Do you recall seeing the watch on or near his body?"

I had no recollection of the watch being anywhere near the body. Furthermore, I didn't recall Shane showing any abnormal behavior when the watch had been brought up in conversation earlier in the day. Nary a blush, sidelong glance, or a tense up. Yet now...something was off. The silent conversation between mother and son. What did it mean?

"Miss Winter?" Quinn pressed.

"No, Inspector." I shook my head. "I do not recall seeing the watch. Nor did I witness Shane stick it in his pocket."

"Are you sure?" Lady Aisling questioned with hostility.

Shocked by her antipathy, I waspishly replied, "I beg your pardon?"

But she wasn't looking at me. Instead, she scrutinized her son, and they seemed to carry on another silent exchange. "How did you hide it from our guest, Shane?"

"Really, Mother!" Cormac reproached.

Shane hurriedly explained, "She wouldn't have seen. The watch was lying on the far side of the body...I mean Brian." His fingers shook as he crushed the half-smoked cigarette in the ashtray. "I didn't notice it myself. Until I went to check his pulse. Ariadne had gone to...uh, tell her cousin to return to the house for help. So-so, she wouldn't have seen it," he stammered.

"I," he gulped, stared into his lap, and reluctantly murmured, "slipped the watch into my pocket."

Quinn chewed on Shane's revelations. "Very well. You'll need to come with me to the station to make a statement." He made one last note on his pad, then turned to the waiting Garda. "Take the watch back to the office. Enter it into evidence."

"I believe I will accompany my son to the station, Inspector Quinn." Lady Aisling delivered a thin-lipped scowl. "To make sure he is treated fairly."

"I assure you, I am conducting this inquiry by the book," Inspector Quinn defended.

"I'll be fine, Mother. You needn't trouble yourself."

"Nonsense," she said dismissively, "it's no trouble."

"You should stay home and get some rest," Shane restated.

"I insist."

With great effort, Lord O'Connell rose to his feet. "He's right, darling. *You* stay. *I* will go with him," he said in a curt manner that brooked no defiance. "Quinn, lead the way."

Chapter Twenty-Five
Julia

Lady Aisling stared, unmoving, after her son and husband with a worried frown. As the entourage exited, she moved woodenly to follow. A sobbing gasp escaped, and she collapsed, sinking to the floor.

The room filled with motion.

"Mother!" Cormac cried as he rushed to her side.

Julia and her mother also went to Lady Aisling, while her father hurried out of the room, calling for help.

"Mother?" Cormac cupped a hand against her cheek.

"Lady Aisling, dear lady, can you hear us?" Julia's mother rubbed the other woman's hand between her own. "She's quite cold. Julia, fetch that afghan on the sofa."

Julia did as her mother bade and laid the red wool across Lady Aisling's body. Julia didn't blame her one bit for fainting dead away. How shocking! She couldn't imagine being in Lady Aisling's shoes. A mother who discovered her son was a murderer.

For that's what Shane was. A murderer.

Julia had no doubt. Not for a moment did she believe a word he said about finding the watch on the dead body. Shane, the black sheep of the family. The son who couldn't hold down a job. It must have been he who pushed poor Brian to his death.

Julia was sick about it. Look at how his actions affected the strong Lady Aisling.

What will it do to the family's reputation? Julia's

mind began to spin with worry. *How will this affect our wedding? Ballyford is a small village. People talk. Perhaps Cormac and I would be better off marrying at home in DC. A dream come true for Mother.*

"Everyone move back," said Ariadne, the only person in the room who had not dashed to the lady's side. She stood above the concerned tableau with a cup of tea in her hand.

"What on Earth?" Julia cried.

Cormac shifted position, allowing Ariadne direct access to her target. *Splat.* She threw tea into her future mother-in-law's face.

Lady Aisling gasped.

Some of the tea splashed onto her mother's sweater set. "Ariadne! Really!" she admonished, shaking the liquid off her arm.

The older woman's eyes fluttered open.

"Unorthodox method, but that seems to have done the trick," Cormac muttered.

"Sorry, Aunt Maggie," Ariadne said regretfully.

"What happened?" Lady Aisling asked in faded tones.

"You fainted," Ariadne replied in curt tones, returning the teacup to its saucer with a clank. Having little sympathy for the matriarch, her features were set in hard lines of irritation.

The older woman touched her cheek, and her sleeve fell back, revealing a pattern of bruises around her wrist. Feeling the dampness, she asked, "Am I bleeding?"

"It's only tea." Cormac used his handkerchief to wipe the liquid from his mother's face.

"Can you sit forward?" asked Julia's mother.

"Of course." Julia and her mother pulled Aisling into a sitting position.

She took the handkerchief from her son's hand and finished the job. Glancing at the stained white linen, she asked, "Why am I covered in tea?"

Before anyone could respond, Julia's father and Mrs. Briggs rushed onto the scene.

"My lady!" Mrs. Briggs cried. "What happened?"

"It would appear I fainted," she replied with a touch of asperity.

"And no wonder. It's been too much for you," Julia's father blustered. "Why don't you have your lady's maid here, take you back up to your room? You could use a little lie-down. Obviously, it's been an overwhelming day. Pumpkin, you go up with her," he encouraged his daughter.

The more her father spoke, the redder Lady Aisling's face became. "Nonsense. I don't need coddling. I'm fine!" she snapped. "*Cormac*, help me to my feet."

Her son and Julia's mother pulled Lady Aisling to her feet. She swayed for a moment in his arms.

"Whoa! I think Mr. Brennan is right. Let me take you up to your room," Cormac coaxed.

She blinked and finally capitulated, "Very well. I will go and lie down. Briggs, be sure to inform me when the men return home."

"Yes, ma'am. Um, where have they gone?"

The room went silent, as they Mrs. Briggs had been unceremoniously dismissed from the conversation.

Ariadne smoothed over the awkwardness by stepping into the breach. "To the station. Shane needs to give an official statement. They'll be back in time for dinner. Aunt Maggie, why don't you help Cormac escort Lady Aisling to her room? Mrs. Briggs, Lady Aisling, didn't get her tea. Perhaps you can send up a fresh pot with a little something for her to nibble on?"

Briggs tsked. "You know you get a little off when you don't have your afternoon tea, my lady. I'll bring up a pot directly."

"Thank you, Briggs," she replied.

174

Lady Aisling must really be out of sorts, thought Julia. It was the first time she had seen Lady Aisling's icy exterior falter. And she'd *never* witnessed the matriarch thank her housekeeper for *anything*.

"Uncle Gerald, the tea in here has gone cold. Can you find Daisy and have her remove the tea things?" Ariadne directed the group of adults as if she were the mistress of the house.

It seemed so natural coming from her cousin, and Julia wondered if she'd ever do as well as Ariadne or Lady Aisling when the time came. She fiddled with her pearl necklace in thought.

Can I be as decisive as my cousin, or authoritative as Lady Aisling?

Neither were the character traits Julia innately possessed, and she wondered if she'd learn them over time. The ticking of the grandfather clock invaded Julia's thoughts, and she realized she and her cousin were alone in the Library.

Julia stared at the darkened tea stain on the carpet, and a giggle burbled up her throat. "I can't believe you threw your tea at Lady Aisling."

"It seemed appropriate at the time," Ariadne commented drily. "But it's not why I cleared the room."

"Yes, I noticed that." Julia strode over to a side table to retrieve a cigarette from the pack Shanc had left behind. A book of matches from the Green Pub was tucked inside the box. With a rasping scrape the match flared, and Julia greedily sucked in the unfiltered tobacco.

"I could use one of those."

Julia tossed the pack to Ariadne, and tucking the back of the skirt beneath her she sat in a leather club chair. After her first puff Ariadne set to pacing in front of the fireplace where the logs had burned down to a smolder. Her lips moved, but nothing came out of them.

"Are you going to tell me why you cleared the room?"

"Do you believe Shane?" Ariadne halted her pacing and loomed above her.

Julia turned her head, blowing the smoke over her shoulder. "That cock and bull story he fed about finding the watch? Absolutely not! He's a degenerate and...and an inveterate liar from what Cormac's told me."

Ariadne's lips curled. She paced away, pivoted, and the two cousins spoke at once.

"I think he killed Brian," Julia stated unequivocally.

"I don't think he did it," said Ariadne.

Julia's spine stiffened. "You can't actually believe that story he told us, about finding the watch next to the body?"

"I do not." Ariadne shook her head, and Julia relaxed into the folds of the cushion.

Her cousin continued, "I don't believe he found the watch next to Brian, because when the watch was discussed earlier, Shane showed no reaction whatsoever." She flicked her palm out in a stop motion. "None. How did he think he'd be able to pawn it, without getting caught? The O'Connell family is well known in this area. I don't believe he'd be able to sell something like Mr. Byrne's watch without raising suspicion."

"My thoughts exactly," Julia agreed, pointing the cigarette at her cousin. "I think he was hiding the evidence and planned to destroy it once the hubbub calmed down."

"No-o." Ariadne tapped cigarette ash onto the glowing embers. "I believe Shane *did* 'find' the watch."

Julia frowned. "What do you mean? You just said—"

"Let me clarify. *I believe*, Shane took—" her ruby-tipped fingers plucked a miniature figurine off the mantel "—the watch from the person who *was* with Mr. Byrne...when he died."

Julia sucked in a breath and delivered a skeptical

176

reply, "If that's so, why didn't he unmask the person? Why make up the story?"

"Because he is using it as leverage to get what he wants," her cousin enunciated each syllable.

"I'm not following." Julia uncrossed her legs and sat forward.

Ariadne placed the figurine on top of a stack of books. "Why did Lady Aisling call her son 'the new estate manager' today?"

"Well, I suppose the family agreed to put Shane into the position."

"I thought that position was still under debate." Ariadne gave her the side-eye.

Julia simply shrugged, tamping out her cigarette in a crystal ashtray.

"So, why didn't she call him by name? Why use that *particular* title? He's her son, not a servant."

Julia's mouth twisted, and her forehead wrinkled. "Now that you mention it, the exchange did seem a bit odd. I just assumed she was putting her wayward son in the hot seat."

"She was communicating with him." Ariadne pulled a Queen Anne side chair in front of Julia and sat on it.

"In what way?"

Ariadne crossed her legs and leaned an elbow on her knee. "She was assuring Shane that if he kept his mouth *shut* about where he *acquired* that watch, she would make sure *he*...would become...the next estate manager."

Ariadne's hypothesis baffled Julia. It made no sense. "Why would Lady Aisling want Shane to hide what he knows from the police? The sooner we identify Brian's killer, the safer we will all be."

Ariadne rested her chin in her palm and stared at Julia in askance.

Then it hit her—what her cousin was driving at. "Oh, *surely* you don't believe Shane is covering for one of the family members?" Julia scoffed.

She didn't answer. One of her perfectly shaped eyebrows lifted.

Julia jumped out of the chair and began her pacing in front of the fireplace, wringing her hands, her brows drew into a frustrated V. "No! Come now, Ariadne. You can't be serious. Why on Earth would anyone in the family want Brian dead?" Julia watched her cousin's curls bounce as she shook her head.

"That's the problem." She turned her chair around, her features troubled. "The one person I know who has a motive, Shane, strikes me as the one person who did not do it. He showed genuine shock at finding Mr. Byrne. I was there. I remember." Ariadne slammed her fist into her palm.

Julia halted her pacing and rotated to face her cousin. "What did you say? What do you mean, Shane had a motive?"

With a sigh, Ariadne confessed to eavesdropping outside the Billiard Room last night. She told Julia about the argument she'd witnessed between Brian and Shane.

"That's a lot of money." Julia whistled between her teeth. "So, Shane *did* have a motive. And what did he mean about telling his father? Who *is* this fellow he saw at the pub with Brian?"

"I've no clue, but I have a gut feeling that this man Cormac and Shane witnessed Brian speaking to in Galway, and again in Doolin, is the key to this entire mystery."

"If you believe Shane is covering for someone in the family, who would that person be?"

Ariadne stared at her cousin with pity.

Julia's stomach lurched, and she let out a hard little laugh. "Surely, you don't believe it is Cormac?" Julia let out a hard little laugh.

"I didn't say that, Julia. What I *can* tell you is that I

had a bit of a fright down at the cliffs."

The memory of how close Ariadne came to the edge popped into Julia's head. "But...Cormac saved you from falling, dear," she soothed.

"Yet, it was *he* who backed me into that precarious position to begin with," Ariadne pointed out.

Julia huffed and crossed her arms. "You're talking nonsense. Cormac's been torn up over Brian's death. He's out of sorts. Whatever you *think* happened on the cliffs is simply in *your* imagination. Cormac was *not* trying to hurt you."

Ariadne's spine stiffened, and she shot back, "Maybe just to scare me?"

Julia felt as if she'd been slapped, her mouth sagged, and her face burned.

In her haughtiest voice, she articulated each word, "You are being ridiculous. Just because you solved one murder, it does not make you a professional detective. And you are going to get yourself into plenty of trouble if you keep throwing out ridiculous accusations, such as the one you just intimated."

Chapter Twenty-Six
Ariadne

Immediately, I allowed my face to go slack and shuttered my blazing gaze away from Julia by turning my back on her. My feelings, like my cigarette, still smoldered. With shaking fingers, I smashed the butt into the ashtray to calm my nerves.

A chilly silence descended, as the two of us remained unmoving, separated by nothing more than a square coffee table, but it might as well have been the Grand Canyon. I hated arguing, especially with Julia. As an only child, she was the closest thing I had to a sister. I valued our friendship above all else. I understood then—Julia would never think poorly of Cormac. If I continued to pursue that line of thinking in front of her, she would choose her husband-to-be's side over mine. Her newfound love would be blind to any of his faults.

In stiff, repentant tones, I apologized to Julia. "My imagination has run amok."

She grunted an acknowledgement and asked, "Did we ever find out where Shane went after he left the Billiard Room last night? Does he have an alibi?"

I tucked a curl behind my ear and shook my head. "Not that I'm aware of."

"So, maybe he *did* meet with Brian, and their argument continued...and it led them to the castle. Where Shane—"

A gasp and the crash of broken crockery startled both of us.

"Oh, dear, Mrs. Briggs will have my head for that." Daisy crouched to pick up the broken pieces of a blue and white ceramic vase that had been resting only moments before, on a decorative plinth just inside the doorway. The matching vase stood on the opposite side. "She's going to sack me," her voice wobbled tearfully.

"Here now, don't cry, Daisy. It's only a silly vase." Julia strode over to help the young maid pick up the broken pieces.

"But it's a matched set, and probably worth more than I make in a year. Mrs. Briggs told me everything in this house is worth more than my salary," the girl cried.

I sucked in a breath and stated, "*I* broke the vase."

Daisy's trembling hands paused. "Miss?"

"We will tell them *I* broke the vase. I bumped into it on my way out of the room. I'm the clumsy American."

Julia realizing the kindness I was bestowing in this poor girl for taking the blame spoke up, "No. I'm about to marry into the family. We can tell them, I broke it."

"Nonsense." I dismissed Julia's idea. "That dragon is already trying to find things wrong with you. To prove to Cormac and anyone who will listen that you're not worthy of the O'Connell name. We can't give her further ammunition. I'm a guest. I'm not related to, or trying to become related to, anyone in the family. What can they do to me, except ask me to leave?"

"Oh, she'd never do that, miss." Daisy pursed her lips. "She'd never be so rude to a guest. Even one who broke a valuable item in the household."

"See, there." I held my hand toward the maid. "As Daisy said, I wouldn't receive any punishment, except for the cold shoulder from Lady Aisling and probably Mrs. Briggs. Which wouldn't be much different than what I've already experienced. I'm certain to be in Lady Aisling's black books already, for throwing the tea on her."

Daisy's mouth bobbed like a cork in water. "Oh,

miss, you didn't," she said in disbelief.

"Indeed, she did." Julia couldn't help the giggle that escaped.

"In my defense, the woman had fainted dead away. She needed reviving. There was no water to be had, so the next best thing was the tea. Luckily, the carpet is dark, but I do feel bad about staining Aunt Maggie's peach sweater. I hope she can get it out." I tapped a finger against my chin. "What was it my mother told me to use when I spilled tea on the linen tablecloth. Was it baking soda?"

"Don't you worry about that. I once got a tea stain out of a silk gown. It was cream colored. The key to it is vinegar."

I crouched down to the maid's level. "Tell you what, Daisy, if you promise to clean up my aunt's sweater, I'll make sure your secret is safe with me."

"I don't know, that doesn't seem like an even exchange." Her eyes brightened. "But I *can* tell you a secret."

"What's that?"

Daisy checked over her shoulder. "I know where Shane went last night after he left the Billard Room."

"Where?" the pair of us asked as one.

Daisy's face turned bright pink, and she chewed her lip, as if rethinking her initial enthusiasm.

"Daisy, it's vitally important. You won't get in trouble. I promise." Julia gripped her hand. "Did you see Shane leave the manor? Was he out at the castle last night?"

Daisy shook her head. "Oh no, miss. Nothing like that. I found him in the Solarium."

"What time?" Julia asked.

"Where did he go after that?" We peppered the poor maid with questions.

"He was...he was..." She finally whispered, "With me."

"I'll be damned," I murmured rolling my lips in to keep from grinning.

That sneaky boy, taking up with the maid. Like a story from a bad soap opera. I could see from the glimmer in Daisy's eyes, she believed he would take her away from a life of servitude. Who knows what lies Shane had told the pretty maid to get her into bed?

"*He was with you? All night?*" Julia said in a squeaky high voice.

Hesitantly, Daisy nodded.

Julia passed a hand over her eyes. "How...how long has this been going on?"

"S-since he arrived home," the girl confessed. "You-you won't tell? Will you?"

Julia's mouth turned down in disgust, and she gulped, as if swallowing down a glob of bile. She snarled, "It would be just like Shane to mess around with the staff and take advantage of an innocent young girl like you. Why he ought to be hung by his thumbs—"

Daisy interrupted Julia's tirade, "We're in love."

Julia and I shared a knowing look. It would be so easy for swashbuckling Shane to smooth-talk Daisy into believing he loved her.

"I'm sure you are, dear." I patted her shoulder. "Now, you must realize Inspector Quinn may wish to speak with you. Shane's gone down to the station right now, and he might have to tell them about your tryst."

Daisy's eyes widened with fear, and she jumped to her feet, wringing her hands. "Oh, but he mustn't. I'll get sacked! *Immediately.*" The girl turned her sad cow eyes onto my cousin. "You don't think he'd tell the Gardai, do you?"

"Well...I-I don't know." Julia picked an invisible piece of lint from her sweater. "Um, he might have to."

"But, *why?*" Daisy wailed in distress.

Julia's eyes pleaded with me.

I cleared my throat. "You see, Daisy...the police, they, uh, found Brian's watch in Shane's room."

Daisy's hands flew to cover her mouth, and her head rotated back and forth. "It's a mistake. The real murderer must have put it in there. To throw suspicion on Shane. You don't understand, his father hates him. He's always blaming the family's troubles on Shane. Oh!" Her fingers went from twisting each other to twisting her apron, leaving behind deep wrinkles. "I must speak to Inspector Quinn. I-I have to see him. They can't put Shane in jail. He'll never endure it."

I wasn't quite sure about that. If it came to it, I imagined Shane would find a way to endure in jail. He was a scrapper and quite cunning. From the few remarks the family had made, I got the impression Shane had spent his fair share of time skirting the law. Between the two brothers, I believed it would be Cormac who would struggle to survive in such a harsh environment.

Daisy swung toward the doorway. "I must go."

Julia grabbed her elbow. "Daisy, wait. Where are you going?"

"My bicycle is around back. I-I have to go. Down to the station. I must save Shane." Daisy broke free and blundered onward.

"Daisy!" I called. "Stop!"

The maid didn't heed the demand, and soon we heard the front door slam.

Julia spun on her heel to face me. She grinned from ear to ear, and her eyes danced. "Can you believe it? It's like a Victorian romance novel. Or a real-life soap opera."

"You think this is funny?"

Her features sobered. She scooped up the pack of cigarettes and lit a fresh one. "No, you're right. It's not funny at all. That poor girl. I could throttle Shane for dallying with her. Clearly, he doesn't love her. I'll have to speak with Cormac and have him put a stop to it.

Goodness, if that girl becomes pregnant...well, I-I can't even imagine the fallout."

"It would cause a scandal," I said drily.

She pointed at me with two fingers. "Exactly. Not something we need on top of Brian's death."

"You know what this means?" I picked up a crystal paperweight off Lord O'Connell's desk.

"What?"

I studied the facets of the cut crystal, watching the light shimmer, creating rainbows against my hand. "If Shane *was* with Daisy last night, he's got an alibi. He couldn't have murdered Mr. Byrne."

Julia blew out a stream of smoke. "So, he was telling the truth about finding the watch?"

"Or he's lying about where he found the watch."

Chapter Twenty-Seven
Gavin Turnbull

Clouds of smoke drifted above the patrons, and the wood floor was sticky. The scent of cabbage and cooked meat flowed from the kitchen as the red-headed waitress burst out of the door carrying a loaded tray of food. The pub had yet to reach full capacity, but the dark paneling and tight tables made it feel cozy on this cold night.

"It'll be shoulder to shoulder in the next few hours." The sandy-haired bartender was covered in freckles across his nose and cheeks. Even his hands were spotted with freckles, Gavin noticed as the man placed a pint of Guinness in front of him. He'd watched as the tap gently filled the angled glass, leaving a half-inch creamy white head of foam at the top. "If you like music, the local band will start up about nine."

"I expect I'll be gone by then," Gavin replied.

"Are you staying nearby?" The bartender put another pint beneath the tap and began to pour.

"I'm waiting for my ride. A fellow from Ballyford Castle is supposed to pick me up."

"Did you say you were headed to Ballyford Castle?" The nasal intonation of a Boston accent interrupted their conversation.

Gavin glanced over his shoulder, coming face to face with a dark-haired man. He had a narrow, pointed, ferret-like face. His hazel eyes took in Gavin and the bartender.

"As a matter of fact, I'm waiting for my ride." Gavin sipped the dark malty beverage, enjoying the afternotes of coffee and chocolate. "Do I hear a Boston accent?"

"Guilty." The American nodded. "From Dorchester." He ordered a Guinness from the bartender before returning to Gavin. "What about you? That's no Irish accent."

"Originally from upstate New York, but I've been living in the city for the past five years."

"Harry." The ferrety man stuck out a hand.

"Gavin."

Harry slid onto the empty barstool. "What takes you to Ballyford, Gavin?"

"I'm a photographer with *Ladies' Lifestyle Magazine*. I was flying back to New York from a Paris shoot, when our plane had to make an emergency landing in Shannon. My, uh, co-worker, who is a writer at the magazine, is staying at Ballyford. Visiting her cousin. I rang her up and wangled an invite until I can get on a flight home Monday." Gavin wiggled his brows and grinned.

The barkeep polished the bar with a rag. "I hope you're not going there for the annual party. Heard it's been canceled. On account of the death."

"Death?" the two men said as one.

The bartender nodded. "A man was found dead this morning near the castle ruins."

"That's terrible," Gavin said.

The other American leaned forward, resting his forearms on the bar, and asked in a slightly sharp tone, "What man?"

"The estate manager. Name of Byrne. I didn't know him personally, but everyone around here knows Ballyford. Titled, fancy sort of toffs. The last lord was the mayor for bout twenty years."

"You say the man was found dead. This morning?" Harry pressed.

"That's what I heard." The bartender returned to

Harry's Guinness turning off the tap just as the head became even with the top of the glass.

"How did it happen?" Gavin asked.

The barkeep shrugged, placing the glass in front of Harry. "Dunno. Guess we'll have to wait for the inquiry."

"An inquiry?" Harry cleared his throat. "Does that mean they're investigating his death? Do they think there was…"

"Foul play?" Gavin completed Harry's thought.

The bartender threw the towel over his shoulder. "I shouldn't think so. Standard procedure to investigate a death when the person hasn't been ill."

"Paddy, three pints of Guinness, a glass of Smithwick, and a TK Red Lemonade!" the wide-hipped waitress hollered before disappearing through the swinging door to the kitchen.

The bartender moved down the counter to prepare the drinks.

"How do you know the O'Connell family?" Harry asked.

"I don't. I hope they aren't upset, my girl—" Gavin cleared his throat. "I mean, my co-worker invited me to stay. I spoke with the housekeeper. She said there was plenty of room."

"I imagine so. The mansion is quite extensive."

"You've been?"

Harry shook his head. "Stayed nearby, but I've, uh, heard about it." He sipped his Guinness in thought.

"Which of you chaps is the Yank I'm supposed to take back to Ballyford?" A lanky man wearing a newsboy cap, with an olive green vest beneath his black woolen coat, stood behind the two men. His lined features looked like sunbaked shoe leather.

"That's me." Gavin gave a two-finger wave. He glanced around the bar, which was now close to capacity. "How did you—"

"Know you two were Yanks? Didn't take much. Just looked around for the men in the fanciest kit." He indicated Gavin's gray suit and tie. While Harry wasn't wearing a suit and tie, he was wearing a busy, red and brown, plaid sport coat that stood out among the duller gray and beige colors worn by the locals.

"I'm Gavin. This is Harry," he said above the increased din of voices.

"Dougray." The men shook hands.

"Thanks for coming all the way out here to fetch me."

"It's nothing," Dougray dismissed.

Gavin held up his half-drunk pint. "Do I have time to finish my drink?"

"Of course. Not going to let a pint of Guinness go to waste. I think I'll join you. It's been a hell of a day." He held up his hand and waved at the bartender. "Paddy, a half pint of Smithwick's red." The man grinned at Gavin. "I better keep it light, since I'm driving."

"Speaking of, I was wondering if I could get a ride. I'm headed in your direction to—" The rest of Harry's mumbled comment was cut as he took a gulp of Guinness.

"I can certainly give you a lift."

Harry wiped the foam off his upper lip before responding, "Much obliged. We heard about the death at the castle. Sorry for your loss."

Dougray rubbed his eyes and frowned. "A terrible accident. Brian was a good man."

"The bartender mentioned there is an inquiry?" Gavin said.

Dougray's head bobbed, and he took the open stool on the other side of Gavin. "Yes, Inspector Quinn, from Lisdoonvarna, is conducting it. He's a worthy man."

Paddy placed a glass of red ale in front of Dougray. The waitress burst out of the kitchen carrying another loaded tray, shoulder height, her hips swaying in a rhythm that kept the dishes from toppling. Gavin wasn't sure what captured his attention more, the delicious scents wafting off the tray, or the skilled dance of the copper-haired woman. Gavin wasn't the only one mesmerized by the waitress and her tray.

"Supper will probably be over by the time I get you back to Ballyford," Dougray said, watching the redhead pass out the meals to a nearby table. "Might want to get your meal here."

Paddy must have the ears of an owl. In two shakes, he pulled a couple of menus from beneath the bar and spread them out in front of the three men.

"What do you suggest?" Gavin asked, perusing his options.

"The Corned Beef and Cabbage, or the Irish Stew, with brown bread, is the most popular," Paddy replied.

"I'll have the Corned Beef and Cabbage." Harry handed the menu back to the bartender.

Gavin and Dougray ordered the Irish Stew with brown bread. Paddy wrote the order down on a pad of paper and passed it to the waitress on her way to the kitchen.

"To better days." Dougray raised his glass high. "Sláinte."

"Better days," echoed Gavin.

"Cheers!" Harry lifted his glass.

The three men drank deeply.

Dougray plunked his glass on the bar and announced, "Be right back. Must visit the toilets. Save my seat."

Once he was gone, Gavin turned to Harry. "Tell me, what do you do for a living?"

Harry's eyes darted around the bar. "I'm a private investigator."

Gavin kept his face neutral and nodded with interest. "Must be interesting work."

His shifting gaze didn't look Gavin straight in the eye. "It can be."

Gavin glanced over his shoulder but saw nothing of particular interest. A young couple sitting close and whispering to each other. A family with grade school children sat behind them. A man wearing coveralls, his face craggy with drooping eyes, sat at the bar next to another man in coveralls. The pub was filled with average Irish folks enjoying a pint and some food at the end of a long day. When his attention returned to Harry, Gavin found him studying a deep groove scratched into the bar. His dirty thumbnail picked at the channel.

Gavin sensed that Harry was reluctant to discuss his work. Or perhaps he suffered embarrassment. Private detectives didn't always have the best reputation, often portrayed as morally ambiguous or having attachments to criminal elements by Hollywood studios. What little Gavin could conclude, Harry was not like the handsome but brooding Sam Spade, nor the highly intellectual Sherlock Holmes, nor the fussy and dapper Hercule Poirot.

No.

The man with his ferrety features, slicked hair, and darting eyes fit the definition of a dodgy character. The type who snuck around taking photos of men cheating on their wives.

Gavin sipped his beer and decided on a safer line of questioning. "What are you doing here in Ireland? Vacationing?"

To Gavin's surprise, Harry admitted, "Actually, I've been conducting some business."

"Really? All the way from America? What kind of business?"

Harry drank deeply. The glass returned to the bar with a distinct clunk. "A client asked me to research an old inheritance claim. Going back over one hundred and fifty years."

"Really? An inheritance claim, here in Ireland? Or in America?"

"Ireland. An inheritance claim that included a title."

His curiosity piqued, Gavin encouraged Harry to continue. "Fascinating. And what did you find?"

Harry leaned closer and dropped his voice so low, Gavin strained to hear. "There was an ancestor who came to Boston, via New York, and ended up in Maine. An ancestor who feared for his life and that of his wife. He even changed his name." Harry allowed for a dramatic pause before delivering, "To hide from men that had been sent from Ireland to kill him."

"Don't tell me, an illegitimate love child that would take away the king's crown if it had been known." Gavin wriggled his eyebrows and grinned, making light of the intrigue Harry hinted at. *Really, the man should be on stage.*

Perhaps sensing Gavin's taunting tone, Harry leaned away, sipped his beer, and wiped the foam from his lip with the back of his hand, intoning, "Something like that."

Gavin straightened his brows, replacing jocularity with a serious demeanor. "And now you're here. To tell the fellow what you found?"

Harry gave a quick jerk of a nod. "I'm on my way, from Dublin, to provide the final evidence of the bloodline and the title."

"Wow!" Gavin's impression of Harry's skills marginally improved. "I bet he'll be a happy man once he finds out he's got a title."

"And an estate."

Dougray suddenly appeared, leaning between the two men. "Where did you say you needed me to drop you off?"

"Lisdoonvarna. I need to visit an inspector," Harry

192

said the latter under his breath.

Gavin heard the statement and gave the P.I. a queer glance.

Before Gavin could ask Harry what he meant by it, the man said in a loud jovial voice, "Dougray, tell us, what is your favorite pub in Ireland?"

After that, the conversation turned to barrooms, beers, and eventually horses—selling, racing, stables, all things horse-related. Dougray had plenty of stories to share, and soon he had the two Americans laughing about a jockey who refused to wash his lucky socks and ultimately ended up sleeping in the stables with the horses after the tavern refused to accommodate him.

Gavin didn't forget about Harry's muttered comment. However, the rest of the evening, the pair were accompanied by Dougray, and Gavin sensed Harry didn't want to discuss his client, or subsequent findings, with the Irish stranger from Ballyford.

Chapter Twenty-Eight
Lord Callum O'Connell

Shedding his dripping coat, Callum followed his errant son through the mudroom. The ride home from the station remained frosty and detached; only the sound of the windshield wipers and the rain hammering against the roof of the car interrupted the silence.

Inspector Quinn had taken Shane's statement and was in the process of interrogating him further when a commotion broke out. Daisy, the maid from Ballyford, drenched from head to toe, burst into Quinn's office and, in a manner worthy of the stage, announced, "Shane couldn't have murdered poor Mr. Byrne, as he was with me all night!" She furthered the statement by claiming they were "in love."

If Callum expected Shane to be mortified by the maid's confession, he would have been disappointed. Callum, however, knew better. The boy simply smirked. His story about filching the watch was now on record. While Shane appeared genuinely humiliated about getting caught with the watch, dallying with the maid had caused him no such mortification.

The inspector took Daisy's statement and sent them all home. Shane stuffed Daisy's bike in the boot and dropped her off at her parents' house. Callum suggested the maid take the day off to recover from her soaking.

As the men hung up their coats, Callum struggled to understand Shane's motives for taking what did not belong to him. *Why is it so difficult for the boy to ask for money?*

Granted, in the past, Callum had forced Shane to justify his monetary requests. After all, Shane had had a perfectly good job. One that made him decent money. Obviously, Callum had made mistakes along the way; what parent hasn't made a few? Instilling the need to save his punts was one of them.

Money flowed through Shane's hands like water. Travel, women, the racetrack, not to mention the pubs. Any time Shane rolled into a pub, he had to behave like the lord of the manor and buy rounds for everyone in the bloody place, throwing money at the barkeep as if it he could wave a magic wand and produce more.

Oh, Shane had tried to hide his spendthrift ways, but word got back to Callum.

It always got back to Callum. The O'Connell name was known far and wide in Ireland.

He hoped, by putting Shane into Brian's role, the boy would at last comprehend how costly the manor and all the lands were to maintain. Perhaps his jealousy over being second-born would wane. And maybe, just maybe, he'd learn the value of money, so that when he came into his trust fund, he wouldn't piss it all away in the first six months.

Callum slipped off his wet boots and slid into a pair of loafers.

Brian's death was a terrible blow. The man had been a brother in arms. When Callum came into his inheritance, he was still young and feared making a mull of it. He didn't rub well with Brian's father, the former estate manager. However, once Brian took over the role, there was no stopping the two of them. They worked together to increase the land's income, and for many years, Ballyford prospered. Luckily, Ballyford came out of the war unscathed. Some of Callum's neighbors had dealt with German bomb damage, even though the Nazi's denied it. It was only within the last half-dozen years that the finances turned south, forcing Callum to take out a mortgage.

Callum blamed Brian's mismanagement of the tenancies, refusing to raise rents. Brian claimed the homes needed repairs and renovations before he would do so. When Callum argued against Brian's recommendations, the tenants moved out, leaving vacancies and a decreased income for the estate. Now, with no one to maintain them, the homes had truly fallen into disrepair. Oo, it made Callum's blood boil when he thought about it. With the estate manager gone, Callum could get back on top of the situation. Dig into it, and direct Shane to put the manor to rights and the finances back into the black.

Still, Brian had been a friend and confidante to Callum...and the family. Often, Brian handled Shane's peccadilloes better than Callum. He wondered how Brian would have handled the business with Daisy.

Or if the man had already known.

Callum prayed Shane would settle into the new role and get off this latest scheme of becoming a photographer. The boy was meant to work with horses and the land. He never saw a better seat than Shane's. Though Callum would never admit it out loud, Shane was better on a horse than Cormac ever could be. The boy had a naturalness about him. If he'd been five inches shorter and weighed thirty pounds less, he would've made an excellent jockey.

The other thing Callum hoped would come out of Shane's stint as estate manager would be for him to learn to stick with something. One of Shane's weaknesses was his inability to stick with any of the jobs he'd held. Even now, Callum couldn't understand why he'd come home. His former position seemed a perfect fit for Shane. A job in which he would thrive until he received his trust fund.

The boy reminded Callum of a cork floating on a river. Bobbing back and forth from shore to shore, going nowhere in particular, simply drifting down the stream of his life without real purpose. He simply did not know why the boy couldn't find happiness. Aisling blamed him for cutting Shane out of the estate business when the boys were younger. However, Callum saw it differently. Shane needed to understand, at an early age, that Ballyford would always be his home, but would never be his inheritance.

The staircase rose above them. Dragging his feet, Shane mounted the steps, shuffling his foot upon each step.

"Shane—"

His son's back stiffened, but he didn't turn to attend to his father.

Callum blundered on, "If you needed money..."

Shane let out a bark of laughter that held no humor. Without facing his father, he quipped, "I'm sure I'll be fine. After all, I have a new job."

"Speaking of the estate manager job . . ."

All humor was gone as Shane spun to face Callum. "What about it?"

"If you're going to take on the role, you can't...you can't..."

"Yes?" he ground out.

"You can't go around having affairs with the help," Callum lectured.

Inch by inch, Shane returned to the landing, giving his father a steely stare. "Agreed. My dalliance with Daisy is at an end. I would appreciate it if you would speak to Mother about making sure the girl has a decent reference when she's released from her position."

"Why would she be released?"

Surprise flittered across his son's features. "I simply assumed... Once Mother hears of this...come, you know she'll never keep her on."

Shane was right. Another thought occurred to Callum, and his gaze narrowed. "You'd better pray that little ginger doesn't come back with a bun in the oven."

Shane shook his head. "Shouldn't be a problem. I've been careful."

Callum's lips pinched together. "Very well, but I'm not sure I can get your mother to agree—"

"Never mind," Shane cut off his father's words and said with self-assurance, "*I'll* speak to her about it." One of Shane's self-satisfied smiles crossed his face. "She'll come around...once she sees it my way."

Without a backward glance, Shane bounded up the staircase as if receiving a direct infusion of energy—wicked laughter echoed against the walls.

A foreboding shiver ran down Callum's spine. He had a sudden premonition that Shane would be the downfall of Ballyford and all that the O'Connell family name stood for.

Chapter Twenty-Nine
Ariadne

Shane dashed toward me, skipping steps as he went, jubilant amusement lighting his features.

"Shane." I paused on the top step, holding the thick wooden rail. "How did it go down at the station?"

"Brilliant! Magnificent!" He continued hurdling up the stairs.

"I was wondering about Dai—" I expected Shane to stop, but instead he came directly at me. I flinched.

He jumped to his right, barely dodging around me. "Another time." He let out another wicked belly laugh and continued down the hallway without a backward glance.

Lord O'Connell remained at the bottom of the steps, watching as his son disappeared from sight. Clasping hands behind his back, he stared at the floor and began to walk away.

"Excuse me, Lord O'Connell." I'd already changed for dinner into a navy blue velvet dress with a sweetheart neckline and full skirt, and my heels tip-tapped down the wooden planks.

He glanced up expectantly. "How can I help you, Miss Winter?"

Reaching the bottom of the staircase, I stopped on the last tread to rest my hand upon the carved newel post. "I, uh, was wondering if Daisy arrived at the station?"

"You know...about Daisy and..." His gaze flickered to the top of the stairs.

"Shane? Yes, when she found out that he'd been taken down to the station, she confessed to the affair to us."

He eyed me. "Tell me, Miss Winter, to whom did Daisy confess?"

"To Julia and me. She came in to clean up the tea service. She heard us talking about Shane and the watch, and she...well, she became quite distraught and insisted on bicycling herself over to the station house to, um, clear Shane's good name. We were concerned for her well-being considering her agitated state and the deteriorating weather, but she refused to listen to reason, and went haring out of here like her apron was on fire."

"You'll be happy to know Daisy arrived in fine form—though a tad wet—and did indeed, um, clear my son's good name."

I uttered, "Oh, that *is* a relief."

"Miss Winter, I would consider it a personal favor if you did not spread around the information you've just revealed." With a shaky hand, Lord O'Connell wiped his forehead with a handkerchief.

I noticed a new bruise on the back of his hand. "About Daisy and Shane?"

"Yes, that. You see, it's rather a...delicate matter—"

I lifted my palm in a stop motion. "Say no more. It is *none* of my business. I am happy to hear that Daisy is safe, and Shane has been cleared of any suspicion when it comes to Mr. Byrne's death. And let me take this moment to deliver my own tardy condolences. I understand Mr. Byrne was practically family. I'm sure you're devastated."

Lord O'Connell's sickly features sank at the mention of Brian. "Yes." He cleared his throat. "It's been quite a shock. I believed Brian would be with us until he retired."

"A tragedy." I placed a hand on Lord O'Connell's bony shoulder. "Please let me know if there is any way I can help the family during this terrible time."

"Thank you, Miss Winter." He patted my hand, and I let it slide away. "You're very kind. I'm going to have a drink before dinner. Would you like to join me?"

"Yes, but I've forgotten my handkerchief. I'm going to run up and get it."

"Join me in the Library when you return."

At the top of the stairs, I turned left instead of right toward my room. I wanted to have a moment to speak with Shane about Gavin's arrival. Also, to pump him for information regarding Daisy and their affair. I'd overheard Shane's discussion with his father before he came upstairs, and I was concerned about Daisy's position at Ballyford.

"You will do as I ask, Mother!" Shane's strident words stopped me in my tracks. His voice came from Lady Aisling's chamber. "Or I will reveal the truth to Inspector Quinn."

I sidled closer to hear Lady Aisling's response, but with the door closed, I couldn't make out what she said.

Lucky for me, Shane was on a tear and continued in a raised voice, "You're no longer calling the shots. *I am.* If you want this secret buried with Brian, you will do as I say, and make sure my brother and father fall in line."

More unintelligible murmurs by Lady Aisling.

"I don't know. But make sure Daisy leaves with a good reference." He paused. "No. Wait. I want you to find her a new position and make sure she's installed there. And I want no hint of scandal to go with her."

"I can't do that!" Lady Aisling cried loud enough for me to hear.

"Of course you can, *Mother. You're* Lady Aisling O'Connell, mistress of Ballyford Manor, one of the most prestigious estates in County Clare. Figure it out!"

Stomping footsteps neared the door. I sprinted to the hall bathroom, slipping inside, as Shane threw open Lady Aisling's bedroom door so hard it slammed against the wall with a crash.

I hid behind the door, holding my breath, praying

Shane wouldn't enter.

He didn't.

When I could no longer hear his foot falls, I let out the breath in a whoosh. My heart hammered in my ears and my thoughts raced.

What secret about Brian Byrne is Shane talking about? What truth is he alluding to and now holding over his mother's head? Does Shane know who murdered Brian?

If Shane knew his brother or father murdered Brian Byrne, what would Lady Aisling do to silence the truth?

Dinner was a sumptuous but subdued affair. Lady Aisling, Shane, and Imogene were all feeling poorly and chose to have supper on a tray in their rooms—a message delivered by Mrs. Briggs.

If I had known having a tray in my room was an option, I would have exercised it. Gavin had yet to arrive. And, when I asked Mrs. Briggs about it, she assured me Dougray had left to pick him up. Furthermore, the housekeeper assured me that Lady Aisling had been informed of his imminent arrival and looked forward to greeting him tomorrow. At least Gavin had a twelve-hour reprieve from meeting with the formidable Lady Aisling, giving me time to prepare him for the introductions.

The aroma of seafood and spices assailed my senses when I stepped into the Dining Room. Dinner, like lunch, was set up buffet style along the massive sideboard. The dishes looked as pretty as they tasted. I started with the rich seafood chowder filled with shellfish meats, potatoes, and lightly flavored onions. Smoked salmon surrounded by toast points spread across a gold-rimmed platter. Flaky crab cakes melted in my mouth, while tender scallops lay in pools of butter in their pale shells.

Since we were so few, the staff removed leaves from the table, so we were not spread as far apart. Without the intimidating presence of the lady of the house, we felt comfortable talking across the table. Julia regaled the ensemble with our visit to the cliffs, turning my own fearful experience into a heroic moment for Cormac.

As Julia recounted the incident, I studied Cormac. He pulled at his collar, as if it was too tight, and sought to downplay his "lifesaving" role, commenting, "You make too much of it, darling. It was nothing."

Did he purposely avert his gaze from mine?

Aunt Maggie put down her knife and fork and turned to me, her features set in shock. "How awful! Thank goodness for Cormac's quick thinking. Are you suffering duress from those terrifying moments, Ariadne?"

Before I could answer, Julia scoffed, "You must be joking, Mom. Ariadne? Suffer unduly? From what I've observed, the streets of New York City are far more dangerous than a little fright at the Cliffs of Moher. Right, Cousin?" She chuckled expectantly at me.

I couldn't muster the same nonchalant attitude Julia seemed to expect. Instead, I dabbed my lips with a napkin before responding, "Thank you for your concern, Aunt Maggie. While the incident was certainly frightening, I have fully recovered my wits. Though I don't plan to return to the cliffs anytime soon."

"Goodness. It seems you owe Cormac quite a debt." Uncle Gerald sipped his wine.

Cormac continued to stare at his plate, his face and neck now red as the wing of a cardinal. He must have lost his appetite, because he shoved the food around without taking a bite.

My lips lifted ever so slightly. "Oh, I'm sure Cormac knows exactly how much I owe him." *So much, I'll be locking my door and sleeping with one eye open tonight.*

"As I said, it was nothing," Cormac said waspishly, slugging back the last few gulps of his wine. "Anyone else like another glass?" He stood up and retrieved the bottle from the sideboard.

Julia, finally sensing her fiancé's discomfort, turned the discussion away from his heroics and onto bird watching. Lord O'Connell seemed to be almost as well-versed as Shane and got into a lively discussion of Irish ornithology.

Following dinner, Cormac complained of a headache, and left our company. Julia made up an excuse and followed Cormac from the Dining Room. Uncle Gerald suggested a game of billiards to Lord O'Connell, and the two men left Aunt Maggie and I to our own devices.

Upon Mrs. Briggs' suggestion, we settled into the Music Room, which held a black baby grand piano, a harp in cherry wood, and other sundry stringed instruments such as a violin and mandolin. Two brocade wingback chairs flanked the fireplace, and other sundry occasional chairs were littered around the room. The crackling hearth fire threw eerie shadows on the gold silk damask wall coverings, but we welcomed its warmth. Mrs. Briggs brought us a tray of coffee and flaky apple tartlets.

Aunt Maggie and I pulled the wingback chairs closer to the fireplace, and I proceeded to tell her about our adventures in Brian's cottage and the cave system. She expressed deep concern about the unknown assailant in the tunnels and vowed to discuss it with Julia in the morning.

Chapter Thirty
Gavin

"Here they are," chirped the elderly woman escorting Gavin through the massive mansion. She wore all black like a crow, and her gray, streaked hair was scraped back into a tight bun. The woman had introduced herself as the housekeeper, Mrs. Briggs, the woman on the phone. Though she appeared intimidating, her kind smile and warm Irish lilt put Gavin at ease.

Ariadne—elegant as ever in a velvet dress that flared at the waist with a set of pearls around her neck—rose to greet him, tucking a dusky curl behind her ear to reveal matching pearl earbobs.

Halfway through their trip, Gavin realized he hadn't wanted Ariadne to leave Paris. Even though he'd been busy with additional photo shoots after she'd left to meet up with her cousin, he'd missed her calm, but inquisitive presence by his side. He deemed the plane's diversion to Ireland, and subsequent invitation, providence.

Her face broke into the smile he'd come to adore—straight white teeth outlined with deep cherry red lipstick partially rubbed off from dinner. "Hello, Gavin. Welcome to Ballyford." She held out her graceful hands, placing warm fingers into his cold mitts.

Normally, he'd pull her in for a kiss.

However, Ariadne kept her arms stiff as she held him at length. "Oh! Your hands are freezing. Here, come closer to the fire."

"I'll fetch another cup, for coffee, shall I?" Mrs. Briggs suggested.

Having put back a few pints at the pub with Dougray and Harry, Gavin felt a bit woozy and welcomed the offer. "The largest mug you've got, please." He gave her his most charming smile. At least he hoped it was charming and not a leering grin.

It took all of Gavin's concentration not to weave his way to the chair Ariadne suggested. He feared he landed rather hard on the elegant chair; it creaked beneath his weight. He found himself across from a middle-aged woman, in a black chiffon frock, scrutinizing him with her crystal blue gaze. Make-up enhanced her features and concealed her true age. However, her hands spoke a different story, fine lines and wrinkles etched across her knuckles, and age spots dotted the landscape. She replaced the dainty blue and white coffee cup on its saucer.

"Beg your pardon." His bottom rose a few inches off the seat, and he held out his hand.

"Aunt Maggie," Ariadne said, "this is Gavin Turnbull, my—"

"Co-worker." Gavin interrupted.

"*Just* a coworker, you say?" Her cheeks dimpled, and her eyes danced as they shook hands. "Oh! Ariadne is *right*, your hands *are* freezing. Here, hold them to the fire." Her fingers pushed him in the direction of warmth.

"Um..." Gavin's gaze darted to Ariadne, who dragged a chair closer.

It occurred to him, he should have done it for her, however, he wasn't sure he'd accomplish the task without falling flat on his face. As a matter of fact, her aunt's image blurred in front of him, and he had to blink to clear it. Deciding it was safer, his bottom returned to the silk seat. Those Guinness pints packed a wallop like no beer from home.

Where is that woman with the coffee?

Ariadne appeared not to notice his lack of manners.

She placed the chair between the two and plopped down with a sigh. "The jig is up, Gavin. Aunt Maggie dragged it out of me," she said, eyeing her aunt. "She knows we're...dating?"

"Dating?" That comment kind of hit him in the face. Gavin believed they were well beyond the dating phase—he had fallen in love with Ariadne and saw himself as part of a couple, even referring to her as his "girlfriend" outside of work. He assumed she had similar feelings—or was he making assumptions?

She surreptitiously winked at him.

His befuddled brain realized, perhaps, she wasn't ready to share that with her family. He played along. "Er, yes, that's right, Mrs. um? Sorry, I didn't catch your name."

"Oh, right, this is my aunt, Margaret Brennan."

"It is quite a treat to meet you before my sister has done so." Mrs. Brennan looked pleased as punch.

Since Gavin didn't know how to respond to Mrs. Brennan's delight at getting a leg up on her sister, he remained mute. His head bobbed up and down like a seal at the circus.

"Aunt Maggie." Ariadne sighed. "You *know* how Mom can get."

While Gavin had met Ariadne's other aunt and her father, he'd yet to be invited to meet her mother. When he'd asked Ariadne about this discrepancy, she promised they would meet "soon." Ariadne had different ideas from Gavin when it came to the meaning of "soon."

"Yes, I do." Mrs. Brennan put her cup and saucer down on a silver tray with the gleaming silver coffee pot. "What you must realize, dearest, your mother is simply looking out for your best interests. She wants you to settle down. Find a husband. Have a family. She worries you'll end up all alone."

"I know. It's simply that...my life doesn't align with

her ideals of marriage and children. I want an exciting career. Something you and Mother could only dream about is within my grasp. Besides, Aunt Ruby isn't married, and she's quite happy with her life."

Mrs. Brennan patted Ariadne's leg. "Trust me, the women of my generation understand the independence that comes with a good-paying job. So many of us went to work during the war. I worked at the Navy hospital, you know."

A stricken look flashed across Ariadne's face. She dropped her head in shame. "I'm sorry. You're right, Aunt Maggie."

Mrs. Briggs broke the tension, arriving with Gavin's cup and saucer—a match to the petite, refined china cup Mrs. Brennan was using. He eyed the silver coffee pot in Mrs. Briggs' hand and wondered how many times he'd be returning for a fill-up.

"Cream or sugar?" she offered.

"Black is fine." He greedily gulped half the liquid, burning his tongue as the steaming brew went down.

"Tell me a bit about yourself, Mr. Turnbull," suggested Mrs. Brennan.

"Call me Gavin." He blew into the cup to cool the hot drink.

"Very well." She inclined her head and asked, "Where are you from, Gavin?"

Through two more cups of coffee, he proceeded to tell Mrs. Brennan about his upbringing, his two sisters, and how he'd become a photographer—a fallback job after his dreams of becoming a professional baseball player were dashed when he injured his shoulder. He realized much of the information was as new to Ariadne as it was to her aunt.

At the end of the baseball tale, he commented, "Your aunt is quite the interrogator, although her touch is so light, you don't even realize what's happening." Gavin chuckled. "She could work for Scotland Yard."

"Well, I think that is enough interrogation for tonight." She winked. "I'm going to retire." The older woman rose, with a slight groan, her joints popping.

Gavin too rose, and Ariadne jumped out of her chair to kiss her aunt on the cheek. "Goodnight, Aunt Maggie."

"Goodnight, Gavin. Ariadne. Be good." She nodded at each one in turn, then strolled out of the room humming "Take Me Out to the Ball Game."

Ariadne eyed him. "Did you have fun at the pub?"

"It was pleasant," he drawled.

"You smell like the dregs of a beer glass." She poured him another cup of coffee.

His head now much clearer from the first cups of the strong brew, Gavin joked, "Don't blame me. That chauffeur your housekeeper sent, Dougray, kept ordering pints. At least he had the sense to have us order dinner, or else I would have slid off my stool straight to the floor." He gave a cheeky grin.

Ariadne rolled her eyes.

Gavin blew across the steaming dark liquid, and asked with nonchalance, "When were you going to tell me about the dead man?"

She exhaled heavily, slumping down in the chair until her legs stretched out in front of her and her shoulders pressed against its curved back. "Can you believe it?"

"Honestly? No, I cannot. How Ariadne? How does this happen? *Twice?*"

"I don't know." She picked at a hangnail. "It's only been a few months since my last run-in with a dead man. I hadn't been here more than twenty-four hours when we came across Brian Byrne, the estate manager, dead at the base of the castle."

"What happened?"

"Fell from one of the turret windows." She waved

her hand in the general direction of the castle. "Maybe the archer's platform. The inspector claimed he saw footprints in the moss."

"An accident?"

Her head rotated side to side. "The local inspector is investigating the death under suspicious circumstances."

"Murder?"

"Perhaps."

"And have you solved it, yet?" he teased.

"I don't know what you mean?" she hedged, looking everywhere but at him.

"Give over. I know your inquisitive nature. You're not going to sit around and let someone else solve the case...like the police. Tell me what you've found."

Ariadne went on to tell him about locating the journal and maps in Mr. Byrne's office.

"You played a dangerous game, snooping through his office. What would you have done if you'd been caught?"

Her face reddened. "We almost did get caught."

"We? You and Julia?"

"Aunt Maggie and me."

"Aunt Maggie was snooping through this man's personal effects with you?" Gavin let out a low whistle. "I never would have guessed it."

"Well, she came in to warn me..." Ariadne tapped her nail against her teeth. "...or perhaps it was to scold me. Either way, yes, we were almost caught. I would have talked my way out of it. This place is a veritable rabbit warren of hallways, doorways, and rooms that connect to one another. Claiming you got lost in Ballyford Manor is not so unbelievable. Although it's nothing compared to the caves."

"Caves? What caves?"

Ariadne described her afternoon with Julia—finding the cottage open and the cat in the kitchen. Then her own discovery of the cave, and subsequent exploration.

"Cripes!" He bobbled the saucer and cup, grabbing both to keep from spilling. "What were the pair of you thinking, swanning around a cave system neither one of you knows? I doubt you were even wearing proper gear for spelunking."

"You're right about that," Ariadne agreed with regret. "I had on my Keds, and Julia was wearing loafers. Both were ruined by the mud. A sturdy pair of boots would have been better. But that's not the worst of it." She told him about the pearl and someone grabbing hold of Julia, and the blackout they experienced when dropping the flashlight.

Gavin's features tightened, and he deliberately placed his cup and saucer on a table. Because, if he didn't put them down immediately, he might very well throw dishware across the room in anger. "Let me get this straight. While the pair of you were knocking around this cave system, someone followed you, and what? Attacked you?"

"Well..." Ariadne's lips twisted in thought. "He didn't exactly attack us. He simply got hold of Julia, who, in turn, panicked. It was Julia who attacked me. She screamed and slammed me up against the rocks."

Through gritted teeth, he asked, "Did you get hurt?"

"A few bruises from that incident." Ariadne's hand automatically went to the back of her head. She couldn't help a wince when her fingers touched the tender lump. "It's not too bad."

Gavin's hands clenched into fists. Unfortunately, there was no one to take out his frustration on, and they remained balled on his lap in frustration. "What about the pearl?"

She snapped her fingers and pointed at him. "That's the point, isn't it? What happened to the pearl? Julia dropped it. In the match light, we couldn't find it.

Moreover, Julia was in a panic to leave." She grimaced. "Honestly, so was I. Luckily, Julia remembered she'd taken the candle from the broken lantern, and we were able to find our way out. Unfortunately, the light by the candle was nothing compared to the flashlight, and we didn't recover the pearl."

Gavin uncrossed his legs and stood up. Placing his hands behind his back, he pushed his stomach forward, stretching his spine. "So, the pearl is still down there? And you think it's a clue to unraveling this murder."

"No."

"No?"

"I mean, yes. I think it's a clue. No, I don't believe the pearl is still down there. I believe whoever followed us went back to retrieve it...after we were gone."

Gavin jammed hands into his pockets and paced, back and forth, the length of the music room. He paused and his fingers brushed against the harp, its warm cascade of notes, like raindrops of water on a lake, resonating through the chamber.

When his temper abated, he inquired, "So, that's the worst of it? You and your cousin got lost in the bowels of a cave system? No one held a gun to your head, like last time?"

Her lips rolled inward, her chin dropped, and her eyes drifted down to the fingers in her lap, which Gavin noticed she wrung.

Through his nose, he sucked in a big breath. "Oh, lord. What happened?"

"I don't wanna talk about it," she mumbled in a small voice.

"Ariad-ne," he drew her name out. Getting down on one knee in front of her, he took her hands in his own and cajoled, "Come now, you can tell me." Her delicate fingers curled so tightly around him; he could feel her painted nails against his flesh. *What on earth is she hiding?*

Visibly, she swallowed. "I noticed the same mud on Cormac's shoes. When I confronted him and accused him of being the man in the caves who grabbed Julia, he...um...kind of walked me back to the edge of the cliff."

Gavin stared at her as if she'd grown horns on her head. "You mean to tell me, you confronted a man nearly twice your size? And you did it down by a cliff?"

"Cormac isn't *twice* my size," she scoffed, as if to make light of it, but her voice was thin and thready.

"Correct me if I'm wrong, that picture on the mantel in your apartment, it's you, your cousin Julia, and Cormac."

She chewed her lower lip and nodded.

"The man is four inches taller, and at least fifty pounds on you. If he'd wanted to, he could have easily picked you up and tossed you over the edge."

"I, uh, guess I didn't think things through." She shook her head as if to shake away the memories of the hazardous interaction. "It doesn't matter, when Julia and Shane saw the danger I was in, Cormac grabbed me and pulled me away from the ledge."

It was Gavin's turn to squeeze her hands. "Only after witnesses were watching!"

"Mm-hm. Too tight." She tried to pull away.

Gavin's grip immediately relaxed. He stared at her taut features and wary eyes. She must have been frightened out of her wits, and she was putting on a brave face for his sake. He kissed her forehead and returned to the wingback chair.

Clearing his throat, he leveled his tone, "So, you think Cormac is the one who murdered Brian."

"Perhaps. At first, I thought it was Shane, because of the argument and the watch. But now, I believe he got the watch from someone else."

"Argument. What argument are you talking about? What watch?"

Ariadne explained the argument between Shane and Brian the night before. "But Daisy, the maid, gave him an alibi. The pair of them have been conducting an illicit affair, and he was with her last night."

"So, we're back to Cormac." Gavin rose to pour the last of the coffee into his cup. "A man who seems to like putting people in precarious positions in high places."

"I suppose." She chewed her bottom lip.

Gavin could tell the gears were turning in that beautiful head of hers. "You're struggling to pin it on Cormac. Why?"

"There are a few reasons I have trouble attaching Cormac to the crime. First, I doubt the pearl we found belongs to Cormac. I've never seen him wear jewelry beyond his signet ring and gold cufflinks with his monogram. Additionally, the blue fabric swatch matches nothing he wore last night."

"He could have changed."

"That's true. But, most importantly, *what is the motive?* Shane's motive would be obvious—to hide the theft. But Cormac? I can find no motive. He's the heir to the estate. If he had problems with Mr. Byrne, he could have had his father dismiss him. What earthly motive could Cormac have to murder the caretaker?" Ariadne flipped open a brass cigarette box. "Would you like one? They are filterless and a bit strong for my tastes, but I've run out of my Chesterfields."

"Here, take mine." Gavin reached into his jacket pocket and pulled out a crumpled pack of Chesterfields. "There are a few left."

"Oh, you are a saint! Thank you! Thank you!" Taking the package from him, she leaned over and delivered a fat kiss on his lips.

"If that's my thanks, I'm sorry, I didn't pack an entire carton." He grinned.

The flame from an intricately cut glass lighter flared.

"You have no idea. This investigation has put my nerves on edge. Here." She held out the pack.

"I'll try one of those Irish cigarettes." Gavin took it and wandered to the fireplace allowing Ariadne to light the fag. The coffee cleared off the blurry effects of the beer, and his mind raced a mile a minute, replaying all he'd learned since Harry sat down next to him at the pub.

Staring down at the smoldering peat logs, Gavin recalled Harry's muttered comment, *I need to see the inspector.*

What if . . .

"Today, I heard an interesting story at the pub while waiting for Dougray."

"Oh, yes?" Ariadne said, faintly distracted by her thoughts.

"Yes, the man is a private investigator from America. He told me about a line of inheritance that was in question. One that included a title."

"Mm . . ." She picked up the coffee pot and, realizing it was empty, placed it back on the silver tray.

"Interestingly enough, the man knew about Ballyford."

She returned to the wing chair. Crossing her legs, she placed the cigarette in the ashtray. "What did he know about Ballyford?"

Gavin went on to tell Ariadne the story Harry revealed. As he spoke, she uncrossed her legs, straightened, and leaned forward, studying him with full attention. The forgotten cigarette burned down to the filter, going out in a final puff of smoke. Finishing his story, Gavin tossed his burned-to-the-nub cigarette into the fireplace.

Ariadne's features crunched together in thought. "What did you say this man's name is?"

"Harry."

"Harry, what?" Her hand moved rapidly with the

palm facing upwards and fingers curved in a come-hither gesture. "Did you get a last name? Business card?"

Gavin shrugged. "Can't say as I did."

The chair squeaked as she deflated.

"But I can tell you, he caught a ride with us as far as Lisdoonvarna. A town a few miles from here." He paused before adding, "Where your Inspector Quinn works."

Using the arms of the chair, Ariadne pushed to her feet. "Harry. That name can be short for Harold?"

"Yes. So?"

Muttering under her breath, Ariadne spun away to pace to the end of the room, then pivoting to face Gavin, she blurted the name, "Harold Kendall!"

"John Thomas!" Gavin jokingly shot back. "Is this the part of the evening where we make up names and shout them at each other?"

She flapped her hand at him. "Harold Kendall was a name in Mr. Byrne's journal. He had an *American* address."

The light bulb went on. "Ah, and you believe Harry-from-the-pub and Harold Kendall are one and the same?"

Her brows drew together, and she silently counted on her fingers. "You say this fellow is a private investigator?"

"Correct." He clasped his hands behind his back and strolled over to Ariadne.

"An investigator would have to be paid. Right? Paid quite a bit for traveling up and down the East Coast. Paid for traveling across the ocean. Paid to travel to Dublin to research family lineage records."

"I suppose he would." Gavin rubbed his pointer finger on that wrinkle between her bottle green eyes and whispered, "What's going on in that brainbox of yours?"

"I think your Harry is the man Cormac and Shane saw Mr. Byrne giving money to on two different occasions. And, if what you say Harry told you about an inheritance refers to the O'Connell family...then...the entire family has a motive for murder," she breathed the last sentence.

Chapter Thirty-One
Ariadne

Footsteps in the hallway set my heartbeat galloping, and my breath quickened.

"Still up?" Mrs. Briggs entered the room. Her black uniform, wrinkled and limp, hung off her hunched shoulders. Her features blank with exhaustion, she offered half-hearted, "Shall I make another pot of coffee?"

Gavin peeled my fingers off his forearm. "I don't think that's necessary, Mrs. Briggs."

Relieved it wasn't any of the O'Connells, I mustered a small smile. "We were just about to retire. Do you know if my uncle is still in the Billiard Room?"

"Oh, no, miss, they turned in half an hour ago. You're the only guests still up."

We heard the mild censure in her tone and realized Mrs. Briggs wouldn't go to bed until the silver tray was cleared and the room put back to rights.

"Apologies, Mrs. Briggs, for keeping you from your bed. We got to talking and lost track of time," I said by way of apology. "Where will Gavin be sleeping tonight? Have you been to your room yet?"

He shook his head and straightened the sleeve I'd crushed. "I was just about to ask Mrs. Briggs."

"You've been assigned to the Lord Bakewell suite. If you'd like, I can show you the way," the housekeeper offered, placing the last of the used coffee cups on the tray.

"No need. Just point me in the direction of the stairs.

I'm sure I'll be able to find it on my own."

Mrs. Briggs frowned with skepticism.

I couldn't help the unladylike snort that escaped. "Gavin doesn't understand the expansiveness of the manor. Tell me, where is the Lord Bakewell suite in comparison to my own?"

"Three doors down from the bathroom you've been assigned." She swept black bits of ash back into the hearth with the small brass-handled broom and straightened the scrolled iron fireplace screen.

"Then I'm confident, I'll be able to direct Gavin to his suite."

"The room was made up for Mr. and Mrs. Chapman, from Kilkenny," she explained. "Luckily, I reached them before they left home this morning."

"I'm surprised we didn't have guests arrive who didn't get the message that the party was canceled in time," I murmured.

"News travels fast in these parts. Especially bad news. I began phoning the guests coming from far away first." She lifted the heavy tray, her back creaking.

I saw the wince she tried to hide. If I didn't think it would offend her, I would have offered to carry the tray to the kitchen. However, I imagined Mrs. Briggs simply wanted the pair of us to get out of her hair so she could finish her duties and turn in.

"Ah, yes. Smart thinking on your part, Mrs. Briggs." Gavin nodded his head with approval and gave her one of his heart-stopping smiles.

At least it made my heart stutter. Gavin must have had thoughts similar to mine, because he made an automatic movement, which I stayed with a gentle grip around his bicep.

"It was nothing," she brushed off the compliment.

Not to be deterred in his efforts to win the housekeeper over, Gavin shook off my hand. "Mrs.

Briggs, please allow me to carry that tray for you."

Immediately, her spine went rigid, and the fatigue left her features to be replaced with stern pursed lips. "I'm perfectly capable of carrying it."

Realizing his mistake, Gavin backpedaled, "Yes, of course you are. I didn't mean to cause offense," he stammered. "My mama taught me to respect our elders—" I elbowed Gavin in the ribs, and he quickly course corrected, "er, um, I meant, to be respectful of ladies, and such."

If possible, this made Mrs. Briggs stiffen up even more.

I took a stab at smoothing things over. "What my co-worker is trying to say, he isn't used to having loyal retainers, such as yourself. Many Americans don't have live-in help, and it's easy to unknowingly step out of bounds. Not understanding the proper etiquette, you understand."

"Just so, Mrs. Briggs, I apologize for my gaffe." Gavin cleared his throat. "By the by, I didn't properly thank you for giving me directions for public transit and sending your man to fetch me."

Mrs. Briggs wasn't completely immune to Gavin's charm, for her visage relaxed. "You're quite welcome, young man. But it was nothing. We've plenty of space."

"It was *absolutely* something. If it weren't for you and the O'Connell's hospitality, I would be holing up at one of the run-down hotels near the airport, or a room above a noisy pub," he blustered.

"Or worse, on an uncomfortable chair at the airport," I added for good measure.

I wasn't sure why Gavin was buttering up the housekeeper, but I figured he had a good reason and did my best to help him out.

Practical as ever, Mrs. Briggs pointed out that the airport closed at nine, and Gavin wouldn't be allowed to sleep there, and that an airport worker would have taken pity on him and likely would have offered him a bed. The thought that someone would provide housing to an absolute stranger boggled our minds.

Her arms gave the slightest shake from the weight of the tray.

I tugged Gavin's sleeve. "We won't keep you further, Mrs. Briggs. Good night."

"See, Lord Bakewell," I whispered, pointing to the gold and black brass plaque. "I told you I could find your room."

It took less than five minutes of wandering through the Ballyford maze, before Gavin realized I'd spoken the truth about the vastness of the manor.

As we made our way to the west wing, he kept asking, "Are you sure this is the right direction?"

The door swung open, revealing a clover green chamber dimly lit by a white hobnail glass hurricane lamp. An electric heater in the fireplace emitted a red glow, warming the cozy room. Lord Bakewell didn't rank as high as the Viscountess Valentina, and his bedroom reflected the difference. About half the size of my bed chamber, Gavin's teak, Corinthian four-poster bed with crème damask curtains overwhelmed the space. A carved walnut chifforobe sat opposite the fireplace. The only other furniture was a small cedar chest at the foot of the bed and a ladderback chair in the corner. Gavin's suitcase rested on top of the chest.

"Well, well." Gavin eyed the room. "Doesn't this look cozy?"

He pulled me inside. Wrapping his arms around my waist, his lips descended upon my own. I slid effortlessly into the kiss, relishing his hard body against my softer curves. He tasted like coffee. The scent of cigarettes and beer clung to his clothing. I nosed his collar, sensing the slightest whiff of the morning's woodsy aftershave—my favorite smell. Gavin nibbled his way to my earlobe, and I melted with a delicious sigh.

When we came up for air, Gavin rested his cheek against my forehead and breathed, "Good heavens, I missed you."

"Me too," I whispered, not realizing until that exact moment how much Gavin's arrival meant to me. How relieved my entire being felt upon seeing him, even in his initial intoxicated state.

A slight noise had me pulling away from him. Neither of us had closed the door. The scrape of a drawer and rustle of paper drew us back into the faintly illuminated hallway.

Gavin gasped. My own throat went dry as I uttered a small gurgle of shock. The ethereal specter gradually rotated in our direction, and I realized earthbound feet and hands were poking out of the alabaster nightdress.

What we faced was no ghost.

I swallowed, wondering if she'd witnessed our intimate moment or expected an explanation for my presence in Gavin's room. Cautiously, I inquired, "Lady Aisling, did we wake you?"

Something felt amiss about the matriarch. She spoke not a word, but her mouth moved silently within her milky features. Hands fluttered aimlessly in the air as if searching for nonexistent pockets. A ribbon of braided hair draped across her shoulder.

"Lady Aisling?" I approached, reaching out. "Is everything all right?"

Gavin seized my arm and hissed, "Don't."

Confused, I frowned at him.

"Waking a sleepwalker can give them quite a fright." He pointed at her sightlessly staring eyes. Open but uncomprehending.

Does she do this often?

Or, like Lady Macbeth, did the weight of guilt lie heavy on Lady Aisling's heart and mind, sinking into her sleeping subconscious? Her lips continued their wordless movements.

"Lady Aisling," I whispered, "do you know who murdered Brian Byrne?"

Her hands dropped to her sides, but she made no acknowledgement of my presence.

I tried again, a little more forceful, "Aisling? Who killed Brian?"

She began to shuffle down the hallway, her bare feet rasping against the carpet, in the direction of the stairwell.

Fearing she might tumble down the steps if she reached them, I gently took her arm and guided her footsteps back toward her room. "Not that way. This way."

Gavin sucked a breath between his teeth, but Lady Aisling showed no sign of waking. Like a pliant child, she shambled beside me. Once we reached her enormous, curtained bed, she climbed into it without further assistance. I pulled the counterpane up to her chin. Her blind eyes closed, and her thin lips fell still.

Built-in wardrobes lined the wall. A faint shaft from the hallway sliced a pie wedge of light into an open cupboard.

"Watch her," I whispered to Gavin, who stood only steps inside the room. With his back to the light, I couldn't read his facial features. Nonetheless, I could feel the confused disapproval emanating from him.

Recalling Shane's trick from earlier in the day, I screwed in the second lightbulb on the two sconces flanking Lady Aisling's room. It wasn't much, but it did brighten the room enough for me to see into the open closet.

A jewelry chest, with a key, gaped open, revealing a gamut of jewels—pearls, diamonds, emeralds, and more. A tiara winked at me, while a sapphire as large as a bottle cap hung from a tiny brass hook on a thick golden chain. I closed the lid over the tiara, shut the wooden hatch, and turned the key, leaving it in the lock. Then I closed the wardrobe. Surveying the wall of doors, I wondered which access held the blue dress Lady Aisling had worn the night of my arrival.

I tugged the closest one open. Garbled mumbles came from the bed, and I froze, barely breathing. The jackrabbit pulse of my heart pounded in my ears.

My name, merely a sigh from Gavin, drifted across the room.

After a moment, I realized our Lady Macbeth spoke gibberish. However, deciding not to push my luck, I left off from snooping, and glided across the carpet to the open entry way.

Gavin pulled the door shut, allowing only the slenderest snick of the latch. He opened his mouth, but I forestalled his questions with a gentle finger upon his lips and a headshake. Indicating with my other hand to follow, I began to lead the way to Viscountess Valentina's corner suite.

Chapter Thirty-Two
Gavin

Ariadne led him past the Lord Bakewell room.

"But—" He tugged at her hand.

"My room is further down," she whispered.

He couldn't resist her plump, heart-shaped lips, and his mouth once again descended upon hers. She didn't hesitate to snake her arms around his neck. The spicy floral notes of the Givenchy L'Interdit perfume he'd gifted her in Paris enveloped his senses.

Regrettably, once again, the sound of an opening door halted their tryst. Ariadne pulled him into the alcove of the nearby doorway.

A man about Gavin's age tiptoed into the hallway—his hair mussed, wearing only trousers, socks, and an undershirt with a tie thrown over his shoulder. Over one arm, he carried his dress shirt and coat. His shoes hung by their heels from a pair of fingers.

Ariadne stiffened and placed her fingertips to her mouth, but Gavin still heard the slight gasp she released.

A young woman's voice called, "Good night, darling."

"Good night, Julia," he whispered. Silently closing the door, he tiptoed away.

"That is Cormac," she murmured directly into his ear.

"Should I follow?"

Stepping into the light, Ariadne watched, with downturned features, as Cormac rounded the far corner. She chewed her bottom lip in thought. Eventually, her head shook. "No...I think he's going back to his room."

The door across the hall opened.

"Ariadne?" Her Aunt Margaret clutched a shawl around her flannel-clad shoulders.

Ariadne jerked with surprise. "Aunt Margaret?"

The older woman squinted. "Is something the matter, dear?"

"Not at all. We were searching for the room Gavin has been assigned," she said with aplomb. "Sorry to have awakened you, Aunt Maggie."

Gavin came out of the shadowed alcove, pointing a thumb over his shoulder. "Not that one."

"What's the name of the room?" asked Aunt Margaret.

"The Lord Bakewell room. I believe I've spotted it." Ariadne pointed to the half-opened doorway. "Look, they've left the door open for you."

"So, they have." He and Ariadne stood apart, watched by her aunt. He cleared his throat. "Well then, ladies, I...uh, bid you goodnight. Mrs. Brennan." Gavin gave a slight nod of the head. "Ariadne...erm..." Giving an awkward peck on her cheek and blushing like a schoolboy, Gavin scurried into his room and closed the door with a distinct click.

Leaning his head against the heavy wood, he sighed with regret. Any sort of rendezvous was thoroughly quashed by Ariadne's aunt, who would, no doubt, keep her ear open for further nighttime shenanigans.

Well, there is always tomorrow.

Kicking off his shoes, Gavin flopped onto the welcoming bed. The eiderdown practically enveloped him as he sank into its fluffy softness.

Chapter Thirty-Three
Ariadne

"Best be off to bed, dear. I imagine tomorrow will bring another busy day." Aunt Maggie delivered a knowing glance. "You wouldn't want to look pulled for your beau."

I dropped my head in defeat and retreated to my large and very lonely Viscountess Valentina suite.

Twenty minutes later, I flopped onto my back and tugged the counterpane up to my neck. Imagining Gavin's lips upon my own, my body warmed, and I threw the heavy comforter off with a huff.

"Damn, Aunt Maggie!" I hissed into the darkness. The only relief from the obscurity, the light emanating from the hallway beneath the door and the glow from my travel clock on the nightstand. The radiator ticked and creaked as the hot water flowed through its coils, keeping the room warm. Rolling onto my left side, I sought to distract my mind by replaying the incident with Lady Aisling.

Where was she going? What was she doing in her jewelry chest? Blindly searching for a lost pearl?

I bolted upright. "The paper."

Moments later, I was tiptoeing across the carpet in my pink silk pajamas that did little to ward off the chilling drafts. Foolishly, I hadn't bothered to put on socks or search for my slippers, and my toes were turning to icicles. Reaching the console table where we'd encountered Lady Aisling, I tugged the drawer. Something seemed to have jammed it, and it took some doing before I could work it loose without making too much noise. Inside, I found a handful of candles and a crumpled piece of paper that must have been the reason for the drawer jamming. As silently as possible, I removed the paper and slid the drawer closed.

A toilet flushed.

Someone else was awake. Fear sliced through my body. I darted back to my room as quickly as my frozen feet could carry me and dove into the bed, stuffing the paper beneath my pillow.

A shadow dropped across the crack of light beneath my door. I slammed my eyes shut as the turning doorknob creaked. My heart hammered, and I made an effort to slow my breaths. Dim light teased my eyelids until the person's silhouette stepped in front of it.

Focusing on the tick-tick of my clock slowed the pulsing of my heartbeat, then the intruder's breaths reached my ears.

At first, I wondered if it was Gavin or even my Aunt Maggie. I thought about opening my eyes and saying, "Boo!"

Then I realized Gavin would have knocked as would my aunt. Both would likely whisper my name. Gavin may have climbed into bed next to me, and I would have welcomed him.

Whoever stood upon my threshold did neither. They remained still.

Watching.

Waiting.

Is it the manor's nighttime sleepwalker, the lady of the house? Cormac? Shane? One of the house staff? Or perhaps the person whom I feared the least is the one I should fear the most—Lord O'Connell. The man who had the most to lose if Brian Byrne usurped his position as head of the household.

A tingle of danger slithered down my spine.

Intuition told me the person in the doorway did *not* have innocent intentions.

Perhaps I should open my eyes and let out a scream to wake the household. How would my intruder explain this nighttime visit? Then I remembered my little suite, tucked away at the end of a shallow corridor. The walls were thick.

Can I scream loud enough to wake anyone before the intruder is upon me?

Should I open my eyes, the watcher would only be visible through my peripheral vision. I could not stand it any longer. With a sigh, I rolled onto my side, intending to peek through my lashes and catch a glimpse of my visitor.

As soon as I moved, the door creaked shut. Unsure if the person was now outside or within my room, my eyes popped open wide, searching the darkness. I held my own breath, straining to hear another's.

I thought I heard a creak of a floorboard, but it could have been the radiator. Or the simple creaks and groans of an old house. My body began to shiver with fear, and I clenched my hands so hard, I felt the nails digging into my palms.

Unable to bear the suspense any longer, in a sweeping move, I grabbed the book on the bedside table and turned on the lamp. The flash of light initially blinded me.

Reflexively, I put a hand to my forehead. Hooding my eyes, my gaze swept the room like a hawk on the hunt for prey in search of my intruder. The book in my hand raised high to strike out or throw at someone's head. Every nook and shadowy corner might reveal danger.

Nothing. My nemesis had retreated.

I was alone.

My head bounced onto the pillow in relief.

I pulled the counterpane up to my chin and breathed

deeply.. In...and...out. I'd once read about breathing exercises a claustrophobic doctor had enacted when he was accidentally trapped inside a closet.

In for five. Hold for five. Out for five.

Did the person in the bathroom witness my flight? If so, why not knock and ask after my well-being? That would be the courteous thing to do. Why open the door without knocking? Or am I being silly? Was it simply Gavin, hoping to pick up where we left off, but upon noticing I was asleep, chose not to disturb me?

Gradually, the shivering stilled. My racing thoughts slowed. I didn't know who had entered my room, but it didn't feel curious or accidental.

It felt malignant.

I couldn't bear to turn out the light.

Eventually, I fell into a restless sleep.

Chapter Thirty-Four
Ariadne

The tapping on my door had me bolting upright. Bright morning light splintered through the window while dust motes danced upon the shafts. I'd forgotten to close the curtains. The doorknob twisted.

"Ariadne? Are you awake?" Julia's voice filtered through the heavy wood. An insistent pounding ensued. "The door is locked. Let me in."

"Not by the hair of my chinny, chin, chin," I croaked.

When the knocking didn't stop. I threw off the covers and raised my voice, "Fine! I'm coming, Julia!"

I whipped open the door. *"What is it?"*

"Whoa." Julia jerked back at my savage greeting. She'd dressed in a gray and pink striped skirt, matching it with a pink cashmere sweater set. "What happened to you? Looks like you did a few rounds with a tiger." She sought to peek around my shoulder. "Did you have a visitor last night?"

Yes, but not one I'm telling you about. "If you're insinuating Gavin spent the night, you're mistaken. Not all of us entertained our beaus last night," I grumbled.

Julia's mouth dropped, and she played dumb. "I don't know what you mean by that."

Retreating to the bed, I pulled the covers over my head. "Go away."

"Ariadne!"

She unceremoniously whipped off the covers. "Explain yourself."

"Fine! Gavin and I saw Cormac exit your room *en*

déshabillé last night."

Sucking in a breath, Julia piously cupped her hands at her waist. "You-you won't tell Mother or Father...will you?"

"If you leave me alone, my lips are sealed." I whisked the sheets over my head.

The mattress shifted as she sank next to me. "And just what were you and Gavin doing up at that time of night?" she teased.

"He didn't arrive until late. We were searching for Lord Bakewell's room, where he'd been assigned to sleep," I grumbled.

"Oh." She didn't say anything. Yet, she didn't leave either.

Groaning, I shoved off the covers and caught my cousin staring at her reflection in the dressing-table mirror. "What *is* it you want, Julia?"

"Do I look different to you?" she asked, stroking a finger down her cheek and tilting her head.

"No. Why?"

"I-I just wondered," she murmured faintly.

Then, it occurred to me, her dalliance with Cormac last night may have been her first time. In softer tones, I asked, "Julia, perhaps there is something you wish to talk about?"

Tentative bright blue eyes gauged my sincerity.

Sitting up, I fluffed my pillows to lean back against them, then straightened the sheets across my waist. Once comfortable, I turned to my cousin, and, taking her hand in mine, invited her to confide in me. "Tell me all about it."

Indeed, Cormac had deflowered my cousin, and Julia was all aswoon.

"Did he use protection? Or will this turn into a shotgun wedding?"

Julia flinched but assured me Cormac had seen to it.

He *did not* want her to become pregnant before they married. The man was in my black books, but I gave him credit for protecting Julia.

After finishing her story, she asked, "What about you and Gavin? Has he..." She waggled her brows at me.

"I don't kiss and tell," I said, my tone acerbic.

"Ariadne!" Her hands went into a praying position at her chest. "Come on," she wheedled. "I told you about Cormac."

"Be that as it may. I do not gossip about my boyfriends."

She sniffed and tossed her hair. "Fine. I assume it's because you haven't gone all the way."

What I'd done would probably make Miss Goody-two-shoes stutter and blush. I lived in New York City, for goodness' sake, whereas Julia was still living at home. Granted, it was in Washington, DC. However, she lived a more sheltered life than I did. Furthermore, I wasn't looking for a ring to tie me to a man. As much as I loved Gavin, and I did love that man, I was not interested in walking down the aisle with him.

At least, not right now.

My cousin couldn't stay mad at me. "I met your Gavin. He's quite handsome," she gushed, patting my leg. "By the way, you'd better get dressed, or you'll miss breakfast. It's in the Morning Room." She flounced across the chamber but paused, staring at the doorknob. "You locked your door."

"Yes." I didn't elaborate.

Her brows turned down along with her mouth. "Were you afraid Shane might...I know he can be a bit of a lecher. I mean with the maid and all...but if he's been pushy with you, I can talk with Cormac about it."

I could hardly tell her I feared Cormac more than Shane. "It's nothing. I thought I heard someone prowling the halls last night and locked up for good measure."

"Probably your imagination. This old house creaks and groans all the time, I've noticed. Unless..." She spun back to me and in hushed tones teased, "Maybe it was Gavin coming to, you know...." Her lips puckered, and she made kissy noises.

I threw my pillow at her.

Julia gave a little shriek and left, slamming the door.

Since I'd taken a bath before dinner last night, I didn't need to worry about bathing this morning. However, amid the hubbub, I'd completely forgotten to pin my hair into curlers. After brushing it and looking this way and that, I couldn't get rid of the flattened right side and knew it wouldn't do. Deciding to pin it back into a French twist, I allowed a bit of fringe to lie against my forehead. Sleepless bruises of dark circles rimmed my bottom lids, and I took time to cover them and pinken my cheeks with makeup. Taking a cue from my cousin, I dressed in warm clothing, pairing a black wool pencil skirt with a forest green sweater and a yellow polka dot scarf.

When I entered the Morning Room, Aunt Maggie, Julia, Imogene, and Gavin were having a lively discussion. Imogene must have gotten a good rest last night, for her perky demeanor was back, and her cheeks plumped as she laughed at something Gavin said. She even fluttered her lashes flirtatiously at him. Shane sat at the opposite end of the foursome, gingerly cupping his morning tea...or perhaps it was coffee. An untouched buttered piece of toast sat in front of him. His features were pulled, and every time his sister laughed, he winced. None of the other men in our party, nor Lady Aisling, were present.

We greeted each other with good mornings, as I piled a plate with sausages, some sort of fish, and toast, and then sat next to Gavin. "What is so funny?"

"Gavin has been amusing us with tales from the photography trenches," Aunt Maggie said.

"I can imagine." Gavin and I shared a knowing grin.

At a photo shoot in Paris, one of the models drank too much of the free champagne becoming so inebriated she could barely stand, much less walk in her sky high heels. Gavin ended up photographing her elegantly draped—a kind way of saying passed out—across an antique sofa.

Surveying the company, I asked, "Where is everyone else?"

"You know your uncle, up with the sun." My aunt sliced a sausage as she spoke. "He dined earlier with Lord O'Connell and Cormac. I believe the two men had a meeting this morning with the priest to discuss the—" her gaze darted to Imogene, who was polishing off a pile of eggs "—er, the arrangements."

Imogene looked up, but Aunt Maggie rushed on, "I don't know about Lady Aisling. Imogene, do you know where your mother is?"

I heard the distant sound of the phone ringing.

Imogene shrugged and swallowed. "If she took one of her sleeping pills, we won't see her for a few hours."

Hm, sleeping pills. Is that what caused the sleepwalking? Which reminds me, the paper I retrieved from the console in the hallway must still be jammed beneath my pillow.

With the ensuing room intruder, I'd forgotten all about it.

Yesterday, the house had been full of maids, footmen, and other staff hired for the big party. I wasn't clear which ones worked here regularly, and which ones were temporary. The only two I'd formally met were Mrs. Briggs and Daisy. Leaving me to wonder, who would be cleaning the rooms? I imagined such a chore beneath the housekeeper. *When would Daisy clean my room? Or had she already been dismissed?*

My thoughts were interrupted by Mrs. Briggs, looking ten years older than she had yesterday. "Inspector Quinn phoned. He'll be arriving shortly and has asked everyone to gather out front. He suggested a coat and good walking shoes." She exited as abruptly as she'd entered.

We exchanged glances with each other.

"Good walking shoes? Are we going on a hike?" Julia giggled.

"Well, I've got my riding gear on. I suppose those will have to be good enough," said Imogene.

Pushing my half-eaten plate aside, I gulped down the hot tea and rose. "I'd better change. These pumps are no use if we're hiking around outside," I said by way of explanation for my hasty exit.

Charging up the flight of steps, Gavin called my name, "Ariadne, wait up."

I didn't stop but slowed my pace, allowing him to catch up with me near the top of the staircase.

"What do you think this is all about?"

"I haven't the foggiest." Before he could ask any further questions, I put a finger to my lips and shook my head.

Chapter Thirty-Five
Gavin

He entered her room, still in disarray, untouched by the maids.

"Close the door," she ordered.

"Wow. This is much larger than my room." Gavin spread his long legs across the sofa and joked, "Very nice. I can see where I fall on the pecking order around here."

"That doesn't matter at the moment. Now, where is it?" She threw the bed pillows to the floor. She tugged the sheets all the way to the foot of the bed and grunted in dissatisfaction. She checked under the bed, and when she didn't find what she was searching for, Ariadne belly-flopped onto the bed, and peered down in the crack between the headboard and the wall.

"Ah, there it is." She retrieved a crumpled piece of paper and held it high.

"What is it?"

"The piece of paper Lady Macbeth was hiding in the drawer."

Gavin sat up from his reclining pose. "What are you talking about?"

"Remember, the sleepwalking?" she said with a touch of asperity.

"Of course," Gavin deadpanned. "I was there. Why are you talking about Lady Macbeth?"

"Listen, Lady Aisling wasn't just out for a stroll. It was more than that. She stuffed *this* piece of paper—" Ariadne waved said paper aloft as if it were a prize at the county fair "—in the drawer of the hallway table."

"Why did she do that? What does the paper say?"

She studied the document. "I don't know. I forgot about it . . ."

"Until Imogene mentioned her mother," Gavin filled in her half thought.

"Correct," she mumbled.

"Well? What does it say?"

"It's a mimeograph of a..." She flattened the crumpled document on her dressing table. The right bottom corner had been torn. "It looks like a birth certificate. A boy born July twelfth, 1808, in Boston, Massachusetts. He was named Patrick Ruairí. The mother is Fiadh McKeough O'Connell, and the father...it's tough to make out the handwriting." She walked to the windows and held the paper close to her face. "I think it's Ruairí...something with a B...O'Connell. Here, you take a look. The script is quite narrow and fancy."

Gavin mimicked her actions, moving the paper closer and farther away. The black strokes of the pen were so faint. "It's definitely a birth certificate. But the names...I'm not sure . . ." He frowned. "Does that say Byrne O'Connell?"

Ariadne gasped, snatching the paper back. "I think you might be right. Is this it? The information your friend Harry indicated?"

"Dunno. I'd think Mr. Byrne would need more than an old birth certificate to prove a lineage of ancestry."

She chewed her bottom lip. "Yes, like a whole swath of birth certificates, marriage licenses, family tree. Something more than this." Ariadne kicked off her shoes and sat down to pull on a pair of socks.

"What are you doing?"

"Mrs. Briggs told us to put on good walking shoes. I'm taking a page out of Imogene's book and putting on a pair of riding boots." She eyed Gavin's new two-tone leather oxfords that he'd purchased in Paris. "You might want to do the same."

"I don't have any boots, riding or otherwise."

"There are boots in the mudroom, I'm sure we can find you a pair."

Gavin frowned. "I thought these would be perfect. Very Lord of the Manor. No?"

"I don't know what Detective Quinn has planned. But I'm taking no chances. I've already ruined one pair of shoes on this trip. It rained again last night, and I won't be ruining another." She pulled on a pair of black riding boots to her knees and tied the laces at the top. "Now go fetch your coat and meet me at the top of the stairs. Then we'll find you some boots."

Chapter Thirty-Six
Ariadne

We huddled in the front hallway, wrapped in our coats, chatting as if it were a summer tea party. Three were missing. Cormac and Lord O'Connell hadn't returned from their visit with the priest, and Lady Aisling had not yet come down. When the doorbell rang, Imogene seized the opportunity to answer it before Mrs. Briggs could come bustling down the hall.

"Good morning, Miss Imogene."

"Hello, Inspector Quinn. Everyone is here except my mother, father, and brother. Father and Cormac have not returned from the parish," Imogene babbled, wringing her hands. "And I don't know where Mother is."

"She'll be down in a moment." Shane slouched against the front parlor doorway, smoking a cigarette. He wore a pair of work trousers and boots, which I assumed were part of his normal uniform when he worked at the stables. "What's this all about, Inspector Quinn? Are we going on a picnic?" he drawled sarcastically. Blowing smoke up into the air.

"Nothing so exciting as that, my boy. But we'll wait until everyone can join us."

The front door opened, pushing the inspector out of the way, much to the surprise of Cormac and his father. Lord O'Connell's eyes widened at the crowd standing in front of him.

"What's going on here?" Lord O'Connell asked. "Inspector Quinn, I didn't see you there. I wasn't expecting you to arrive so early. We've been meeting with Father Michael about the funeral arrangements. Brian's family will be arriving today. You haven't been waiting long, have you?"

"It's no problem. We're simply waiting for the housekeeper and your wife."

"No need to wait any longer. Here I am, as requested. Or should I say, demanded?" Lady Aisling clomped down the stairs in a pair of green Wellingtons, a sturdy blue and gray woolen skirt, with a matching coat, and a colorful silk scarf tied around her hair. She reminded me of a photograph I'd once seen of the Queen at her Scottland Estate. However, Lady Aisling's face looked more like that of Queen Elizabeth I. Her features were pasty white, and the makeup she'd used to cover the circles beneath her eyes had not been put on with a steady hand. Caked powder cracked and flaked beneath her lashes onto her cheeks.

"And Mrs. Briggs?"

"I'm here, Inspector Quinn," Mrs. Briggs faintly called. From the dark hallway beyond the staircase, Mrs. Briggs appeared like a lurking wraith. Dressed in a light trench coat, her hair was also wrapped with a headscarf, only hers a cotton one in dull gray. She must not have gotten much sleep either, as she looked almost as pale as her employer.

"There's been a break in the case. Follow me." Quinn led the way out of the front door.

Once we'd herded into the circular driveway like a flock of sheep, Lord O'Connell called out, "I say, Inspector Quinn, this seems a bit strange. Where are you taking us?"

Quinn counted heads, pointing at each person as he mouthed the numbers one through eleven. "It seems we have an extra person." Detective Quinn zeroed in on Gavin. "And you are, sir?"

I stepped forward. "This is Gavin Turnbull, my, uh, coworker. He arrived last night."

Quinn's bushy mustache jiggled. "Mr. Turnbull, it's nice to meet you. Since you were not here the night Brian Byrne died, your presence is not required."

"But I've changed into these walking boots and donned my coat," he pointed out, unwilling to get left behind. "It's a nice day for a walk, sunny out. Don't mind if I tag along, do you?"

The inspector opened his mouth to respond, but before the words came out of his mouth, a man exited the inspector's car, and Cormac pointed with an accusing finger, "There's the man. That is the man I saw with Brian at the pub in Galway!"

We traced Cormac's pointing finger to a wiry, weasel-like man with eyes set too close together and an upturned nose. His slick-back hair only emphasized the way his ears jutted out from his head.

Gavin strode over to the newcomer, who shifted his weight uncomfortably from one foot to the other. "Harry! Good to see you."

The man allowed a faint lift of his mouth and shook hands. "Gavin."

"Shane, is this the man you claim to have seen at the local pub?" Quinn asked.

Shane weaved through the crowd, flicked his cigarette to the ground, and snuffed it out with his toe. The grating crunch of pea gravel scraped the air like nails on a chalkboard. "That's the man."

"Very well." Quinn said nothing further about the man, nor did he introduce him. "If you are a little patient, all will soon be explained. Follow me, please."

The detective led us up a pathway toward the stables.

"Aisling?" Lord O'Connell offered his arm to his wife, and the pair took their place behind Inspector

Quinn. My aunt and uncle followed, game as a pair of rabbits going on a jaunt through the countryside. Then Julia and Cormac followed behind them. Imogene glanced from one brother to the other before deciding to catch up with my cousin. She looped her arm around Cormac's empty elbow. Shane strolled after them, as if he hadn't a care in the world.

About a dozen steps behind, beyond the earshot of the first group, Gavin, Harry, and I brought up the rear.

"Harry, this is my...uh, coworker, I told you about, Ariadne Winter."

"Don't tell me, let me guess. Your name is Harold Kendall."

The smile transformed the man's pinched features. "That's correct, but I don't recall giving Gavin my surname. How did you know?"

"I have my ways," I said mysteriously.

"What are you doing here, Harry?" Gavin asked.

"I spoke with Inspector Quinn this morning." At our looks of quiet confusion, Harry saw fit to elaborate, "The case I told you about?"

"You were working for Brian Byrne. The case is about the O'Connells, isn't it?" I pushed.

Harry glanced at me. "I shouldn't say anymore. I promised the inspector I'd allow him to handle it his way."

The group passed the stables and continued along the track that led to Brian's cottage.

"Does it have anything to do with a birth certificate from the 1800s?"

Surprise filtered through his features. "How would you know about that?" he asked rather loudly, garnering the attention of Shane, who stopped to wait for our group to catch up with him.

"Shh. Not so loud," I replied in muted tones. "And not in front of Shane."

"So, Gavin, are you going to introduce me to your American friend?" Shane asked in that drawl that I found increasingly irritating.

"Harry Kendall, meet Shane O'Connell."

The two men shook hands.

"What brings you to our neck of the woods, Mr. Kendall?"

"Doing a spot of work here and there," Harry hedged.

"Any idea what the Inspector is up to?" Shane indicated with his chin, as Quinn veered right at the fork in the pathway, which led beyond Brian's cottage directly toward the castle.

I drew in a quick breath, realizing where Quinn was headed—Mr. Byrne's death site. I didn't know how I would feel about returning. Moreover, I worried about Imogene's reaction to seeing it, and was frankly surprised Quinn had insisted she come along with the rest of the family. *What does innocent young Imogene O'Connell have to do with Brian Byrne's death?*

As we walked, I scrutinized Imogene. Her hand dragged on Cormac's elbow, and he kept speaking kind, comforting words to her.

Is she a blind spot in my investigation? This young woman might lose her home and her beloved horses if the Byrne family members are the true heirs to Ballyford. Her dramatics yesterday showed a bit of a violent streak. Did she find out something? Did she draw Brian up to the tower? Is Imogene a master actress?

244

Chapter Thirty-Seven
Ariadne

Clouds scuttered across the deep blue skies. We huddled closer to each other as the Atlantic winds lashed at our coats and whipped at our scarves. What started as a breeze at ground level increased fivefold standing atop the circular turret. To my surprise, Quinn had not guided us to Brian's death site but instead trudged the entire crew step by agonizing step, round and round to the top. He must have had something big up his sleeve, because the climb came with quite a bit of groans, moans, and downright refusals to go any further without an explanation.

To all complaints, Quinn simply replied, "All will soon be revealed," and "You won't want to miss this." Occasionally, almost in a begging tone, "Humor me, won't you, Lady O'Connell?"

I must admit, the view was nothing short of breathtaking, offering a spectacular panorama of Ireland's rugged west coast. The castle overlooked the windswept landscape of a vast limestone expanse stretching out in rippling gray waves, its rocky terrain softened by patches of green grass and delicate wildflowers.

To the west, the ocean dominated the horizon, its endless blue waters meeting the sky in a seamless blend. I glanced at the Cliffs of Moher towering over the ocean, their sheer faces standing strong against the crashing waves below.

Turning inland, the rolling countryside of Clare

unfolded, a patchwork of emerald fields bordered by winding stone walls and dotted with grazing sheep and cattle. Small country roads snaked through the hills where whitewashed cottages and traditional pubs nestled against the landscape.

I witnessed these vistas through the empty window casings as we climbed the circular stone steps.

"Now that you have us here, Inspector Quinn, do you mind telling us what we are doing?" Cormac demanded.

"As you can see, here is where I believe a scuffle happened between Brian Byrne and his killer two nights ago." Quinn pointed to a section where the moss had been ripped away and stones were missing, leaving a gap in the wall large enough to push a body through. "And someone shoved Mr. Byrne through that opening where he fell to his death," he stated baldly.

Imogene and Mrs. Briggs gasped.

"I say, Inspector, is it quite necessary to bring the ladies out to see this?" Uncle Gerald scolded.

"He's right," Lord O'Connell huffed. His yellow skin was more noticeable in the bright sunshine.

"I believe it is. Most important, sirs. If you'll let me continue."

Uncle Gerald and Lord O'Connell begrudgingly nodded.

"Now, for the past twenty-four hours, I've been scratching my head trying to hit upon a motive. Was this an accident? Why would someone want Brian Byrne, the estate manager, dead?" That wrinkled blue gaze pierced each of us in turn, silently waiting for someone to speak. "Then this morning, the break I've been waiting for arrived upon my doorstep in the form of this gentleman." He indicated Harry. "For those of you who don't know, this man is Harold Kendall."

All eyes turned to the new man among us, some with curiosity, others with blatant animosity. Harry responded with nothing more than a defiant glare toward the family.

"Mr. Kendall, can you please tell us what you do for a living?"

"I'm a private investigator...from America," Harry supplied.

"And what were you investigating?" Inspector Quinn groomed his mustache, pressing it down with his fingers.

"Brian Byrne hired me to investigate his family's origins." Harry's gaze held no one but the Inspector's.

"And why did he do that?"

Harry scratched the stubble along his jawline. "He believed his ancestry stemmed from right here at Ballyford."

Cormac didn't exactly gasp, it was more like a deep sucking breath, which he immediately affected to cover up with a cough.

"It was my understanding that Brian's family emigrated to America in the seventeen hundreds. His great-grandfather returned to Ireland after the American Civil War," Lord O'Connell said with asperity. "I fail to see the connection with his death."

"An interesting story indeed. Mr. Kendall, can you please tell the audience what you found?" Quinn encouraged.

Harry shuffled in place and cleared his throat before beginning the story. "Once upon a time, there were two brothers born eleven months apart. So close in age and looks, many times they were mistaken for twins. The elder brother died before his twentieth birthday without issue. The younger brother, Ruairí O'Connell, was set to inherit the lands. However, his older sister from their father's first marriage, Brianna, had four boys. She was widowed at the age of twenty-eight and returned home with her children, along with a man she referred to as her faith healer. Although many believed he was her lover."

Harry's cheeks turned pink from the winds, and a chunk of his slicked hair tried to take flight like the wing of a crow. He quickly patted it in place.

"Please continue," Quinn prodded.

"Right, um . . ." Harry cleared his throat again. "Three years later, the father was on his deathbed and begged his remaining son to marry his affianced before he died. Granting his father's last wish, the son married the girl, and the father died the following day. It is rumored, Brianna wanted her children to inherit the land. She and her faith healer tried to poison the younger brother —"

"Yes, yes, I've heard this old rumor. Father told me when I was a child," Cormac dismissively cut in. "Brianna murdered her brother and buried him in the walls of the castle. It's my old ancestor, Lord Ruairí O'Connell, walking the halls a night and stirring up trouble. Woo. Spooky." He clapped his hands together. "Come now, Inspector Quinn, is that why you've dragged us up here? To have this stranger relate a family fable."

"You've never told me the story, Daddy." Imogene gave a delightful shiver. "It sounds like quite the scandal."

"I don't believe I've heard it either," Shane commented thoughtfully, rubbing his jawline.

I raised my hand. "I'd like to know the story Mr. Kendall has to tell. Perhaps it's a bit different."

"Yes, me too," Gavin chimed in.

Cormac tsked and rolled his eyes.

Realizing he had a willing audience, Quinn encouraged the PI to finish, "Go on, tell us the rest, Mr. Kendall."

Harry screwed up his mouth. "Yes, where was I?"

"Brianna poisoned Ruairí," Aunt Maggie helpfully supplied.

"Right. Ruairí realized his sister had turned his own men against him. Except for a young footman who warned the lord that his life was in danger. When the poison plot didn't work, Brianna sent men to kill Ruairí and his wife. They barely escaped Ireland alive. The pair landed in New York. Thinking they were safe, they settled in Boston, Massachusetts. However, Brianna heard they survived the trip, and her lover sent an assassin to murder them."

At this point, the crowd hung on Harry's words. The PI paused to rub his bare hands together, then cupped them around his mouth and blew into them to warm them up.

To my surprise, Uncle Gerald piped up, "Don't stop now, son. We're invested in the story."

"Yes, what happened next?" asked Aunt Maggie.

"By this point, Ruairí's wife had birthed their first child. The assassin tracked Ruairí to Boston and located his farm. However, a letter of warning from the footman reached the couple just in time. They fled the same night the assassin attacked. Unfortunately, the wet nurse was mistaken for Ruairí's wife. She was murdered in her sleep. The family managed to escape to Maine, where they changed their name to hide from Brianna O'Connell and her new husband...the faith healer."

"That's quite a fairy tale," Lord O'Connell commented.

"Isn't it?" When Harry grinned, his two front teeth stuck out—a bit like a beaver.

"And you expect us to believe that Brian Byrne is the long-lost ancestor of Ruairí O'Connell, and the true heir to Ballyford? Like a real Anastasia Romanov?" Cormac scoffed, his gaze darting between his mother and father, who were decidedly quiet on the matter.

"What's not a fairy tale is the paperwork I have found linking Brian Byrne to this castle." He tapped his toe on the stone floor. "Right here."

Lord O'Connell's brows knit together as he crossed

his arms over his chest. "What are you insinuating?"

"I insinuate nothing. I'm telling you the facts," Harry stated.

"Thank you, Mr. Kendall. I think that is enough." Inspector Quinn stepped forward. "What Mr. Kendall brings to light is something I've been wrestling with for twenty-four hours. *Motive.*" His lips enunciated the final word like a gavel striking the block. "If what Mr. Kendall said is true, excepting Miss Winter, her associate, and Mrs. Briggs, everyone standing here now has a motive to want Brian Byrne dead."

"Why, that's preposterous! Surely, you can't believe my wife and I have any reason to wish the man dead," blustered Uncle Gerald. "Why, we hardly knew him."

"Your daughter is about to marry into the family. Gaining a title and this vast estate would be a significant advancement for her," Quinn asserted.

To which Aunt Maggie simply burst into laughter. "You must be joking! We're from America, we don't give a fig for your high-falutin' titles. We held a revolution to get rid of kings and queens. If the Byrnes are the true heirs to this crumbling castle, good for them. Speaking frankly—" she leaned toward Inspector Quinn and put a hand to the side of her mouth, as if imparting a confidence "—if there's no grand inheritance, my daughter and her husband could come make their fortune in America, where I'd be able to see my grandbabies more often."

"My wife is correct, Inspector. You'd have to come up with a much better motive for us to cause harm to the estate manager. Moreover, it seems you've forgotten, my wife and I have an alibi." Uncle Gerald wrapped his arm around Aunt Maggie's shoulders. "We were with each other all night."

"You make a good point." The inspector studied his shoe for a moment. Then his head popped up. "Very well,

Mr. and Mrs. Brennan, I'll give you and your husband the benefit of the doubt...for now." He strode in front of us from one end of the group, then turned to march back to his starting place. "I believe that Mr. Byrne was slowly revealing this information to the family. At some point, he revealed it to the wrong person."

"That's quite an accusation!" Lord O'Connell puffed.

Adjusting his cap, pushing it down tighter in the wind, Quinn addressed Cormac, "Mr. O'Connell, when we ran your banking statements, we found regular withdrawals from your accounts in the amount of three hundred and fifty pounds. Can you explain those withdrawals?"

"Spending money." Cormac shrugged.

Shane barked out a laugh. "And you complain about my spending habits."

Cormac's gaze narrowed. "I fail to see how this matters, Inspector."

"Within twenty-four to forty-eight hours of your withdrawals, we saw the exact same amount of money deposited into Mr. Byrne's account. Why do you think that is? Coincidence?"

"As you say, Inspector." Cormac tugged at his collar. "Coincidence."

"You know what I think?"

"I'm sure you're going to tell us," Cormac shot back.

"I believe you *did* ask Mr. Byrne about the meeting he had with Mr. Kendall in Galway. Furthermore, Mr. Byrne confessed to you. Realizing what this meant to your lifestyle, *you* offered to pay him off."

"That's daft. Why would Brian take my money? He could have the whole estate according to you and that-that..." Cormac searched for words as he waved his hand in Harry's direction. "Weaselly shamus."

Quinn thoughtfully fiddled with his mustache. "Perhaps, Brian was willing to make a deal. But on Friday night, something triggered you to act. And *you,* Cormac O'Connell, drew Brian Byrne *here.* Fought with him. Pushed him over the ledge!"

"Don't be absurd," Cormac said in derisive tones. "I was nowhere near the castle that night."

"Can you prove it?" Quinn barked.

"Prove what? I was with my fiancée discussing wedding plans, then I escorted her to her room."

"But what about afterwards? Where did you go after saying goodnight to your fiancée?"

Cormac rubbed his neck. "To bed, of course."

Quinn continued to press, "Can anyone verify that?"

"Can anyone verify if you were in bed last night, *Inspector*?" Cormac shot back.

"As a matter of fact, yes." He grinned at Cormac. "Mrs. Quinn."

"There's a Mrs. Quinn?" Shane said in disbelief.

Julia stepped forward and in a small voice confessed, "H-he was with me."

"Julia," her mother scolded.

Lady Aisling tsked. Shane whistled and hooted.

"Shut it, Shane!" Cormac snarled.

Julia chewed her lip and tugged her earlobe. That motion was like a punch to the gut for me. It was a tell I'd learned when we were teenagers playing card games.

Why did Julia lie to the inspector? Surely, she has nothing to do with Brian's death.

Harry Kendall's investigation could blow apart this entire family. The inspector was on a fishing expedition...and things weren't going the way he'd expected. He paced back and forth in silence.

My gaze flittered over each person in turn.

Cormac solicitously placed his arm around Julia and possessively pulled her to his side. While Julia's eyes remained downcast with embarrassment.

Lord O'Connell rested feebly against the interior

wall, his breath still uneven from the climb, even though we'd been standing around for at least a quarter of an hour. *Would he have been able to muster the strength to tussle with and push the healthier man off the parapet?*

Lady Aisling remained stoic, seeming detached from the events unfolding before us. However, her gaze darted about everywhere but the opening from which Brian fell. Subconsciously, she placed a hand around her wrist.

Shane simply looked bored.

Aunt Maggie and Uncle Gerald showed nothing but curiosity.

Imogene had pulled her braid forward and chewed on the ends. Her avid gaze flicked between the inspector and her parents. She rocked back and forth from her heels to her toes.

Mrs. Briggs pulled the collar of her coat tighter around her neck. "Why would Brian have come up here in the first place? You said the teens had not come back."

Inspector Quinn halted mid-stride. "An excellent question, Mrs. Briggs. Why did Brian Byrne come up here?"

Lord O'Connell pulled himself upright and admonished, "If you don't know Inspector Quinn, then why the devil did you drag us all the way up here? Is this some sort of circus stunt? It is bloody freezing up here. My wife and poor Briggs are shivering with cold!"

Indeed, Lady Aisling had begun a full-body shiver. The biting wind numbed my ears, and I jammed my cold fingers deeper into the pockets of the borrowed peacoat.

"I, for one, am finished. Come, darling, let us leave this grim place." Lord O'Connell turned to make his way to the doorway.

Lady Aisling finally stared at the ruined opening, shuddered once, then turned away.

"I'm not finished," Quinn blustered.

"I am!" Lord O'Connell thundered at him. "This is

my home, and you're floundering around like a haddock on the dock. If you wish to discuss this further, we can do so inside the house. Out of the cold! NOW!"

Down, down, down and round and round we went. At one point I stopped to find Imogene immobilized staring out of one of the window casings. Gavin and Mr. Kendall backed up behind me.

"Imogene?" I touched her freezing hand.

She jerked out of her reverie. Her eyes—enormous and dilated—gazed at me.

"Dearest, I understand this is upsetting. We need to keep moving." I indicated the fellows behind us.

"Is something wrong?" Gavin asked.

Imogene said not a word but continued the downward spiral.

A cloud shifted, and I observed faint lines of candle wax drippings in the window casing.

An important puzzle piece clicked into place.

Once we reached the driveway, Lord O'Connell pointed at Harry. "That man is *not* welcome in my home."

Harry jammed his hands in his pockets and shrugged. "Shall I wait in the car?"

Quinn studied Lord O'Connell's mulish expression. "Very well, if you don't mind. I'll send for you if I need you."

Harry, realizing there were very few friendly faces amongst the crowd, grinned. "I don't mind a bit."

Chapter Thirty-Eight
Ariadne

Divested of our coats, we were back in the fussy Front Parlor. Lady Aisling stood in the center of the room, practically catatonic, as people passed around her.

"Brr, there's a chill in here." Mrs. Briggs pulled back the curtains, allowing the sunlight to pour into the room. Dust danced upon the shafts.

Taking charge, Aunt Maggie rang for the maid. "I think we could all do with a cup of coffee, or tea, and maybe refreshments. Shane, be a dear and set about lighting a fire. Here, Lady Aisling, why don't you take a seat by the hearth? We'll have you warmed up in no time."

When Lady Aisling didn't move, my aunt gently guided her into an apricot armchair near the fireplace, then turned to Lord O'Connell. "Lord Callum, you look tuckered out. Why don't you sit by Lady Aisling?"

It didn't take much persuading. His skin was pale and clammy, and looked as if a stiff breeze could knock him down. A young maid I'd never seen before arrived, and Aunt Maggie directed her to bring tea and refreshments.

As the family members took seats, I approached the inspector and murmured, "Inspector Quinn, I believe I've put the missing puzzle piece together."

"Oh, you have, have you, Miss Winter? And what missing piece would that be?" Quinn checked his pockets and found the pad and pencil he was searching for.

"I know why Brian Byrne went to the castle in the first place."

Quinn scribbled today's date on a fresh piece of paper and distractedly responded, "And why was that?"

I tucked my hands behind my back. "If you'll give me a few minutes, I believe I can explain what happened to Brian Byrne on Friday night. Including who the murderer is."

Looking up from his pad of paper, his startled gaze assessed me.

"I promise you'll find it interesting," I tempted.

"Very well. You may have five minutes."

"Ladies and gentlemen, if I could have your attention, please. There is a murderer in this room. And *I* know who it is," I stated dramatically.

"What is she playing at?" Cormac groused.

"Sh, Brother. I'm intrigued. Please, do go on, Ariadne," Shane smirked as he said my name like a caress.

"First, I'll begin with the blackmail." I watched Cormac's gaze turn to slits. "On the day you drove Mr. Byrne into Galway and caught him speaking to our friend Mr. Kendall, you said you stayed quiet in the car. Didn't mention it."

"That's right."

"That's a lie. You *did* ask Brian about the strange fellow he'd met at the pub. Furthermore, he told you the story that Mr. Kendall related to us on top of the castle just now. And you believed him, because he had just enough information to make you concerned. You offered to pay him off to keep him from talking. Made some sort of deal."

"Again, why would Brian make a deal for a few hundred punts when he could have the entire estate?" Shane asked.

"Good question. Perhaps, he had some of the pieces required to make a claim, but not enough. Not enough to take it to the courts." I turned to Cormac. "Am I right?"

256

Cormac shook his head. Admitting nothing.

I paced away, turning in a wide circle. "However, knowing how noble your father is, you knew he would look into Brian's claims...if he were told. And with your father's failing health, you feared the news might kill him."

"There's nothing wrong with my health," O'Connell declared.

"Come now." My brows rose with skepticism.

He shook his head in denial.

"Fine, I'll lay it out. You've a yellow tinge to your skin and in the whites of your eyes. There are spider veins on your hands, you're prone to bruising, and your clothes are overly large because you've recently lost weight. Not to mention the extreme fatigue you exhibit." I listed his symptoms off on my fingers. "I would guess it's a malady with your liver."

At that point, all eyes in the room were on Lord O'Connell, his neck reddened, and his mouth hung open.

"Daddy?" Imogene squeaked.

I softened my tones, "My college roommate's father passed five days before graduation, of a similar affliction. I'm very sorry."

The man deflated, sinking deeper into the sofa. Aisling gripped his hand, stroking it.

"You've made some astute observations, Miss Winter," Inspector Quinn said in measured tones. "But I fail to see what Lord O'Connell's illness has to do with Brian Byrne's murder?"

"I'm getting to it. Where was I?" I ran through the key points in my head again.

"Brian was blackmailing my brother. And Cormac murdered him for it," Shane suggested tongue in cheek.

Cormac's face twisted into anger.

"Initially, that is what I believed." I pointed at Shane. "But...no."

His smart-aleck grin faded.

"Shane, when you saw Mr. Byrne with Mr. Kendall at the local pub, you unknowingly witnessed Mr. Kendall providing him with the final documents. One document in particular that would allow Mr. Byrne to go to the courts to prove his claim on the O'Connell estate."

"So, now you're saying that *I* murdered Brian?" Shane drawled.

"No." I shook my head. "Poor Daisy provided you the perfect alibi for Friday night. Didn't she? And, while I believe you're a thief and a scoundrel who takes advantage of innocent young ladies, you have not added murder to your crimes. Have you, Shane?"

"As you say." His lips curled around a lit cigarette.

"However, when you threatened Brian in the Billiard Room on Friday—"

"I never did so," Shane challenged.

"Oh, but you did. Brian was angry you'd pilfered money from the estate. In retribution, you threatened to tell your father about the interaction you'd witnessed at the Green Pub." His gaze narrowed as I spoke.

"So, you *were* sneaking around, listening at keyholes..."

I clasped my hands at my waist. "Nothing of the sort. I went searching for a bathroom. Got lost. It was quite by accident that I overheard your conversation. Your threat unknowingly put Mr. Byrne's plans into motion. Plans, I am willing to bet, he would have waited to enact. Instead, you forced him to confide in another family member."

Shane defensively responded, "I did nothing of the sort."

"Oh, but you did. That night, Brian decided to tell Lady Aisling about what he'd discovered. If you recall, Mrs. Briggs told us he was quite insistent on speaking with her."

Inspector Quinn flipped through his pad of paper.

"She's correct. Mrs. Briggs said the victim wished to speak with Lady O'Connell."

"Mr. Byrne did this for two reasons, first to have her silence Shane on the subject until after the party. Perhaps until Lord O'Connell . . ." I didn't finish my thought. Clearly, the family had not told Imogene how advanced her father's illness was.

Lady Aisling said nothing.

"I did hear raised voices in Brian's office," Mrs. Briggs recalled.

"My guess is, Lady Aisling didn't believe him...at first." I pivoted to face her. "But then he offered to show you the paperwork, which was back at his cottage. Isn't that right, Lady Aisling?"

Her mouth worked. "He said he had birth certificates, marriage licenses . . ."

"So, you went with him to the cottage. But while you were there, you spotted the candle in the castle tower window. Didn't you?"

"He spotted it," she corrected.

"What candle? We didn't find a candle in the tower," said Inspector Quinn.

"There was a candle burning in the middle window of the tower," I explained. "Someone had left it burning, perhaps as a signal?"

"Who would have done such a thing?" Aunt Maggie asked.

I zeroed in on Imogene, who was staring quite hard at her boots and scratching at a dirt mark on her jodhpurs. "You said you were late because your horse threw a shoe. Yet when I mentioned it to Dougray, he said Peanut was fine and didn't need a new shoe. The stable master had no reason to lie to me."

Her shoulders hunched, and she scratched harder.

In dulcet tones, I continued, "You weren't late because of the horse. You were late because you'd been climbing the tower. *You* left the burning candle. Didn't you, Imogene?"

"Yes," she whispered.

"What was it? A signal to your friends? Were you planning another séance?" When she didn't respond, I continued, "Brian stopped the first one before it had even begun. Before you'd had a chance to meet up with your friends?"

"They weren't supposed to do it that night! I told them I wouldn't be able to come. But stupid Jacob Gilbert tricked them into doing it without me," she cried, her lower lip trembling. "Fin and I were supposed to conduct the séance on Friday night. But after dinner, Briggs gave me a message from Fin. She'd gone to the tournament to see Jacob instead!"

"Then what happened, young lady?" Inspector Quinn prompted with steel in his tone.

Tears sheened the girl's eyes. "I figured the candle would burn out. I didn't know Brian would go and investigate. Or-or what would happen after," she said the final sentence in a stricken voice. Then the waterworks erupted, and Imogene wailed, "I killed Brian! I killed him!"

Whoa! This is not where I thought the conversation would go.

Apparently, neither did anyone else, for the room remained paralyzed in shock. That is until Aunt Maggie's maternal instinct shifted into gear.

"Imogene, Imogene! Child, calm down. You don't know what you're saying," she soothed and tried to clasp the wretched teen to her breast.

But Imogene would not be consoled. She pushed my aunt away and howled, "*If-if I hadn't lit tha-that candle he would s-still b-be alive!*" Holding forth her wrists, she dropped to her knees. "T-take me to j-jail. It's all m-my fault."

Lady Aisling stared at Imogene, aghast, unable to comfort or perhaps comprehend her daughter's guilt-ridden revelations.

Lord O'Connell went to his daughter. "Imogene! Imogene! Stop this." He grabbed her by the shoulders and gave her a shake. "You didn't kill Brian."

"I did! I did! I left the candle b-burning. If I'd g-gone b-back to b-blow it out . . ." she blubbered, wiping her nose with a shirt sleeve. "I'm a-a horrid p-person! *A k-k-k-killer!*" The hysterics began in earnest. An uninterrupted wail came from her wide-open mouth, and tears coursed down her flaming cheeks.

Lord O'Connell looked to his wife for help. Finding none, he gave his youngest child a forceful shake and slapped her across the face.

The rough treatment appeared to bring Imogene out of her spiraling mania. Her mouth closed, and she put a hand to her injured cheek.

"Imogene," I said in gentle tones, handing her my handkerchief. "You did not kill Brian Byrne. Yes, he went to investigate the candle, but that is not the reason he fell from the tower."

She sniffed and hiccupped. "It isn't?"

"Not at all." I bent at the waist to be at eye level with the teenager. "You didn't push him, did you?"

"*No!*" She shook her head with vehemence.

"I didn't think so. Now dry your tears. You are not to blame."

Imogene blew her nose, making goose-honking noises. Finally, she calmed down to snuffling and nominally shuddering.

The squeak of the tea trolley captured our attention.

"I've coffee, tea, and a nice lemon pound cake made for the par—" the maid realized all eyes were on her. She took in Imogene's penitent distress and the general tension in the room. "I'll..." She gulped. "I'll just leave it here. Shall I?" she squeaked. Not waiting for an official dismissal, she beat a hasty retreat.

While Lord O'Connell and I assisted his wrung-out daughter to the loveseat, Julia poured her a cup of tea. "Here, take this. It'll make you feel better."

Once Imogene was ensconced with her tea and a small throw across her knees, Inspector Quinn asked, "How did you know about the candle, Miss Winter? Did you see it on Friday night?"

"No, but on our way down today, I did see the melted wax on the sill. And recalled that Julia and I found a white candle in the tunnels that matched the wax on the sill."

"That still doesn't explain what happened to Mr. Byrne," Inspector Quinn reminded me.

Chapter Thirty-Nine
Ariadne

"You are correct, Inspector. While Brian went to deal with the candle, Lady Aisling took the time to read the papers." Pivoting on my heel, I aimed my attention at the lady of the house.

"Like this one," I said, pulling the birth certificate from my pocket, waving it in the air. "She must have realized what Brian had."

Staring into the fire, Lady Aisling made no demur to my suppositions. The only sense I had that she'd heard my accusations was her nails digging deep into the silk damask of the chair's arm.

"What have you got there?" Quinn asked.

"A birth certificate." I handed it to him and grilled the older woman. "Did you go after him in a panic, or was it always your intent to kill?" When Aisling didn't respond, I continued, "You went up the steps, catching your blue dress on a sharp stone. When you got to the top, you found Brian. There at the top of the tower, you confronted him. You argued."

"Now hold on a minute." Lord O'Connell straightened in his chair, becoming agitated. "You can't actually believe . . ."

When I didn't deign to look at him, he turned to the inspector. "Quinn, I insist you put a stop to this. The girl is out of line."

Quinn studied Lady Aisling as her fingernails shredded the shimmery silk damask. "I'd like to hear what Miss Winter has to say."

Driven to provoke the matriarch, I hurled my accusations without pause, "At some point, he grabbed you, which accounts for the bruising on your wrist." I pointed to where the sleeve had fallen back. "You wrenched away from him. He stumbled closer to the edge. And you saw your chance to make it all go away. You realized the opportunity to finish him off. And you *took* it! *Pushing* him over the ramparts! You watched him fall to his death," I expounded. "In the scuffle, his watch fell off, and you picked it up before descending the stairs."

"*NO!*" Lady Aisling came alive, thrusting to her feet. "That is not how it happened! Yes! I followed him to the tower. I feared Imogene had gone up there, when I realized she was the one who placed the candle in the window. When I got to the top, Brian was the only person there."

"Aisling, you shouldn't—"

She continued as if her husband had not spoken. "I asked Brian what he intended to do with the estate. He had it all worked out. Oh, the man had thought long and hard about his plans." She tapped her temple. "He told me he'd bring his brother and sister back to the West Coast and build homes for them on the northern part of the land. He'd sell off the southern portion to the Dunlavys to pay off the loan. I asked what he expected us to do. He said Cormac and his new wife—" she pointed to the pair "—could stay on and take over *his* role as estate manager."

Cormac made a disgusted grunt.

"Shane could live at the manor until he came into his trust fund, *if* he closed the deal with the Hollywood men."

Shane grinned.

His mother continued, "And *if* he stopped stealing from the estate."

The grin fell from his face.

"Imogene could stay on as long as she liked. He

generously offered to pay for her training to become an equine veterinarian," Lady Aisling scoffed, as if educating her daughter to become a vet was a grand joke.

A little hurt cry came from Imogene, which her mother ignored.

"Then he said..." Lady Aisling swallowed hard. Turning to her husband, she sank to her knees before him, resting her hands gently on his legs. "He said we could stay on until your death."

Without a word, he reached out and touched her arm. His eyes softened, brows pulling together in quiet sorrow. No judgment. Just the ache of witnessing someone else's suffering.

"My, darling," he whispered.

"Callum. You. You were born here. In this house. The rightful heir. I couldn't fathom *the idea* of it being taken from you. And-and the blackguard said, once you'd passed, he'd find me 'other accommodations.' He had the gall to suggest, I take one of the crofter's huts! *Me*. Living like a common *peasant*."

"Oh, my dearest," Lord O'Connell whispered, laying his hands atop hers. There was a silence between them, but it was heavy with care. His pity wasn't condescending. It was tender, human, full of sorrow that wanted to heal.

With surprising dexterity, the older woman rose to her feet and spun around, practically spitting out the next words at Inspector Quinn, "He spoke as if I meant *nothing*. Do you understand? Me! When it was *my* dowry—" she pointed to her chest "—which kept this place from falling down around our ears. Without *me*, Ballyford would be *nothing*! Enraged, I slapped him with all my might. He grabbed my wrist." She pulled away her sleeve revealing the purpled skin beneath. "And told me it was finally time for his happiness. He blathered on about marrying the love of his life. I remember laughing..." she trailed off. Her gaze darted to Mrs. Briggs, then away.

Mrs. Briggs, a woman who'd spent her career schooling her features, now gazed at her mistress with undisguised malice.

But Lady Aisling didn't witness the housekeeper's hatred, for she turned her back on the woman. The matriarch's face hardened, and a steely glint entered her eyes. She growled through clenched teeth, "He said I always was a cold-hearted shrew, and he pitied Callum for *having* to marry me."

"Oh, Aisling...that's not at all true," Lord O'Connell murmured in comforting tones.

However, Lady Aisling no longer paid attention to her husband. She spoke, as if in a trance, "I saw red and shoved him away from me." She made a shoving motion with her hands.

Someone gasped, but I didn't see who, because my attention remained riveted on Lady Aisling's next words.

"He lost his balance. Rocks fell. His arms windmilled. When I realized what was happening, I grabbed for him." Her fingers clawed in the air. "But the only thing I gripped was his watch." She stared down at her empty palm. "It came off in my hand."

"Then what happened?" Inspector Quinn quietly prompted, "Tell us."

"And then...then the opening was empty. He was gone," she choked out, her voice fading into silence as her eyes widened, her pupils dilated in disbelief.

"Aisling?" Callum breathed her name, shaken to his core.

Her mouth fell open in a silent gasp, and her breath caught mid-inhale. A tremble rippled through her shoulders all the way down her spine. It became obvious that the matriarch no longer perceived the people in the room.

Under our gaze, Lady Aisling relived the harrowing moments when Brian fell to his death. Her skin turned pale, lips trembled. A low, involuntary whimper escaped her throat—the kind that comes from somewhere deep and primal. Then she simply collapsed, crumpling to the floor. A long tortured moan escaped and turned into dry heaving sobs of remorse.

Callum crawled to her side, wrapping an arm across her shuddering shoulders.

Chapter Forty
Ariadne

The room watched in silence as Lord O'Connell comforted his wife.

The murderess.

I didn't dare go near her, for fear she'd snap and scratch out my eyes. Inspector Quinn must have thought along a similar vein, for he made no move to immediately arrest the lady of the house. The rest of the room remained immobile, either too repulsed or too dismayed by her revelations to offer assistance.

Eventually, the great wracking sobs slowed to quiet weeping.

Cormac got down to one knee and kindly coaxed, "Come, Mother, this isn't good for your health. You must pull yourself together. Father, help me get her to the couch."

The two men hauled Lady Aisling to her feet, assisting her stumbling form to the sofa in front of the fire.

"Here, Lady Aisling, take my handkerchief." Julia held out a lacy robin's egg blue handkerchief. When her future mother-in-law didn't take it, Julia got on one knee, and patted her damp cheeks, and beneath her nose.

"I'll pour you a cup of tea, shall I?" Aunt Maggie offered.

Aisling tilted her head toward Julia. "You really are a lovely girl. You'll make an exceptional mistress of Ballyford." She patted Julia's hand. "I'm sorry I ever doubted you."

Aunt Maggie gave a little huff as she poured cream into the tea.

I, however, was not finished with Lady Aisling's movements on the night of Brian Byrne's murder. "You took the candle in the window, and came back via the tunnels, didn't you?" I inquired in soft tones.

She nodded and took the tea from my aunt. Settling the cup and saucer in her lap, she made no move to drink it.

"You lost a pearl off your broach...or earring?"

"A pearl? I-I don't know what you're talking about." Her face showed genuine confusion.

Perhaps she didn't realize she'd lost the pearl?

When no one challenged me, I continued to probe, "You stole paperwork from Brian's cottage. Why didn't you burn it?"

"I-I didn't have time. I-I mean, how-how did you know . . ." She began to shake. The teacup rattled.

"That is quite enough, Miss Winter!" Lord O'Connell scolded. On a dime, his tone turned soft and gentle, "Come, my darling, I'll take you to your room. You're wrung out and need your rest." He put aside the teacup and pulled his wife to her feet.

At that point, Inspector Quinn stepped forward, clearing his throat. "I'm afraid, Lady Aisling must come with me."

Lady Aisling's mien remained impassive.

"Inspector, my wife is in no shape to sit through one of your interrogations. We'll come down to the station tomorrow and discuss things when Aisling is feeling better."

"You don't seem to understand. Your *wife* admitted murder in front of an officer of the law. And a dozen witnesses. She cannot simply take to her bed," Quinn officiously declared. "Lady Aisling O'Connell, you are hereby under arrest." From one of his coat pockets, the inspector pulled out a pair of handcuffs.

"Why, you can't—" Lord O'Connell sputtered.

"Yes, I *can*," Quinn said sharply.

"Are those necessary, Inspector?" Cormac beseeched. "My mother is in no condition to attack anyone."

The inspector frowned while explaining, "It's procedure, son. It can't be helped." He cleared his throat. "Now, Lady Aisling, hold out your hands."

Lady Aisling, her face a tear-stained, unreadable mask, compliantly held out her hands, and Quinn locked the metal shackles around her thin wrists.

"This is utter nonsense. Cormac, contact Father Michael," Lord O'Connell directed, snapping his fingers.

His son nodded and headed toward the vestibule. "Yes, sir."

"Phone the parish priest, or the Archbishop of Armagh. Or call on the spirit of Saint Patrick, if you must. They won't be much help when it comes to the law. I suggest, instead, you phone your solicitor," the inspector counseled.

"I'm coming with you," Lord O'Connell declared.

"I'm not a taxi service. You will have to follow in your vehicle," responded Quinn. "Can someone fetch Lady O'Connell a coat?"

"I will," offered Mrs. Briggs.

"Don't worry, darling. I'll straighten this out and have you home in time for supper," Lord O'Connell assured his wife. He stumbled and caught hold of the sofa's arm to steady himself.

"Daddy?" Imogene said in a small voice.

My aunt gave a little gasp, placing fingers on her lips. "Gerald . . ." Her gaze pleaded with my uncle.

Always a gentleman, Uncle Gerald straightened. "You're in no shape to go alone. I'll drive you."

Lord O'Connell raised a shaking hand. "It's not necessary."

"I insist."

Realizing the trek up and down the tower had worn him down, Lord O'Connell gave a resigned nod of assent.

Uncle Gerald waited for Lord O'Connell to gather his energy and followed at a sedate pace behind the head of the house.

No one knew what to say, so we waited in silence for Mrs. Briggs to return with the coat. The inspector stood stiff, at attention, next to his charge. Every so often, Imogene sniffed. The mantel clock ticked. Julia fidgeted with her skirt, pleating it and then letting it go. I think we all released a breath of relief when Briggs returned.

With a bowed head, she handed the coat to Inspector Quinn.

Since Lady Aisling's hands were already cuffed in front, the inspector stepped behind to drape the long wool topcoat over her shoulders.

As he did so, Mrs. Briggs' chin came up with an expression twisted into utter loathing. A moment of frightened realization spread across her superior's features, as Mrs. Briggs hauled her arm back and let fly.

Crack!

A collective gasp swept through the room. Lady Aisling's head whipped to the side, and she stumbled into Quinn. Off balance, and tripping over each other's feet, the pair fell to the ground, Lady Aisling landing on top.

From her apron pocket, Mrs. Briggs withdrew a long narrow kitchen knife. Wielding it above her head, she hissed something in Gaelic.

"DON'T!" I yelled amidst a cacophony of other objections and a high-pitched scream.

Abject fear invaded the older woman. Her legs kicked and her bound hands jerked in an effort to scramble away, but like an upturned turtle, all she could do was wriggle futilely atop the inspector. Her hair, unbound from its chignon, flailed in his face. He battled the tentacles away from his mouth and eyes.

Gavin, who had remained silently leaning up against the hearth through the proceedings, jolted into action. Moving past me at lightning speed, his right hand clamped around Mrs. Briggs' wrist, holding it high, while he wrapped his left arm and body around her middle, tackling her to the ground like Pittsburgh Steeler Ernie Stautner. The knife tumbled from her hand, landing harmlessly at Shane's feet.

Imogene's scream finally petered out as Gavin rolled off Mrs. Briggs. Her mouth opened and closed again and again. Helpless. Unable to draw breath like a fish out of water.

Immediately, I realized what had happened. Kneeling next to her I explained, "Remain calm, Mrs. Briggs. You've had the wind knocked out of you. Listen to me, try to breathe in through your nose and out through your mouth." I demonstrated to no avail.

Mrs. Briggs continued to flounder.

Aunt Maggie kneeled next to me. "Pull your arms above your head. And bend your knees up." She helped the housekeeper, placing her feet flat against the ground.

Air whooshed into her nasal passages and rushed out of her mouth.

With sleight of hand, Gavin made the knife disappear beneath a chair cushion.

"There you go. That's the ticket." Aunt Maggie pulled the housekeeper's skirt over her knees for modesty's sake. "Give it a few moments, you'll be right as rain."

While Mrs. Briggs recovered, Gavin and Shane assisted Lady Aisling and Inspector Quinn to their feet.

"I say, what the devil was that all about?" the inspector asked, dusting off his pants.

Mrs. Briggs lay on the floor; silent tears trickled into her hairline. "He was the love of my life," she whimpered, rolling onto her side.

Aunt Maggie and I exchanged a shared look of realization and pity.

Had Mrs. Briggs and Mr. Byrne been secret lovers? Was he planning to claim his rightful inheritance and elevate Mrs. Briggs to be the lady of the manor?

Shane stepped forward. "Brian was very special to Mrs. Briggs. She simply lost her head for a moment."

"She assaulted your mother," Quinn said.

"Who could blame her? My mother has the ability to make people go a little crazy at times." He winked at the inspector, clapping him on the shoulder.

A hint of skepticism spanned the inspector's face. I realized, between the scuffle and Lady Aisling's wild hair, the inspector had not witnessed Mrs. Briggs wielding the knife in an attempt to stab her employer.

"Frankly, I'm surprised it's taken so many years for Mrs. Briggs to give her a wallop. Mother undoubtedly deserved it." At the same time, Shane was insulting his mother, he hung the coat over her shoulders. Gripping them tightly, she winced. Again, an action lost on Inspector Quinn, who was retrieving random items that had fallen from his pockets.

"Don't worry, Mother. I'll sort out Briggs. Obviously, she was simply overcome by your revelations. As are we all." Shane shuffled the pair into the foyer. "You'd best hurry, Inspector, or father will arrive at the station before you."

Chapter Forty-One
Ariadne

Once the front door shut behind the pair, Shane sloped back into the parlor and headed straight for the liquor cabinet. "I don't know about you, but I could use a drink. Anyone else?" He poured a finger of whiskey into a cut crystal lowball glass. "Mrs. Brennan? Julia? Ariadne? Gavin? No takers?"

"I'll take one."

Shane ignored his sister's suggestion.

Julia disdained, "It's barely half past ten."

I helped Aunt Maggie assist Mrs. Briggs to her feet. The housekeeper wiped her eyes and nose with her apron.

"Why don't I take you to your room, Mrs. Briggs?" my aunt kindly offered. "You can compose yourself there."

"How about you, Briggs? A drink before you go?" Shane called. "You certainly earned it."

Mrs. Briggs didn't respond. Aunt Maggie shot Shane a dirty look and placed an arm around Mrs. Briggs' shoulder. The housekeeper shuffled with her shoulders hunched and continued to sniffle.

"To Norah Briggs. Who knew you had it in you?" Shane held the glass up in a salute toward the ladies' retreating backs and downed the amber liquid in one gulp. He then poured another two fingers into the glass.

Julia rolled her eyes. "One thing I don't understand, Shane. How did you end up with the watch?"

"Did Mother hide it in your room?" Imogene asked.

"What do you think?" the young man flippantly asked. "Anyone want a fag? No?" Flopping onto the sofa, he proceeded to light a cigarette.

My gaze narrowed. "You saw her returning to the manor that night. Didn't you?"

Shane gave the cigarette another puff before answering. "From the Solarium. Daisy and I were on the loveseat, and I'd just gotten to the point—"

Realizing Shane would like nothing more than to say something shocking, I interrupted, "Of shenanigans?"

"Oh, it was more than *shenanigans*, Ariadne," he leered.

Julia's lip curled in revulsion.

Redirecting to the question at hand, "But you did see your mother returning from Brian's cottage. After finding him dead, you went snooping in her room. Before we went down to the cliffs. I saw you coming out of there."

"I know all my mother's hidey holes," he drawled.

"I never should have told you about that when we were kids," Cormac said regretfully as he entered the room.

"But you did." Shane sipped his whiskey.

"You've known she was the killer all along?" Julia flung at Shane with dismay.

"I found the watch and realized she knew something about his death." His head swiveled back to Cormac. "Honestly, I suspected *you*, big Brother. Thought Mother was covering a mess of your making."

"Then you decided to leverage your knowledge to gain the estate manager job here at Ballyford. By holding the watch over her head, you knew you could get Mother, and thus Father, to agree to anything you wanted," Cormac accused. "You figured you'd fritter the next few years away until you came into your inheritance?" He took a cigarette from the box on the table and slapped the lid shut with a snap.

One of Shane's eyebrows rose up. He took a deep drag before answering, "As you say, big brother."

"Did you plan to do any work at all?" Cormac sneered, striking a match.

The glass slammed down onto a table, and Shane said through clenched teeth, "What a low opinion you have of me. We made our agreement. I don't wish to see the old place go completely to rack and ruin. It is, after all, the home I grew up in."

It occurred to me that, should the Byrne family follow through on their claim to Ballyford, Shane may end up being the one family member with money. Tapping my chin in thought, I turned to him. "Is your inheritance independent of Ballyford?"

"Aren't you a clever thing?" He tamped out the cigarette. "The trust came from my grandmother's side. It is unentailed to anything belonging to the O'Connell estate. With the watch in my possession, for once, I was the one with the upper hand in this family. And Mother knew it."

Imogene's forehead puckered in confusion. "What does Shane's inheritance have to do with anything?"

"Would you like to tell her...or should I?" Shane stared at Cormac, who frowned in thoughtful silence.

"What it means, little sister, is that once the Byrne family takes possession of the estate, you and the rest of my esteemed family will be thrown out on your proverbial ears. And *I* will be the only O'Connell with any money."

Cormac winced at Shane's plain speaking. "Stop trying to frighten her. We know nothing of the sort."

Shane laughed outright.

Imogene processed what she'd been told. Her bottom lip began to quiver. "But what about the horses? Will all of them be sold? Even Peanut?"

Leave it to a fifteen-year-old to be more concerned about a stable of horses, rather than the roof over her head.

Taking pity on his sister, Shane comforted, "Aw, don't cry, Imogene, I'll let you bring your horses to *my* new home."

The lip stopped quivering as she was offered hope. "Do you promise?"

"Yes, yes. I promise. I won't leave you and your horses without a home." He slugged back the last of the whiskey.

"Now what happens?" Imogene asked, picking at the afghan over her legs. "The Byrnes are supposed to be here by teatime. Do we tell them about Mother and the papers?"

Julia sat next to Imogene and took one of her hands. "I'm afraid that we are going to have to. If we don't, surely the inspector or that private investigator will tell them."

Her face paled, and she whispered fearfully, "Do you think they'll throw us out. Like Shane said?"

Julia glanced at Cormac.

"No one is throwing us out of our home. There will be legalities. Solicitors. Courts. It'll take months if not years for the Byrnes to prove their case," he explained.

"What about Mother?"

That was a tough question that no one seemed to know how to answer.

"I don't know. I guess we'll just have to wait and see," Julia soothed.

Cormac had taken up residence behind Julia resting a hand on her shoulder, and smoking with the other. He stared contemplatively down at his fiancée.

Gavin poured himself a cup of tea and changed the subject. "So, who did the pearl belong to?"

Imogene sheepishly raised her hand. "It's mine. I cut through the tunnel on Friday night. I realized I was late for dinner, and it was faster. It came off my horse brooch."

Confused, Julia asked Imogene, "*You* were the one who accosted me in the tunnel?

"Accosted you? I haven't the faintest idea what you're talking about," Imogene responded. "I haven't been in the tunnels since Friday night."

I stared hard at Cormac. His gaze came up to meet mine, and his cheeks turned pink.

Finally, he confessed, "I'm afraid, darling, that was me. I didn't mean to frighten you. I, too, saw my mother coming back late on Friday night. Then Brian's body... When you found the pearl... Well, I thought. I didn't know *what* to think," he huffed.

"*You?*" Her head swiveled to glare at him. "What were you doing in the tunnels to begin with?"

"Some of my own investigating. I saw a pair of boots in the mudroom with the same mud from the cave system. It was fresh. I thought I might find a clue. Only you found the clue. And when you started screaming, I-I, well..." He inhaled on the cigarette until it was down to the nub. "I'm afraid I lost my head and ran away in confusion," he stated in off-handed tones.

"You...lost your head?" Julia stared in wide-eyed astonishment. Slowly, she rose to her full height and placed her hands on her hips.

I'd seen that pose before—on Aunt Maggie, right before she'd lay into us for whatever trouble Julia and I had stirred up.

"Are you joking? *You scared the daylights out of me!*" she roared.

He glanced at her with a sheepish expression. "Forgive me, sweetheart...I am most terribly sorry for giving you such a fright."

When my cousin didn't respond, he spoke rather cavalierly, "Besides, it all came to nothing anyway?"

Unsure, Julia chewed her bottom lip.

Irritated by Cormac's dismissiveness, I was about to

remind her of the abject terror she felt when we were plunged into pitch darkness.

But Cormac wasn't done downplaying his role. He arrogantly commented, "Come now. Don't you think you're spreading it on a bit thick?"

Angrily, she spat back at him, "And Ariadne? On the cliffs? She told me you backed her into that precarious position! I suppose that was just...what? 'Spreading it on a bit thick,' as you say?"

Cormac jerked at the venom in her voice and finally realized downplaying her fears had gotten him into hot water. "No, no. Sweetheart, you've gotten hold of the wrong end of the stick," he soothed.

"Oh, really?" Julia folded her arms across her chest. "Enlighten me."

"My-my mind was all over the place. Your cousin was putting the pieces together. I feared she would find the answers that *I* didn't want to hear. Because those answers meant I would lose Ballyford and you, in one fell swoop," Cormac said in a rush to defend himself. Coming around the sofa, he edged closer to Julia. "If I did back her up to the edge, I didn't realize it. I swear. It-it was done completely unconsciously. Only when you and Shane called out did I see how close she'd come to the edge, and I immediately pulled her from danger."

He searched for a friendly face in the room. Finding none, he indicated his brother. "You saw it."

Shane contemplated that last bit of whiskey at the bottom of his glass. "I'm not sure what I saw." He swallowed the last of the tawny liquid.

Trying to be helpful to her older brother, Imogene sat forward and interjected, "*I* believe you."

Cormac pivoted, trying a different track. "I do most humbly apologize, Ariadne. It was never my intention to alarm or cause you harm. Please, forgive me," he said, his eyes darting between Julia and me.

"Julia..." Cormac held out his hand. "Please..."

Julia blew out a tense breath as she tucked her hands behind her back. "I-I don't know. You-you just *left* me, I mean us, in the tunnels. You must have heard how frightened I was. And Ariadne...the cliffs." She pushed a hank of hair behind her ear and shook her head. "I don't know Cormac. I have to think about this." She gazed at the engagement ring on her finger.

"Darling, you can't mean..." Cormac gripped her arm as she moved to pass him.

"Let go. I need to be alone. To think."

When he didn't immediately release her, I stepped to her side. Julia yanked free of Cormac's grasp and practically ran from the room.

"Julia!" He spun around to go after her, but it was *my* turn to grab *his* arm.

"Let her go, Cormac."

His face flushed and jaw tightened with pain and fear. I released him and stepped back. Tension vibrated from him like a plucked bowstring.

Providing support, Gavin came to my side and slipped his arm around my waist. "Best let her cool off, mate."

He ran a hand through his hair. "You're right. Of course. She needs to cool off." After another moment, Cormac's stiff body finally eased. "You must believe me, Ariadne, I meant no harm to come to either of you. My head has been a stew since Brian revealed the truth to me. I...I've not been myself."

I wasn't so sure I believed Cormac. But he put on such a penitent hang-dog face, I didn't feel I could rebuff his apology in front of the others. "Very well."

He perked up. "Do you think you could talk to Julia? Smooth things over for me?"

Gavin's arm tightened around my waist, and my gaze narrowed on Cormac. He'd revealed a side that I personally disliked.

When the chips are down, will he be there for my cousin? Tensions for the O'Connell family will only escalate in the months to come. Given what he'd just confessed, asking me to speak on his behalf is a huge request.

"I'm sure she'll come to you when she's ready to talk," I said neutrally.

Epilogue
Ariadne

Four months later

The delicatessen's tables were filling up quickly. The scent of coffee, baked goods, and smoked deli meats wafted around the eatery, helped by a lazy overhead fan. The bell above the door dinged, and I leaned to the side of the booth. A bald man in a checkered suit took a seat at the counter and mopped his forehead with a napkin. It was a stinker of a day; the mercury in the thermometer was going up and up. The newspaper predicted a humid ninety-three. Thank goodness the delicatessen had air conditioning. When I left my apartment, the window unit in my bedroom was whirring away.

The waitress refilled my coffee cup. She wore a scratchy polyester turquoise dress with a yellow apron, and her nametag read Irene. Sweat coated her hairline.

"Thanks. I'm sure she'll be here any minute."

"How about a buttermilk biscuit or a blueberry muffin, while you wait for your friend? They're made fresh every day."

My stomach grumbled. I had been sitting at the table for half an hour. "I suppose a muffin will be nice."

Once Irene left, I checked my watch again—quarter past one.

She was late. I began to worry she had missed her train from Washington. I'd chosen this place because it was half a block from Penn Station, an easy walk, even carrying a piece of luggage. Her train was due at twelve-thirty. She should have been here by now.

I stirred sugar into my coffee. The bell dinged again. I leaned over, and the worried tension withdrew from my body.

Her lilac suit was rumpled, and her hat askew, but her eyes were bright with excitement. I half-stood and waved at Julia. She waved back and wove her way around the tables, maneuvering her brown leather suitcase so it wouldn't bump into the customers.

"I'm finally here!" She dropped her suitcase, and we hugged each other. Her floral perfume mixed with the earthiness of her sweat. "We got stuck behind a freight train outside of Philly. It took *ages* to get moving again. I worried you might leave."

"Never."

"This place smells divine." Julia removed her soiled gloves and stuffed them into a black and lavender polka dot handbag before sliding into the booth. "I'm famished. What's good here?"

I pushed Julia's suitcase under the table and sat across from her. "I'm getting the chicken salad sandwich, but my father raves about the pastrami on rye."

Seeing my guest had finally arrived, Irene bustled over, and we placed our orders.

"You're looking much better than the last time I saw you. How are you holding up?"

Julia loudly exhaled. "It's been four months. Some days it seems like only yesterday you and I were rattling around in those horrid cave tunnels." She glanced at her naked ring finger. "Other days it seems like years."

"Do you still miss him?"

"Yes and no." She drew a circle on the Formica tabletop with a soft pink colored fingernail. "I miss the man I thought he was. I don't miss the person he showed me to be."

"You're well shot of him."

Irene placed an ice-cold glass of water and a cup of coffee in front of Julia, and a blueberry muffin in front of me. "Your sandwiches should be out soon."

Julia chugged half the water in one gulp. "Ah, I needed that." She hungrily eyed my muffin. "What have you got there?"

"Here, share it with me." I cut the pastry in half and shoved the plate into the center of the table. "I didn't know when you'd arrive, and Irene talked me into an appetizer."

Julia dove in, and we made quick work of the tender muffin.

"I read your article." Julia poured a teaspoon of sugar and a dollop of cream into her coffee. "It said the murder trial won't happen until sometime next year."

I gave my cousin a strange look.

"What?"

"The trial won't be happening at all. I'd assumed you'd heard."

She plonked the coffee cup onto the saucer. "I don't understand. Did they drop the charges?"

I shook my head. "She..." I gulped. "She hung herself...in jail."

"Oh." A hand went to Julia's mouth.

"I know, rather dreadful. Now there will be no trial. Maybe for the family's sake, it's for the best?" I gave a pragmatic shrug.

She leaned toward me. "Are you going to write about it?"

I shook my head. "No. It's...too awful."

The table behind Julia burst into laughter, and she waited for the hubbub to die down before asking, "What about the Byrne family? How do they feel about it? Have you heard anything more about their claim to the estate?"

"I'm not sure what their reaction was to Aisling's

death. I understand they've come to an agreement. The O'Connells are going to give them a settlement and a portion of the Ballyford property. Brian's brother and sister are going to waive their rights to the estate and title." I sipped my coffee.

A confused frown rippled across my cousin's face. "Why would they give all that up?"

"It seems they aren't interested in undertaking the care of Ballyford Manor." I ran a finger around the lip of my cup. "They weren't brought up to be lord of the manor, so to speak. That was Brian's dream. They don't want to take on the burden of the entire estate. I understand Brian's brother has a thriving business in Dublin. And his sister, a nurse, doesn't want to leave the clinic where she works. I guess they plan to build a couple of houses on the land where they can vacation and eventually retire. Considering the journal I found among Brian's things, I suppose that is what he intended for them all along."

"How on Earth did you find out all of this?"

My face warmed. "I've, uh, been corresponding with Shane."

Julia's jaw dropped.

"He sent some photos, which I shared with Gavin. They were pretty good," I defended. "The magazine hired him to do some freelance work. That movie deal also worked out. And he's getting paid to do some sort of promotional shots for them."

She collapsed against the seat back. "And he shared all of this...with you? Doesn't he know about the article?"

"I doubt they get the *New York Post-Journal* over in Ireland. Besides, he doesn't know my pseudonym." Only a handful of people knew A.E. Winter, a freelancer who occasionally wrote articles for the *New York Post-Journal,* was a female writer working for *Ladies' Lifestyle Magazine.* Gavin knew, and a few of my family members knew.

I gave a half-shrug. "Honestly, I think he needs someone to talk to. He said, nobody speaks of it around the manor house—perhaps in deference to Lord O'Connell. It's my understanding the family put it about town that she had a massive coronary."

"How can they get away with that?"

"The family claimed she was innocent all along, that Brian's death was a tragic accident. The prison claims they don't know how she got the rope, and they must have realized the family has cause to bring charges of negligence. But a suicide makes her look guilty." I picked a muffin crumb off the table and dropped it on the plate. "Apparently, the news of her death put Lord O'Connell in the hospital. I guess everyone thought it would be best if they claimed she died of natural causes."

"Hmph." Julia slapped her hand down on the table in annoyance. After a few moments of reflection, her features cleared. "Well, I'm sorry about Callum. He was always nice to me. Distant, but nice. What happened to poor Mrs. Briggs?"

"I understand she left the manor shortly after Lady Aisling died."

"I'm surprised she stuck around that long."

I didn't put my suspicions about Mrs. Briggs into words. Shane mentioned that she visited Lady Aisling a day before her death. He claimed it was to make peace with his mother. I wondered if it had been the housekeeper who smuggled the rope into prison. If so, did she do it for revenge or pity?

"Shane said she's working for a Viscount in Northern Ireland. A step up from a mere Baron." I wiggled my brows.

"Wow. Well, good for her." Julia drummed her fingers.

I fiddled with my spoon, searching my brain for a new topic, but the question I feared she would ask came out, "Did Shane say anything about Cormac?"

On my way to the delicatessen, I went over and over in my head how I would answer if she asked. I could tell her, no, Shane hadn't shared anything about Cormac. But the letter that arrived two days ago was still fresh in my memory. And even though it was in the postscript, I couldn't erase the scribbled lines from my mind.

"I can see it all over your face. You know something. Just spit it out."

With a deep sigh, I spilled the beans, "Cormac is engaged to a girl from Galway. Her father is some sort of shipping magnate. She's very wealthy."

It took a moment for Julia to digest that little information bomb. "Well, I suppose it makes sense. They are desperate for money. And I was bringing nothing to the table...as that old witch pointed out more than once!" she angrily snapped.

It was the first time I'd ever heard my cousin say anything negative about how Lady Aisling had treated her. I grinned and began humming "Ding Dong the Witch is Dead" from *The Wizard of Oz*.

Julia kept a straight face and tsked.

I kept humming and bobbing my head side-to-side. Eventually, she burst into laughter.

"We are wretched, wretched girls," she gasped.

With the arrival of our sandwiches, we closed further conversation about Ballyford, its occupants, and the events that happened. I sincerely hoped, for my cousin's sake, that the door would remain closed, and she would get on with her life without any serious repercussions.

"I understand, through the grapevine, your mother simply adores Gavin."

I wiped my mouth with a napkin. "In other words, Mom has been gossiping with Aunt Maggie, and subsequently with you."

"Of course." She gave a cheeky grin. "So, do I hear wedding bells?"

I stared down at my half-eaten chicken salad sandwich. A bit of celery fell out onto the plate. A tiny smile may have formed. "Gavin has been hinting around."

"Yay!" She clapped her hands. "You two are adorable together. When do you think he'll pop the question?"

"Now, now we're not there yet."

Gavin and I had only recently started discussing the future. He understood I wanted to continue down a career path and wasn't ready to have children. We hadn't gone much beyond that discussion, and talking about the M-word made me uncomfortable. Probably because, ever since I turned eighteen, I'd been dancing, dodging, and evading the discussion with my mother. The actual idea that I *may* have found a handsome, lovely man who supported my career goals seemed a miracle. Frankly, I didn't want to jinx it.

Instead, I rotated the tables on my cousin. "Now, *I've* heard through the grapevine that *you've* gone on several dates with a handsome doctor."

"I have." She blushed and grinned. "He's a pediatrician."

I put my chin in my palm. "Tell me all about him."

Author's Note

In 2023, I visited Ireland with my husband. We took a castles and manors driving tour around the southern part of the island. The highlight was visiting Kilkenny Castle, once the home of James Butler, 1st Earl of Ormond, 7th Chief Butler of Ireland. However, it wasn't my husband's ancestral home that inspired *Deadly Secrets at Ballyford Castle*, but rather a charming manor house hotel nestled beside the ruins of Ballinalacken Castle near the Cliffs of Moher. According to the website, "The original house was owned by the famous O'Brien clan—a royal and noble dynasty who were descendants of the High King of Ireland, Brian Ború. The house, castle, and 100 acres of land was bought by Declan's grandfather Daniel O'Callaghan, in 1938 and he and his wife Maisie opened it as a fine hotel." During that time, the hotel hosted gentry and famous starlets of the 1930s, including actress Maureen O'Hara and her husband. The luxury hotel has been run by three generations of O'Callaghan's.

Rising above the hotel on an outcrop stands Ballinalacken Castle, a 15th-century tower house. While the current ruins date to the 15th century, it is believed an original fortress was built in the 10th century "by famous Irish clan, the O'Connors—rulers of West Corcomroe." On our first evening, the hotel's owner took a small group of guests into the crumbling stone castle. The highlight of the tour was the climb up to the top and out onto the narrow archer's platform. Looking down, I realized how easy it would be to push someone over the edge, and my mystery writer's brain went into overdrive. I adored Ireland so much; I decided to set Ariadne's next adventure there. To learn more about Ballinalacken Castle and hotel visit: ballinalackencastle.com.

Acknowledgements

I'd like to the thank the O'Callaghan's, the owners of Ballinalacken Castle hotel for their hospitality and delicious food. And for the wonderful tour of their castle. Without it, I'm not sure where I would have sent Ariadne on her second adventure. Our trip to Ireland revealed the Irish to be warm, generous, and gracious people. I'd also like to thank my neighbor, Gavin McDonnell, a Dublin native, for his invaluable help in making Ariadne's adventure authentically Irish.

Thanks to my new editor Susan for keeping me on the straight and narrow. And a shout out to my beta reading team. Their perspective catches weaknesses in the text and strengthens the storyline.

As always, thanks to my husband for his support, and going with me on our exciting adventure to Ireland. He did most of the driving while I navigated, which kept us both sane and out of automobile accidents.

Read an Excerpt from
Swindler's Revenge

The knock, or I should say pounding, on my door startled me out of the rainy Saturday morning HGTV home renovation coma I'd slipped into. The clock read half past ten, and I realized I'd been watching back-to-back shows for over three hours. I picked up my coffee to finish it, but the half inch at the bottom of the mug had gone cold and skimmed over.

Bang! Bang! Bang!

I clicked off the show. "I'm coming! Keep your pants on!"

The knocking likely came from one of my fellow condo neighbors. Winding my auburn hair into a bun and tightening the knot on my chenille robe, I shuffled to the foyer.

"Who is it?" I asked, peeking through the peephole.

The man on the other side wore a long overcoat opened to reveal a barrel chest in a dark suit, white shirt, and striped tie. He had gray-brown hair and a bulbous nose. Not a neighbor.

"If you're peddling your religion, you can move along. I'm quite happy with my own beliefs. Thank you!" I hollered.

"FBI. Open the door, Ms. Cardinal. I have a warrant to search the premises." He held his badge in front of the peephole. It read "Gerald Newcomb".

Warrant? I turned off the security system, unlocked the deadbolt and the floor bolt, and pulled it open. "May I see the warrant, please?"

The agent, a little shorter than my five-foot-nine height, invaded my personal space as he laid the piece of paper onto my open palm. "We're looking for Michael Finnegan."

"Mike?" I glanced over the sheet. "Your information

is out-of-date. We broke up a few months ago, but feel free to search away." I pulled the door wide, and two other agents wearing Men's Warehouse suits followed Newcomb into my tiny foyer. The first guy was in his late twenties, with freckles and reddish blond hair. I held out a hand to stop him. "Your ID, please."

"He's with me," Newcomb snapped.

My mouth flattened and I delivered him a side-eye. "It wasn't a request. *Identification, please.*"

"Brandon Keller, IRS, fraud division." The freckled fellow held out his card.

The olive-skinned, black-haired man following Agent Keller held up his badge as he entered, but he needn't have. I recognized Amir from the last time he'd been in my home more than a year ago. "What?" I mouthed. Ever so slightly, Amir shook his head. Something slammed in my kitchen. Newcomb and Keller had already begun their search of my two bedroom, two bath condo. Abandoning Amir, my fluffy pink slippers and I shambled over to investigate.

My kitchen was U-shaped with an island in the center. Newcomb opened and closed each cabinet, needlessly slamming them shut with a bang. However, he had no such luck with the soft-close drawers that were put in when I updated my fifty-year-old condo a few years ago.

"Wow, it's ten thirty on a Saturday. Judge—let's see . . ." I scanned the paper in my hand. "Here it is— Judge Robinson must really love you."

The agent didn't respond and started with the lower cabinets along the back wall.

I leaned against the island and drawled, "Mike is six foot tall and a solid 185 pounds. Do you really think he's going to fit in the cabinetry?"

"Please stand back, Ms. Cardinal, and let us do our job," Newcomb stated.

Crossing my arms, I moved aside to allow him to

check out the island cabinet behind me. "I'm telling you—you're barking up the wrong tree. We broke up over two months ago." My volley didn't receive a response. "Agent Newcomb, what division of the FBI did you say you worked in?"

"White Collar," Newcomb replied in a clipped tone as he pulled open the cabinets beneath the sink.

White Collar? Hm, did I just fall down a rabbit hole with Alice? Mike worked in the Cybercrime division.

Newcomb opened the tiny microwave above my stove, and I rolled my eyes.

"You know, Mike once told me that they found an entire safe inside the dishwasher. Maybe I've stuffed him in there." I pulled it open and whipped out the racks. Dirty dishes rattled and clanked. Newcomb jerked upright, putting a hand to his hip in an action I'd seen from Mike. Amir hustled in from the other room.

"Nope, not in there. Don't forget to check the fridge. Oh, and there's a washer and dryer in the pantry." I pointed. "Maybe he's hiding in there."

Newcomb was not amused. "Ms. Cardinal, I can arrest you for interfering in an investigation, or you can go sit down and wait until we're finished," he said in a menacing voice.

"Interfering? Why, darlin', I'm just tryin' to help," I explained in my sweetest southern debutant accent.

Amir cleared his throat and caught my eye. His silent message was clear: "Don't."

"Okay, fine." I threw up my hands. "I'll leave you to it. Let's see what the tax man is up to."

I discovered that Keller had moved from the living room on to my bedroom, and he was searching my dresser drawers.

"Is fingering my lingerie part of the warrant, Mr. Keller?"

His freckled face bloomed like the red tide.

"Then I suggest you get your mitts out of my panty

drawers and check places where an adult male might hide. Under the bed, closet, bathroom. You get the picture," I snapped.

He slammed the drawer shut.

"Leave my shoeboxes alone, too. He's not hiding in them, either!" I delivered the parting shot and strolled across the living room and down the hall to my guest room, where I found Amir searching the walk-in closet.

"Amir," I whispered, "what the hell is going on? Is Mike in trouble? What are you doing with White Collar? I thought you worked in Cybercrime."

Amir put a finger to his lips to shush me. "Ms. Cardinal, I believe Agent Newcomb asked you to take a seat while we finish the search," he said in a normal tone. Then he took my hand and placed a tiny, folded piece of paper in my palm.

Shoving the paper deep into my robe pocket, I harrumphed, "Fine. I'll go wait in the living room." I stomped to the living room, plopped down onto the sofa, and flicked the TV back on to the home renovation show.

A few minutes later, Newcomb came into the living room. I turned up the volume.

Keller also joined us in the living room. "The bedroom is clean."

"Did you check under the dining table?" I snarked, then caught Newcomb staring at the sofa. "Oh, for the love of Pete!" I muted my show, stood, and picked up the cushions one at a time. "He is *not* in my velvet couch. And if he did dare to try and crawl in there, *you* would be the least of his worries!"

Newcomb didn't seem convinced and continued to stare.

"What? Do you need to check behind the couch?" I yanked the armrest and it moved about six inches.

Keller trotted over to give the backside a gander. He pulled it out farther and shook his head. "Nothing back here."

Shoving my favorite piece of furniture back in place, I collapsed down and put my fluffy feet on the coffee table.

Newcomb pulled up the safety bar and unlocked the slider.

I sighed as he spotted the door on the far-right side of the deck. "You'll need the key for the utility closet."

"Please open the closet, Ms. Cardinal," Newcomb requested in a very nice way.

Amir joined us in the living room. "All clear in the guest bedroom and bath."

"Agent Amir, would you please retrieve my car keys from the glass bowl by the front door?" I asked sweetly, copying Newcomb's tone.

When Amir returned, Newcomb indicated I should open the door for them. Instead, I plucked out the key to the closet and held it between two fingers. "I prefer to keep my distance from the creepy closet. Last fall, a copperhead slithered in there while I was replacing the furnace filter. I locked that sucker tight and haven't been in since." I wiggled the key. "It's all you."

With interest, Newcomb took the key. All three men piled onto my tiny deck, standing tense and at the ready, as if waiting for Mike to jump out of the closet like a jack-in-the-box.

"Be careful. That deck gets slippery when wet!" I hollered from the comfort of my couch. I considered shouting "boo!" when they opened the door, but I decided I might get shot.

The agents were doomed to disappointment. The door swung open, revealing my furnace and rusted water heater. Newcomb said something to Keller. The poor guy pulled a small flashlight out and dove into the depths of the three-by-five-foot snake- and spider-infested room. I hated that closet and shivered in disgust just watching him. He returned dusty and holding a dried-up snake carcass.

Jumping to my feet, I cried, "See! I told you there was a copperhead."

"Ma'am, it's just a rat snake. They're good snakes. They eat rodents and vermin."

"There is no such thing as a good snake if it's in my home," I replied to Keller's misconceptions. "There's a dumpster out back where you can dispose of it, please." I added the *please* in a particularly wheedling tone, because there was no way I wanted that snake to be dropped in my kitchen trash.

I guess the show was over, because after closing and locking the closet, Keller and Amir filed through my apartment and out the front door.

Newcomb returned my keys. "Your boyfriend—"

"*Ex-boyfriend*," I clarified.

"—is in big trouble. He's wanted for questioning. If he contacts you, please give me a call." He passed me his business card.

Following Newcomb to the door, I said, "Pardon me, but I'm having a difficult time believing my Boy Scout ex did anything illegal. What exactly is he accused of?"

No one responded.

"Hello?"

Newcomb paused, with his hand on the halfway closed door. "It seems he's scarpered off with one point two million dollars. We need to find out why." The agent shut the door in my mouth-bobbing shocked face.

Visit your favorite online bookstore to read more of *Swindler's Revenge,* a Karina Cardinal Mystery.

About the Author

Ellen Butler is the international bestselling author of the Karina Cardinal mystery series. Her experiences working on Capitol Hill and at a medical association in Washington, D.C. inspired the mystery-action series. *Publishers Weekly* called the Karina Cardinal mysteries, "intelligent escapism." Butler also writes the Ariadne Winter historical mysteries as well as historical spy fiction. *The Brass Compass* has won multiple awards for historical fiction including: a Speak Up Talk Radio Firebird Book Award, Indie Reader Discovery Award, and a Readers' Favorite Silver Medal. The second book in the duology, *Operation Blackbird: A Cold War Spy Novel*, is inspired by true events, and won a Next Generation Indie Book Award gold medal for historical fiction. When she's not writing, Butler enjoys spending time with her family, attending classic car shows, and reading with a cup of tea.

You can find Ellen at:
Website ~ www.EllenButler.net
Facebook ~ www.facebook.com/EllenButlerBooks
Instagram~@ebutlerbooks
Goodreads ~ www.goodreads.com/EllenButlerBooks